C000264861

The Wonderful Discovery
of Elizabeth Sawyer

Best wishes.

Jonathan Vischer

'The perfect marriage of research and imagination, of historical detail and universal human truth, *The Wonderful Discovery of Elizabeth Sawyer* will stay with you long, long after you have turned the last page.'

Glenn Patterson, author of *The International*

The Wonderful Discovery
of Elizabeth Sawyer

Jonathan Vischer

The Book Guild Ltd

First published in Great Britain in 2022 by
The Book Guild Ltd
Unit E2 Airfield Business Park,
Harrison Road, Market Harborough,
Leicestershire. LE16 7UL
Tel: 0116 2792299
www.bookguild.co.uk
Email: info@bookguild.co.uk
Twitter: @bookguild

Typeset in 11pt Adobe Garamond Pro

Printed and bound in the UK by TJ Books LTD, Padstow, Cornwall

ISBN 978 1915352 019

British Library Cataloguing in Publication Data.
A catalogue record for this book is available from the British Library.

To Dolores, Elspeth and Aidan.

Day 1

John Dicker passed the lantern to Henry Goodcole. The two men stood in Limbo, illuminated by a single light. From overhead a grinding noise reverberated through stone from an upper floor; it sounded as if a granite slab had been slid into position in the guardhouse above them. Now, in the bowels of the prison, that sound had nowhere else to go and it echoed dully before subsiding into London clay.

Dicker looked past Goodcole at the guard, then at the dungeon door. "Bang three times when you're done. Maddox, the sergeant here, will stay outside at all times. Meanwhile, I will ride north. First, I will question Reverend Thickpenny at Edmonton Church, then I will examine the parish register to establish the facts." Dicker turned away from the light then froze. "One last thing," he said. "When you have taken the witch's confession, be sure to lift your effects and bring them back out again with you."

"I will pack all into my bag." Goodcole patted the leather satchel in which he kept paper, quills, sand and ink.

"Leave nothing in the cell with that woman — not so much as a hair from your head. Do you understand?"

Goodcole mopped his brow with his wool cap, which he then replaced on his bald scalp. "Worry not for I have hardly a hair left these days," he said.

Dicker raised his hand in farewell. "I will return on the Sabbath."

"Then it will be Holy Week. God speed."

Inside the cell Henry Goodcole waited for the door to lock behind him. Reassured that Maddox was but a knock away, he turned and raised his lantern to the darkness. The prisoner lay on cold stone and was naked except for a blanket and leg irons. The chaplain approached her carefully, much as a doctor would a victim of the plague. He tugged away the blanket and shone the light over her broken body. The woman was old and disfigured – her right eyelid healed shut over some past gouge. She winced from the light and tried to crawl back into the darkness. Goodcole leaned the lantern closer. He played its light over her arched spine and the pustule on her anus. "God sees into our inward parts," he said, "and you, Elizabeth Sawyer, have been found out." So saying, the preacher hooked the lantern onto its stand and settled down at a writing desk close to the door. For a while there was quiet in the room, just the scratching of his quill when he wrote '14 April 1621' at the top of his paper.

Sawyer's slow drawl sounded from the gloom. "Soon I will be stretched between earth and sky. Then all that is base in me will become blessed once more."

Goodcole's pen stopped mid-stroke; a pool of ink blotted the page. "Do you believe that you may yet find salvation beyond the hangman's rope?" he asked.

"That is my discovery," she said.

He wrote down her word 'discovery' and settled himself. Sitting there in the glow of the lantern, he contrasted the corrupt breath blowing out of her mouth with the precise marks he had made on the page, then he thought of God's Word printed in the psalter in his bag, which was eternal.

Over the last five years Goodcole had listened to many confessions. As prison chaplain it was his Christian duty to guide the pitiful and the possessed through their last hours on earth. Experience had taught him that their guilt was useful to the Church. So, if the condemned were prepared to talk, he wrote down their stories however deluded and ignorant they might be. Now, newly promoted to Newgate, he faced his most difficult case yet. The trial of Mother Sawyer for witchcraft at the Old Bailey had caused uproar in the parish of Saint Sepulchre over the past week. Thus a well-judged account of the witch's contrition and conversion would sit well with both the board of governors and the Church. Who knows, it might even secure funding for a new prison chapel.

The woman was watching him through her one good eye. "I will tell you how pride has placed me in this pit," she said.

Goodcole addressed the darkness. "You may tell me what you will but you must first explain the Devil's access to your soul and then confess your guilt. Repent fully or not at all."

"You are right. The Lord sees into our inward parts," she answered, "and He finds us all out in the end."

"Aye, that much is providence," he agreed.

* * *

I was born Beth Cronwell at Wroth's Mill on the River Lea. My father kept a team of cobs there for the master John

Harlow. Harlow was a hard man with a cruel streak but my father was careful and he knew his nags. He loved me with the same diligence that he showed to all.

"You are my first child and you are my last child." Each night my father said these words to me after prayers. Then, while I fell asleep, he took out a studded leather casket and raised the lid. It was nothing to look at, what lay in that box. It was brown and shrivelled like the dried skin of an eel pulled from a pond; but to him, it was fine, wondrous even, for it was all that was left of the silken bubble that had once contained me. My father minded the shock of my first breath, which had greeted my mother's last. Goodwife Wombwell had told him to keep the caul. It would afford us protection and could be prayed to like a holy charm.

Wroth's Mill is used for fulling cloth. It is built of red brick and stands on the high ground overlooking the marshes that spread beyond the Lea. Some might say that it's a lonely spot for a child to grow up but I loved the nags and saw my cousins most days at church. One morning in my eighth year, my father was trundling his cart over the bridge when I piped, "I am the first child and I am the last child."

He pulled up the horses and said, "Soon you will answer to the bishop for catechism and yet already I have ruined you."

So he vowed to teach me to be humble not proud. For a moment he knew not how to do this but when he saw the rolls of cloth bundled in the back of the cart an idea came to him. The cloth was hemp; its rough fibre had been woven on the looms of cottagers upstream. It would be soaked and softened in the mill, then trampled by wooden hammers to render it fit for the garment trade. The process would provide a life lesson for me.

That night he set to work. Folding an off-cut of the coarsest hemp, he chalked out an outline and trimmed it to shape. Next, he sewed the two halves together with woollen thread and stuffed them with horsehair. When he had stitched in eyes and a mouth, he sat back to admire his work: the result was plain and simple like a gingerbread man. Then my father tucked the hemp moppet between me and my pillow and left me to sleep.

The next morning I awoke with a rash on my cheek. My father saw my scoured face and said, "'Twas put there to learn you. Come, I will show you for why."

That day my father showed me how the mill worked. He did this to teach me that, in this world, reward is earned only by suffering. That day was Hocktide. It being April the millstream was full and fast. The flood poured onto the blades that drove the wheel and spattered us in spray that tasted of the marshes. That taste minded me of the mud the horses trod into the stable; it was the muck I licked off my fingers when cleaning my hands.

Inside the mill was a storm of noise. My father held my hand and we stood by the stocks that rose and fell. There were two men working there. The one who turned the crank was Jim Broad. Jim wound the weave on a great roller under the hammers while the other man, Tapper John, topped up the liquor it was dipped in. That day we watched them work, then, to escape the pummelling, my father took me outside to where broadcloths were stretched in the sun. He pressed my hand on the weave so I might feel how it was rendered warm and soft against my skin. He said, "See how the wool turns to felt?"

My father would have told me more that day but a voice cut in from behind. John Harlow said, "M'Lud Wroth would not have you loitering." The mill-master reached out and gripped my hair. He said, "The mill floor's no place for a young'un. What would you do if your one-and-only was pulled into the works?"

At this my father remained tight-lipped. He turned on his heel and led me along the wall, which faces the South Marshes. For a while we leaned on the burred oak with the split trunk and looked below to the county bounds. A tinkling of cowbells came from the herds that grazed down there. Then, from behind, a deeper sound tolled. The bell summoned us to church where we would hear Reverend Gunn read from the Black Book. The Word says,

> *Correct us, O Lord, lest we be consumed and brought to nothing.*

Inside the nave my father fretted that I would forfeit all. On Trinity Sunday I must face the bishop to proclaim the Articles of Faith, the Lord's Prayer and the Ten Commandments, all learned by heart. If I could not do so, I would never be one with my mother in heaven. Amongst the bowed heads, a familiar face turned our way; my uncle Francis Cronwell was back in the parish on business. Francis Cronwell could read the Word of God. He was a learned man who knew the garment trade backwards and had clerked for a beak in Tottenham. Thinking his prayers answered, my father squeezed my hand. He waited to the end of the psalms and pushed through to find his brother. Aunt Mead's red face blotted out all. She scooped me up in her strong arms and said, "When are you going to give this child a Christian home with a mother and a family?"

My father said, "I keep a Christian home Goodwife Mead. Beth has a mother; she has one now, just as she had one before." He prised me from Aunt Mead's fingers, shunning as he did so, the braid of hair looped around her wrist. It was a charm worn to ward off evil. My father held me tight for he distrusted the Meads who practised the old rites.

After we had left church, I ran to my uncle who was waiting by the graves. My father said, "How now, Francis, we need your help."

My uncle ran his fingers through my chestnut hair. He said, "You want me to be godfather to this one?"

"Aye, to prepare her for the bishop."

"I've business at the mill in two days. I'll call round and we can talk it through." He touched my cheek and, noting the rash there, said, "God preserve us all." Then he tipped his hat and was gone.

That evening my father tucked the hemp moppet tight by my side. When I told him it was not soft, he traced the crude stitching with the nail of his thumb. He said, "Only you can make it soft." He brushed my eyelids closed, "'Tis as Reverend Gunn told us today: 'rend your heart and not your garments'."

He left me then and it wasn't long until I heard him open the studded box; the sound calmed me just as it did every night. Soon I heard my father praying; I knew that he spoke the Word to my mother when he said,

Blessed are they that mourn… for they will be comforted.
Blessed are the meek… for they shall inherit the earth.
Blessed are the pure in heart… for they shall see God.

Lying there in my cot I listened and hugged on to the hemp moppet. Although it was rough to the touch I could smell the horsehair within. It minded me of the nags in the byre below; the warmth of their bodies rose up around me and I fell into a deep sleep.

Two days later Uncle Francis dropped by on his fine mount. The sun was setting when he led his mare into the stable. He said, "Have you room for one more?"

I said, "What do you call your horse?"

Uncle Francis loosened the straps and removed the saddle. "My mare is called sorrel which means chestnut like your hair."

Hearing his words, I said, "Sorrel means chestnut like my hair." At that moment my father called my uncle in to eat.

Later, when I had fed and watered the horses, I peeked through the half-open door to where the two men sat. My uncle was in fine form. He said, "At church, I saw how the women hanker after Beth."

My father said, "Did you spot the loop of hair worn around Agnes Mead's wrist?"

"I've heard some still make offerings at shrines."

My father nodded. "So far, our minister is powerless to stop it. Such things have gone on since time out of mind."

Uncle Francis looked around him: the room was clean and dry but it lacked all homely cheer. He said, "You are right to be wary of those scolds but Beth needs companions and you live a life apart here on the bounds."

When I went in to clear their bowls, my uncle pointed to a chair. He said, "Soft, child. Sit with us a while." He looked into my eyes. "Tell me, Beth, have you received instruction from the curate?"

I said, "On Sundays, Reverend Thickpenny teaches us catechism. On Thursdays Mistress Hayes takes us at the Glebe."

"And will I be the only godparent who will stand with you on the day?"

"Mistress Wombwell will be with me. She was at my baptism."

Later, feigning sleep in my bed, I listened as my father and uncle made a pact: now that I had reached the 'age of discretion' I would have a mentor. As godfather, Francis would show me the parish and teach me right from wrong. He would also sharpen my knowledge of Scripture, coaching me on questions the bishop might ask.

Later, I once again heard my father open the studded box. Praying to my mother's spirit, he said, "Let Francis not turn our girl's head for, with all its fancies, the world shows us a false face."

Our first outing took us around the common fields of the parish. We made an odd pair, my uncle and I: together we were youth and knowledge on one saddle. Sitting up high, tucked in front, I marvelled at our mount for riding the sorrel mare was a far cry from the creak and grind of Master Harlow's cart. The horse brought out the best in other travellers, too. Instead of cursing me, traders now made way, some doffed their caps in respect. At Southbury Field the women tending their peas waved their hoes in greeting. I minded some faces from church and spotted my cousins in a clump. My Aunt Mead was wearing a straw hat and stood between her girls, Meg and Eve. When I waved my hand in greeting, I watched them curtsey then bend once more to the earth.

Throughout the journey, above the clack of the horse's hooves, my uncle told me of all we passed. At Potter's Field he pointed at the wives on the slope. He said, "Mothers come here with their firstborn for it is said that the spring water makes for healthy bones. A wealthy widow once owned this land. Her name was Joan Potter and she gave away all she had to help the common sort." He pulled up the horse so that we could look at the lush grass. He said, "'Tis the nature of kind to share God's plenty with those in need." Then he flicked the reins and we rode on.

That night, back in my bed, I pressed my face to my moppet and dreamt of riding on high. I thought of Meg and Eve curtseying to me amongst the peas. Meanwhile, my father and uncle faced each other over a meagre meal. My father said, "I've heard you have been out by the bounds. At evensong there was a deal of talk."

My uncle said, "Aye, but worry not about that for though your child is young, she knows her own mind."

"She is my first and last child."

My uncle said, "Your girl needs only to understand one thing to be confirmed into the Church. That one thing is the nature of grace."

"Grace is God's promise that the meek will inherit the earth."

My uncle said, "For they are 'the salt of the earth'. Now, to teach Beth the nature of divine grace, I must show her how water flows."

"What better place than a mill?"

"Aye, but not just here in Wroth's backyard. We must tour the whole diocese." Hearing this my father was uneasy but he bowed to his cousin's learning.

He said, "You may do it on one condition. You must not go back to Potter's Field. That place is bewitched and has been for ever and a day."

The next morning I set off again with my godfather on the sorrel mare. Once again, we caused quite a stir. At the mill we passed Jim Broad and Tapper John stacking frames by the racks. Jim Broad said, "She should be mucking out stables, not riding high like a princess."

Tapper John said, "He's a sly one that Francis Cronwell. He's checking out the Mill."

"You reckon?"

"That's one of Burghley's thoroughbreds he's riding." Tapper John put down the frame he was holding. He called his mate over to inspect the stream. The works were quiet today, the hammers stilled by the lack of flow. Both men looked up at the weed baked on the blades of the mill wheel, then down at the trickle that ran underneath. Jim Broad said, "Someone's taking our water."

Tapper John said, "Aye, M'Lud Burghley: up in the headwaters and now downstream too." I heard this later from my cousins at church for word gets round and it was common knowledge that my uncle was Burghley's man.

On the road from Durant's Arbour we passed along Bungie Lane. At Bury Farm we turned left, hugging the hedgerows by Old Park to keep away from Potter's Field. Here we crossed the brook that marks the parish line and so passed into M'Lud Burghley's parish: Edmonton. The traffic was busier on this road, the carts stilled by drovers and their cattle. When they had passed, Uncle Francis pointed at the shadow of oaks that traced the edge of the forest.

He told me of the woodsmen who work the coppices in the Lord's Grove. "They cut the second claw off our dogs and cook up great stinks in their bone pits. It is to warn us to keep away." So we rode on until the horse stopped at a mill. Here we dismounted and crossed a bridge.

The miller called, "Ho, Cronwell, welcome to Screwes."

My uncle pointed to the pool. He said, "The water's low."

The miller said, "Water's been down since yesterday." The miller handed my uncle a canvas bag. He said, "These are the orders for Farley's in Tottenham."

My uncle said, "We go there next but first this child needs to see how water runs." He led me to where the flow spilled through the sluice and said, "*Water is like God's grace. It falls on rich and poor alike and cannot be contained.* It runs through us, just as it pours through the ground. Without it, we are dust." At the time I knew not the importance of what he was telling me. Only later did I understand that it freed me from my teachers, even Mother Church.

The moon was high above the marshes when we made it back to Wroth's Mill. Its shine caught on flittermice that darted above the Lea. We found my father standing in the doorway of the stable. He said, "What took you so long?"

Francis said, "We had a deal of business at Farley's Haberdashers at High Cross. Your girl loved the fabrics there: wool, fine linens and damask."

"You showed her *silk*?"

My uncle was too tired to argue; he clapped a hand over his brother's shoulder and said, "Softness never did anyone any harm."

Then my father knew that he had made a mistake because, for all his learning, Francis Cronwell was a vain man.

That night, when I squeezed close to my moppet, I dreamt I was floating in water: the water was held in a silken bubble and the bubble was silver like the moon.

The next day dawned overcast. As usual my father put the horses out to pasture while I checked the tack. First I untangled the harness for the cart, then I laid out traces, halter and tugs. My pet job was treating the saddles and I did my uncle's first. Uncle Francis's saddle was bespoke. It was stitched for him by a lorimer, not bought from a slop-shop like the rest. That morning I worked as usual. First I soaped the hide with slow circles of the cloth, then I rubbed the polish into the scratches like an ointment. The soap smelt of wet wool and beeswax and caught in the outline of a cat that was cut in the pommel. I was licking the soap off my hands, when I heard footsteps. Mistress Wombwell stuck her nose around the stable door. The midwife's face was wrinkled and she had the wide eyes of an owl. She said, "Is your father about?"

I stepped outside and pointed over the river to the marsh. Mistress Wombwell looked at the horses at pasture and then stepped back into the stable. She brushed her fingers over the newly polished saddle then pulled up two stools and bade me sit with her. "Know you, I vouched for you at baptism after your mother died?" I nodded. She said, "I hear you have a godfather now and that you ride a fine horse." I stood up and pointed back to the nags, which were grazing in a clump. I said, "My horse is chestnut like my hair."

The midwife did not look up; she regarded the soaped saddle. Then she pressed her thumb down on the outline of the cat. She said, "A horse like that does not belong at a mill. Its flesh is too fine."

That year April finished as wet as it started. The rain that drove the mills also fed the spite that is a way of life on the Lea. For whether there is a drought or a flood, no man controls the river, whatever his desire.

At that time my uncle Francis was busy fitting out Lord Burghley's house at Pymmes but he still crossed the parish line to visit us by the marsh. Sometimes he brought me presents: snippets of cloth from Farley's at High Cross. Each evening, after my prayers, I would lay these out in a row. Next to the coarse weave of my moppet, the pulls of Flemish wool, silk floss and spun lace looked light, like hare's tail picked from the marsh. Though their finery brought me joy, it also made me sad for it minded me of a world beyond my reach. My father soon put a stop to these gifts. He told my uncle to stick to Scripture. He said, "The bishop's visit is now less than a month away. Beth should fill her heart with the Holy Spirit and be ready to answer to catechism."

Rogationtide falls the Monday before Ascension. It is the time of the 'beating of the bounds' in Enfield, when parish lines are marked and those marks witnessed by all. At Rogationtide, folk in our parish vie to prove their worth: some dress fine while others look for outsiders in our midst. So, borderers from Mimms, Hadley or Edmonton are not welcome and strays from these places are sometimes jumped and left for dead in a ditch; some have been tarred and feathered. The year of my confirmation it had been raining for a fortnight, which made for a soggy show, though still people turned out. First came Curate Thickpenny walking with Churchwarden Wyld, behind them trudged Reverend Gunn, flanked by a choir of five. After these orderly types chased a rabble of children with switches in their hands. Many times Churchwarden Wyld had to act as constable because one thing is certain: give a boy a stick and, sooner or later, he will poke someone's eye out.

When they reached us at the mill, the line came to a halt by the burred oak with the split trunk. First Reverend Gunn stood with his back to the tree, then the choir spread out on either side and sang, "Sing unto the Lord with thanksgiving."

Next our minister turned to Churchwarden Wyld who rested a chisel on the split in the oak and, with hard knocks of a mallet, cut a cross deep into the heartwood. The cross was the size of a man's hand and its grooves were pale and raw. When the churchwarden stepped back, the children surged forward. For a brief while I caught hold of Meg and Eve and we three spun round while the boys and girls of the parish beat the tree.

Uncle Francis knew not to cross the bounds during Rogationtide. The next time he called he brought no presents, just questions for me to answer at bedtime. Before he bade me goodnight, I sat on my cot and described the Trinity, recited the Lord's Prayer and named the commandments Moses brought down from Mount Sinai. Then I curled up with my moppet and listened to the stirrings of the sorrel mare below. I was about to fall asleep when a thought came into my head and once it took hold there was no stopping it. I slipped out of bed, tiptoed over the boards and found the cupboard where my father kept his things. I found the key under a cup and so opened the door and looked up at the shelves. Only by standing on a stool could I reach what he kept there. There was a wooden bowl with river pearls in it, there was a folded cross of reeds such as pilgrims carry on Palm Sunday and there was the brown leather box with studs in it. I knew this was the casket my father opened each night when he prayed to my mother. Had I been younger I would never have been so bold but the 'age of discretion' is the time we must own up to the choices we make. It is the time a child first feels the promptings of the Devil and it is to protect us against this that we are confirmed into the Church. The casket opened with a click but when I peered inside, I found my caul was little more than a matted stain. I had hoped for more so I wet a finger on the blood from my mother's womb, then I leant further to taste it with my tongue. The stool tipped, I fell backwards and the blow from that fall knocked me cold.

For three days I lay fevered in my cot; three days in which the dark river flowed and three days in which spite in the parish held sway. During that time it was Mistress Wombwell who kept watch. She turned me over, sponged water into my jaw and kept vigil with my father each night by the bed. When my fever cooled, I woke to find the midwife holding the studded casket in her lap. It was then that my sin came back to me and I felt shame. Mistress Wombwell saw the guilt in my eyes. She said, "You are your mother's daughter, Beth. Pray to her now and no harm will come." When we had prayed together, the midwife told me that my uncle Francis Cronwell would not be back. Although she did not tell me what was amiss, the mistress assured me that she would vouch for me to the bishop and so all would be well.

The next day my father tightened the bandage around my head and told me that we should attend evensong to hear Reverend Gunn read from the Black Book.

The journey to church was bright with flies. The cob pulled through the lanes while the sun settled into the dusk of May. At church I stood barefoot on the flags. All around I could hear whispers. All around I could feel the heat of people's stares.

The Reverend Gunn read from Luke. The Word says,

> *The Lord hath put down the mighty from their seat. He hath exalted the humble and the meek.*

There were prods from behind, sniggering even.

Later we left church alone. My father said, "They think that you were thrown from your uncle's horse. They say he is a proud man who does not respect the rule of the Church. Worse, they say he is a *dissenter*." I stared at the cob's bony backside and said nothing; its tail swished away a fly and the cart jolted in a pothole. When we reached the mill, I went straight to my bed and fell asleep with my moppet pressed to my face.

The next morning I discovered that the sorrel mare was no more. I pieced this together from the words spoken by Jim Broad and Tapper John. I was up early and about to step into the dew, when I spotted the two men outside the stable. They had a brazier lit and a poker heating in the fire. Tapper John said, "It seems a sin to burn it."

Jim Broad tapped my uncle's bespoke saddle. He said, "Just there, on the sign of the cat." I heard the sizzling sound and held my nose.

Tapper John said, "Harlow's a bastard."

"He can't be seen on a saddle with Burghley's mark on it."

"I mean about the horse."

"It wasn't about the horse. It was a case of 'whose side are you on?'"

"'Twas the pleasure Harlow took in laming that creature."

"Forget it. That nag's dead meat, so will we be if we don't sort out this saddle."

When I heard what had happened I wanted to curl up in the muck. I was about to scamper back to bed when I spied the woollen blanket used to rub down the sorrel mare. I pulled it from its hook and fled upstairs.

That morning Mistress Wombwell paid me a visit. She took a look at me curled up in a ball, then folded my blanket and placed it on my pillow. She said, "Child, it has the horse's smell on it." Then the midwife turned her attention to my moppet. It was wet with tears; she ran her fingers over its softened weave. "What do you call this one?"

I said, "I call her Grace."

She said, "Ah Grace, like your mother. Now, this Grace has your smell on her. She is truly yours." Mistress Wombwell sat with me. When my father came he was diligent to a fault.

He said, "Trinity Sunday is but a day away."

She said, "We're done with Scripture for Beth knows her catechism by heart. It is the truth a person holds in their heart that is important, not words in a book."

On Trinity Sunday the bishop wore black and white. His clothes were of the finest style. He stood in front of the altar table in Enfield Church. Beside him stood Reverend Gunn and Curate Thickpenny; together the churchmen faced children from the parish. Each of us had reached the age of discretion; each had a godparent waiting behind. Eve was there, as was Tapper John's niece Anne. I stood last in the row, eying the bishop's hat as he bobbed closer along the line. Compared to Reverend Gunn the bishop was short, although his girth was wide. He spoke with a voice like stewed plums and, when he gestured, his vestments made the candles flicker. To my right the choir sang Alleluia as I breathed in the scent of beeswax and wet wool. Behind me I sensed Mistress Wombwell; above I heard the drum of rain on the church roof. When the bishop drew close, I touched hands with Eve, then I looked up at the Black Book lying open on the lectern and thought of the secrets locked within its holy script. My uncle had taught me to read only two words. These were written, not in the Black Book but on my mother's cross. They were inscribed outside the church in the flooded burial ground; in grooves chiselled into raw wood they spelled out her name: 'Grace Cronwell'.

The bishop stood in front of me. He wore a cape of sable fur around his neck. He said, "What is your name, child?"

I said, "My name is Elizabeth."

"Who gave you this name?"

"My mother… in whom I was made. I am a child of God, bound for the kingdom of heaven."

The bishop slowed his words almost to a standstill. "What then did your godfather and godmother do for you?"

I said, "They did promise that I would forsake the Devil and his vain pomp."

The bishop nodded to Mistress Wombwell. He said, "And are you bound to do as they have promised?"

I answered, "Yes, verily, I pray God He will return me to my mother, Grace, that I may be with her… after my life's end."

* * *

Henry Goodcole held up his hand for Sawyer to pause her storytelling. He checked through his transcription and, referring to the words he had underlined, he noted down the following paragraph:

> *Your uncle Francis was a dissenter who taught you that divine grace runs free through Creation like water. This is a falsehood; divine grace comes only through Mother Church.*

Goodcole took a moment to read over the words he had written; then, he told Sawyer to continue. Again she spoke out of the darkness.

* * *

It was the year of the Spanish ships. I was sixteen years of age, standing in front of my mother's grave in the churchyard. Now that my father, too, had passed from this world, a stone stood instead of Mother's wooden cross. It was Lammas-time and I could smell the chaff of threshed corn.

Meg Mead said, "Do you really think you are the only one?"

I looked at the stone sunk deep in the long grass; then, I faced my cousin. I said, "I am their first and last child."

She said, "You are not your mother's first. Your mother had a son before ever she met your father." Meg savoured my hurt but I was used to her jibes so I stepped past her and made to go into evensong, only I could not. At the door of the church Mistress Hayes barred the way to a husband and wife carrying a child.

She said to the mother, "You are unclean." Mistress Hayes passed the mite to its father and led the woman away.

As we entered church Meg said, "They are stopovers bound for Waltham. The family name is Ward. She gave birth on the London Road."

Inside we found Eve. A baptism had been prepared and Reverend Gunn read from the Black Book. The Word says,

> *Except you become as little children, you shall not enter*
> *the kingdom of Heaven.*

During the baptism I saw Churchwarden Wyld lift the newborn; I saw Reverend Gunn splash water on his soft scalp; I saw the child's father cross himself when he knew his boy was safe.

Reverend Gunn said, "Now, he is one with Christ Immaculate and is watched over by Mother Church."

Afterwards the three of us walked back through lanes thick with flies. With the harvest on, some commons were full of Welsh Black cattle and dung on the road warned us to be wary of strays. To keep clear of the broken fence at Hammond Leys we took the long way home, which meant we would pass by Potter's Field. The soil there is the richest in the parish and yet, up until that year, it had neither been cropped nor put out to pasture. My cousins had no fear of the spirits there. My aunt took Meg and Eve after their first bleed and they returned each year to make offerings at the shrine. That night, walking between the hedgerows, I lagged behind the girls for I wanted time by myself and knew I would get none at Gonge. Seeing them waiting for me there in the dusk I felt both dread and joy. When I reached the slope I looked up at the Judas tree that grows by the stile, then down at the pods that we crunched underfoot; they were as dry as last year's peas. I said, "What was my brother's name?"

Meg said, "The Church gave him no name but your mother called him Robert."

Eve said, "Our mother keeps a gift of his hair at our home. After prayers we will show you."

By the time we reached Mead's cottage an ochre moon had risen above the marsh. We set about our chores: while Eve picked up sticks and Meg rested, I drew water. Walking to the well in Gonge Meadow, I pondered Eve's news that my aunt kept a lock of my brother's hair. I could not help but wonder why. Was it a keepsake, was it a charm like the caul my father kept, or was it more? When I threw the pail down the shaft I minded a tale of a newborn pushed into a pot and kept within a wall. It spooked me so I returned home with half a bucket of water.

Eve said, "Mother's been asking for you. Go to her now."

I found Aunt Mead propped up on a goose-feather plump. The girls had dressed the room with bay leaves but it still smelt sour of fever. Aunt Mead was dry about the mouth; she waited for me to sponge water onto her lips and said, "Dog days, Lysbeth. I shall not rise before Friday when the weather breaks." The old woman nodded towards the marsh where the Dog Star hung. I pulled up a chair. Aunt Mead said, "Meg says you know little about your mother. I don't suppose your father told you much."

I said, "My father was a good man."

Aunt Mead said, "Your father was a good man but no man loves a child like a mother." She grasped my hand and I felt her failing strength. "Mind that when Reverend Gunn talks of 'Mother Church' for men of the cloth are just the same – they are as flawed as Old Adam." I looked at my aunt's sallow cheeks, her dimples stolen by age. We both knew she didn't have long.

I said, "Tell me about Grace."

Your mother was baptised Grace Mead. She grew up with her father and brothers upstream from Wroth's Mill in a place called Horsepoolstones. Grace had deft hands and a keen eye. She earned silver stitching piecework for a man called John Alabaster. Alabaster hailed from Hatfield. He ran a slop-shop there and employed cottagers across three counties to stitch for him. His agents would ride from Ware to Epping, from Waltham to Edmonton; they carried all in their saddlebags. In them they packed: templates; bolts of cloth; bone needles and fine twine rolls. The agent who came to Horsepoolstones was a man called Thomas Munt. Munt rode a long route and, in the course of each day, he saw many women. As far as Grace was concerned he had a way of suiting himself. Sometimes, he would turn up on the agreed day but often he would just appear without so much as a by your leave. From the start Grace's father kept his eye on this travelling man but Grace's piecework brought in silver that kept the family right in lean years when the harvest failed or their livestock had the canker. After a while the nature of Munt's visits began to change: if Grace was at market or church when he called he would leave a gift. When she returned she would find a trinket or some other sop to sweeten her for the next time. When her father caught wind of this he told John Alabaster to change his agent but it was too late for, though Munt stopped coming, Grace grew sick. Soon it was plain to see that she was great with child.

The sickness that afflicted your mother was more than just the morning kind. It gnawed at her soul and left her in a stupor. The neighbours were quick to spot her sorry state. Some said that she had pricked her hand on a bone needle, others that a marsh sprite had entered her body through bad water from the well. Whatever the cause no one could find a cure. During this time we Meads stood together – as we always do. The men put up with the scorn and scoured the three counties for Munt, who'd become scarce as a hare at a hunting party.

By late November your mother was due to give birth. That year the rains were heavy. In spite of cramps and her waters breaking Grace slipped out of her father's house and started for the Lea. By the time her labour was hard on her she had already reached Norris Lane. By the time the birth pangs stopped her in her tracks she was past East Field. Where the river divides she gave birth to Robert. There on Wyld Marsh where the millstream breaks from the main flow, she leant back on the grass and pushed him out into the cold November air.

After she had told me this much, Aunt Mead grew tired so I fetched a pitcher of all-heal and left her to sleep. Meg was serving up barley broth to her sister at the hearth so we sat and supped. When we had cleared the table I said, "Where do you keep the gift of my brother's hair?"

Eve said, "Leave this for now. We will show you at first light."

The next day, I woke to find a linen purse on my pillow. The purse was all the finer for its slight size. Since I was first up I rubbed sleep from my eyes and placed the pouch in the palm of my hand. By weight I knew the purse must be empty so I did not open it at first; instead, I marvelled at the needlework and cross-stitched sign of the heart on its front face. It was only when I held it by the drawstring that I thought to check within. Inside the lining I found, amongst the bog cotton picked from the marsh, a twist of birth hair. The hair was downy and black; so short that it made but a single curl. Pinching it between finger and thumb I wondered at its softness and held it to my nose for I fancied it still carried the biscuity warmth of a newborn. Across the room Meg was watching me. She said, "She did not love him."

I pressed my brother's birth hair back into the purse and said, "How can you know?" Eve was awake now, too. She rose, checked on Aunt Mead who was stirring behind the draw, then returned. She said, "Did our mother tell you why *Robert was not baptised?*"

Meg gave me a hard look; she said, "The River Lea baptised your brother. The river took his life and gave it to him at the same time."

I squeezed the purse in my fist. I said, "Did she help him suck?"

Meg said, "She didn't help him do anything. Her brothers found her. They carried her back home but within days she was back at the riverbank." She pointed at the crushed purse in my palm. "All that trouble to sew a heart for a child she never loved."

I got up to fetch water from the well. When I returned from Gonge Meadow I found Eve fretting at her mother's bedside. She dipped a cloth and dampened Aunt Mead's brow. For a while we listened to the old woman babbling, then Eve said, "She wants you to take that birth hair back to Potter's Field."

"Why?"

"Because that is where the rest of your brother lies."

We finished our chores and found a neighbour to sit with Aunt Mead. Then we broke our fast and prepared for the hot walk to the Glebe for all three of us had been summoned to meet Mistress Hayes at noon.

Mistress Hayes schools most girls in Enfield. She works in the Glebe teaching the Lord's Prayer and Articles of Faith for catechism and has done so for as long as I can recall. Mistress Hayes is widow to the alderman and has no children on account of her slippery womb. She reads the Word from the Black Book and is a champion of the new ways in the parish.

When we entered the Glebe that hot Lammas Day we were grateful for its stout walls and shadowed hall. The three of us waited in our old school room. Ten harvests had passed since Eve and I sat there, more for Meg. That afternoon the dust from scythed corn caught in the sunlight; it was the same we had washed from our ears and eyes over the past week; its smell minded us of, not just aches and blisters but of malt for beer and bread, too. That afternoon the school bell made us feel seven years old again. Mistress Hayes wore her hair tied under a white coif. As always she wore a robe of black velvet. There, in that schoolroom, the chain around her waist caught my eye for it glinted on hips that could not hold children; now those hips were locked and secure. The Mistress looked us up and down; then, she fastened on Meg. She said, "How fares Goodwife Mead?"

"She grows weaker every day."

"Whilst you, Margaret Mead, grow bigger by the hour." Mistress Hayes turned to Eve and me. She said, "You know this means you cannot stay at Gonge?"

Eve said, "We may still pay the tithe."

"This is not about the tithe." We knew that nothing we could say would soften her for Mistress Hayes had it in for us Meads. She said, "You girls must marry. In the coming weeks I will find a match for each of you. We will start with the First Fruits Procession where you will present the loaves."

Afterwards, we sat in shame in that same classroom where we had learned our catechism. Like my cousins I bridled at the prospect of being offered to another. Meg said, "She takes me for a slattern."

Eve said, "She means to make a show of us at Lammas Thanksgiving."

I said, "She is laying *us* on the altar."

The First Fruits procession falls on the first Sunday of August. It is the time when the new grain from the harvest is paraded around the green. At First Fruits the boys ogle the girls that present the bread for it is known that they will soon be wed.

The journey back home was hotter than the way out. With most of the harvest gathered the drovers were busy moving more cattle onto the commons. At Southbury Field we spied a herd of White Park steers. They had long horns and were finer than any we had seen, even at Barnet Fair. As we watched, a wagon laden with fodder came in from the London Road. Spotting the red livery of the boy who opened the gate I knew that the cart came from Durant's Arbour. I said, "M'Lud Wroth's cattle are straying on our commons, again."

Meg said, "Know you, Mistress Hayes now keeps a herd?"

Eve said, "Where M'Lud's cattle wander, the Glebe's will soon follow."

Back at Gonge the meadow was alive with gnats; they whined around my ears and stuck to me in the hot air. When I dropped the pail into the well I found myself wondering how long I might stay and where I might end up. In the cottage Meg was skinning a hare for the pot. Josh Mead had lamped it on the marsh and it had hung in the wood-store for three days – long enough to be high. Having broken the skin she ran her thumb between fur and flesh and pulled off the jacket with one tug. The body of the hare was blue as clay. Its guts smelt of our life by the marsh: of shit, oil and bog cotton. I brought in fuel and kindled the fire. Eve said, "Tonight, we will prepare candles for Potter's."

I said, "We have plenty of beeswax in the store."

With the hare baked we set about boiling more water on the stove. I took a slab of beeswax and beat it in a hemp sack by the midden. This we melted in a double kettle until the smell of the hive mixed with wood smoke and juice from the cooling hare. To make a wick Eve threaded a strand of hemp through a juniper berry; this she dipped in wax. Meanwhile Meg fetched the linen purse. She said, "You must do this for you are the closest blood-tie." My fingers were sticky so I was loath to touch my mother's fine needlework.

Eve said, "Worry not, for all will be burnt at Potter's. Your brother must rest complete. We will return every last bit of him so he may rise at Last Lammas." I was taken aback.

"He may yet be saved?"

"We shall pray to the Holy Mother for she is immaculate."

I pinched the birth curl between my forefinger and thumb and twisted it around the wick. When I was sure that every last hair had stuck fast I dipped the length of it in molten wax to seal all together. We made three candles that evening – one for each of us. Mine was to petition Mary for Robert's life in the hereafter, Eve's was to charm her beloved and Meg's was for the soul of her unborn child.

That night I dreamt I was back at the mill before my time; I was watching for my brother. It was midnight and a November moon had risen above the marsh. A body bobbed in the millstream and I watched it turn over in the flow. Robert's face was puckered up – his eyes squeezed shut against the darkness. As I watched he was drawn under the shadow of the mill wheel to the steps where my father waited. My father caught the drowned child in safe hands and held him as later he held me. He cradled the lifeless body and waited for the woman who approached from the other bank. It was the first time my mother and father met.

The next morning Aunt Mead summoned the three of us to her bed. Her ire was up. She said, "Alice Hayes needs knocking off her perch." Then she turned from Meg to me. "She was nothing before she met the alderman and she will be nothing again, soon enough."

I looked at Meg, then at Eve. Eve said, "The mistress wants this land for pasture."

Meg said, "Know you, she grew up on Bradley Moor, between here and Potter's?"

The Friday before Lammas Thanksgiving the weather broke. As my aunt predicted, no sooner had the Dog Star left the morning sky than the heavens opened. The rain rinsed chaff from the thatch and dung from the road; it made the brooks flow free and the mill wheels turn. The cooler days that followed minded us of autumn: of picking hazels and crabs. A good harvest should bring joy but that year it brought fear.

Our Saviour said, *Suffer little children, forbid them not to come to me, for such is the kingdom of Heaven.*

When Reverend Gunn read these words in church, Meg Mead scoffed. I saw her hold her belly in one hand and her rosary in the other. During the Psalm, we three girls sang 'Purge me with hyssop', knowing we must submit to Mistress Hayes.

At the Glebe the maid pointed to the washhouse where our teacher waited with her sleeves rolled up. Mistress Hayes held a bar of lye soap in her right hand and a paddle from the washhouse in her other. She said, "Throw your duds in the basket, I have stitched new robes for you all." Because she meant to burn our gowns, which were flea-ridden, we hid our beeswax candles in our shoes. I was last in the line and watched Meg kneel. Mistress Hayes worked up the soap into a lather and told my cousin to untie her hair. Then she plunged her head into the tub before wrenching her up by the scruff and working the lye into her scalp. When she was finished she left Meg to towel herself off and used the lye on Eve and me.

Afterwards, scalded, we sat outside the Glebe with our backs to the church. The clouds had cleared now and, beyond the flint wall, the churchyard was again bright in the harvest light. We looked one to another. Skin smarting from vinegar and dressed in the same ill-fitting gowns we were like corn moppets twisted by our mistress's hand. A cart drawn by two oxen had stopped outside Church Field. We watched the man and his boy unload poles and ropes for the Lammas Fair.

Meg said, "They're the Browns from Bury Farm. Come on, we may cadge a lift to Potter's Field." The Browns' cart was as ramshackle as you could find. Sitting on its bare boards, we felt every stone in the road, so much so we wondered if the axle would break. By the time we reached Southbury Field Meg was bleeding. The blood seeped through the gown Mistress Hayes had stitched and spotted the bare wood of the cart.

The sun had already set when we helped Meg down onto the road. Pa Brown looked wary but he gave us his lantern before prodding his oxen into life and leaving us in the twilight.

For a while we three cousins stood in silence under the Judas tree, then I helped Meg over the stile to where the grass grew wet and long. It was my first time standing on the turf of Potter's Field and I followed a well-worn path to a clump of yews on the ridge. When we reached the hollow that lay behind them, Eve told me to hold the lantern high while she helped Meg. The shrine was small enough: an idol the size of a headstone stood below a rock where water spilled from the earth. I had never seen such a thing and mind how the Virgin held her palms outstretched at her sides. For a while we stepped amongst the half-buried pots there but we could not find a space for the long growth of summer hid more urns. Feeling these underfoot, we were afraid to tread lest we trample a child's remains. So we stepped back from the shrine and made our offerings there.

In the dying light, Eve said:

> *'Hail Mary, full of grace,*
> *Blessed art thou amongst women,*
> *And blessed is the fruit of your womb, Jesus.'*

She pulled up her sister's robe so the spots of blood fell onto the clay. Then she bid me light the first of the candles. Eve said:

> '*Holy Mary, Mother of God,*
> *Pray for Margaret and her child,*
> *That just as they are one blood now,*
> *They may stay together in life everlasting.*
> *Amen.*'

After this, *we lit Robert's candle and asked for intercession.* When the bitter whiff of his kiss-curl was gone I looked around for a sign but there was nothing, only gnats in the dying light. I said, "How shall I know if Robert is saved?"

Meg said, "You shall not know. You must hold that hope in your heart."

Eve said, "Believe it and it will be."

But I could not just believe it, so I said, "*What* will be?"

Then Eve pointed at the urns, laid in Potter's Field for generations. She said, "At Last Lammas when wrongs are put right all these forgotten ones – the unbaptised, the stillborn, the unwanted – will rise and take their rightful place with our Lord."

Then Meg said, "And the wicked, those like Reverend Gunn and Mistress Hayes who have barred them from the churchyard, will pay the price in Hell."

* * *

Goodcole raised his hand to stop Sawyer. "Enough woman. Waste not your time for curses are what brought you here and the Church is your only hope." He checked through his transcription and, referring to the words that he had underlined, he noted down the following paragraph:

Your cousins the Meads did not live within the precepts of the Church. Because your brother Robert was not baptised, you prayed to an idol with them in a field.

He scanned what he had written and then turned back to Sawyer. "You must know that such rites are heathen; they run contrary to Scripture and have led you to the Devil. Tomorrow I will visit again and we will resume. In the meantime pray for your immortal soul."

Day 2

A cold dawn greeted Goodcole when he rose in his lodgings that Palm Sunday. He splashed water on his face and then stood beside the hearth where he intoned a grace for Passiontide. His wife Anne was at his side and, after he had concluded the prayer, she proffered a pax cake. Goodcole accepted but took only a bite before he replaced the broken remains on the pewter plate. Last night the aroma of her baking had promised much but today the biscuit tasted stale. He drained a beaker of mead and moved to the hallway where he pulled on his winter coat. Even with his back to her he knew she was watching him, willing him to succeed against uneven odds. He shouldered his bag, drew back the bolt and without looking back entered the alley.

Out in Newgate Street a chill south-easterly made Goodcole's eyes run. He could smell charcoal from the braziers at the cathedral and sensed the thrill of the start of Holy Week.

Once inside the gaol he made his way down to Limbo where he greeted Maddox and, holding his lantern high, entered Sawyer's cell. For a while Goodcole settled himself at his desk. He wrote the date at the top of the page and was about to address Sawyer when she spoke to him out of the darkness.

"You work the Sabbath," she said.

"This is God's work. Now, explain the Devil's access to your soul and confess your guilt." For a while there was silence, then Elizabeth answered him.

* * *

The first time the Devil spoke to me I was already with child. At Advent, having escaped Mistress Hayes and my parish, I had wed Edward Sawyer and moved to his village of Winchmore. Winchmore is across the bounds in Edmonton; here it sits on the rising ground close to the Lord's Grove. The time of the Devil's coming was in March and all was frozen fast for there was no end to winter that year. That first time the Devil came at night and he chose the shape of a fox. It was the week before Lady Day and I woke to the smell of sulphur for his maw was close to mine, his breath hot in my face. The Devil had red eyes, was silver as shekels in the moonlight and had me pinioned to my cot. I wasn't fooled.

I said, "Who let Satan into my bed?"

The Devil said, "*You* did." Hot coals watched me draw breath, claws pressed my ribs and a silken tongue gave me a great lick. The dog-fox tasted the salt off each pap and looked up when there was no milk there, then he dug his snout lower to my belly, "You are with child, so now you must choose."

"How so?"

"I will either have your soul or that of your child; tell me your choice when I return." With these words the Devil slipped off me and loped into the night. For a while I lay in fright. I could feel the chill east wind under the door and the warmth of Edward asleep in the bed beside me. Though my bump was slight I placed my palm over it and swore an oath to my child, 'I'll have you blessed and baptised before that fiend can get near.' Then I got up and cleansed each nipple with willow water; I did this to rid me of the brimstone spittle that burned there.

A week passed and the cold did not relent. The London Road was busier that March and many in our village warned of bilks and tricksters in our midst. One day, when my work was done, I ventured to the crossroads in Palmer's Green to watch the carts and footsloggers pass by. They came from far afield for there was dearth in three counties and all were City-bound.

Later that day I told Edward what the other wives were saying. I said, "Agnes Barfoot says we are cursed and this winter is sent to punish us." Edward looked at me through clay-blue eyes.

He said, "This cold could be the making of us."

"How so, when nothing grows and even the forest is barren?"

"We have the kilns. They will sustain us."

"If the forest dies, then so will we."

"Worry not, *for the forest will provide*." He said the words like a charm: as if just voicing them made them true. Then, to soothe me, Edward told me again about the coppices where he worked: how this Lady Day last year's timber would first be hewn, then splintered; how he and his brothers would bake all in the firepits and how new grades of charcoal would be carried by packhorse to the City. Edward said, "Prices will make for a fat purse for it's an ill wind and all that." For a while I wondered at my husband's words; I knew Master Estry the woodward paid but a pittance but I was newly-wed and keen to show some cheer, so I hid my doubt and turned to the dark line of trees that marked the edge of the Lord's Grove. I minded how each year trees die back to grow again and told myself that, though the sap be deep in the heartwood now, it might soon rise and with it all God's creatures – that is the bees, birds and beasts that together make the spring a joy. I told myself all this but part of me still worried that the Sawyers had brought the Devil to our door.

In Winchmore, as elsewhere, Lady Day is a busy time for it marks the start of our New Year. Aside from work in the forest there is Bush Hiring Fair to attend, livestock to buy and spring planting to begin. That March winter put a stop to this, for with drifts of snow blocking the lanes and ditches full of ice, there was no point blunting a shovel or breaking a ploughshare on ground as hard as a mason's stone. Lady Day is also a time when tithes are due and forfeits settled. The freeze did nothing to stop this reckoning; instead it heaped debts on those least able to pay, so in Winchmore that March the threat of the bailiff's knock was on everyone's minds. On everyone's but the Sawyers that is, for that year we Sawyers were flush with silver.

It is a strange thing that a wife can be full of hope yet full of dread at the same time; perhaps this is just a mother's lot. On the eve of Lady Day, as a blow-in to the parish with a child in my womb, I was fearful of many things. I knew other wives were watching so the Devil's word that he would come again left me taut.

I thought, *what if they see him entering the cottage; what if they hear his hellish words and what if it is Edward that brought him to our bed?* That night, needing some relief, I lit a candle and addressed myself to the Holy Mother. I prayed, 'Let me too find favour.' In this I used her own words to Archangel Gabriel for I knew that once even Mary had been afraid.

The first morning of the New Year Winchmore awoke to the sound of marching feet. It was not yet light and Sawyers' toft was cold as a corpse. I had risen early to stoke the hearth and had no sooner put kindling on last night's coals than I heard the baying of dogs. These were not the mutts that skulk round the midden looking for scraps but a pack of hounds hot on the scent of their quarry. Behind them came the tramp of armed men. Sensing Edward's warmth in the darkness behind me, I half turned; his mother, too, was standing in the doorway. Ma Sawyer was wrapped in a shawl and was pale as a ghost.

I said, "Is it a hunting party?"

Edward bent his ear low, "It's the nightwatch, most likely from Arnos but 'tis a rare thing for them to use dogs." The pack was passing outside our door now and we could hear the snivelling of snouts and scraping of paws as they skittered over the frozen ground. When the marching feet too had tramped by, my husband opened the latch and we peered at the fiery glow of torches spreading in the mist. "That's Grocer Weld's men and they're making for the Holy Oak at Highwood Gate." A bony hand pulled first me then my husband inside. Mother Sawyer slammed the door and shot the bolt home.

She said, "Stay close, or you'll let the Devil in." The old woman picked a sprig of rosemary from her apron and threw it on the hearth. Then she fished out her bone-bead rosary and spoke the Word from Psalm 58,

> '*Do you judge uprightly, ye sons of men?*
> *Yea, in your heart you work wickedness; ye weigh the*
> *violence of your hands in the earth.*'

Then I knew that it was already too late for her prayer was a rebuke to her sons and all their crooked dealing.

Lady Day dawned clear and still. I had drawn water and was feeding our last goose when Agnes Barfoot stuck her head over the wall. She pointed up the lane.

She said, "They've scorched the Gospel Tree and killed it where it stands."

"Our Holy Oak that marks the bounds?" I dropped the millet and followed her to the bridge. There, where Whappools Brook lay heaped in ice, three stout fellows with staves were guarding the entrance to the chase. Beyond them a crown of branches marked the bounds between Edmonton and Enfield. I turned to our neighbour.

I said, "Who would set a fire in a living tree?" Agnes Barfoot narrowed her eyes.

She said, "You tell me."

Back at the hearth Ambrose and John Sawyer sat at my table. I put out ale and bread but their mood was sour so I left to tend the pigs. Ma Sawyer followed me into the sty. For a while she said nothing, only leant on her stick but presently she took her bone-bead rosary out of her apron and, with her right hand, began to click the beads.

She said, "This business with the nightwatch is a bad do. Your husband is gone. He will not be back… not for a while."

The old woman watched how I took in the news. I nodded to show I was not afraid for I knew better than to ask.

Out in the street a squall was blowing in. Braving the hail I walked back to the scorched tree at Highwood Gate and found the guards gone for no man can tarry in the east wind. The oak was split asunder from root to branch. For a while I moved around its girth and peered within where all was burned, then I stepped inside its blackened shell and knelt where hailstones melted into char. How dark and bitter it was in that hollow. With bare hands I sifted through the ash until I felt, not just dead coals, but shards of bone. Between finger and thumb I picked out a milk tooth. The milk tooth was smooth as a ball of hail, except it had a jag of jaw at its root. I searched but could find no trace of the rest of the child's skull for all was baked and there were only bits. Above me a figure blotted out the light.

Agnes Barfoot said, "Ho, 'tis you, Lysbeth."

Other faces crowded in. "The Enfield woman has her hands in our tree. She means to grind the bone to powder."

"Aye, to make bone char for bone char has made Sawyers rich." When I heard them I knew I must leave for the Devil was due to return and, with the baby growing greater in my womb, I could not risk staying in Winchmore another day.

I entered the Lord's Grove the day after Edward left. I minded his promise that 'the forest will provide' and thought to find him at the kilns where I might confront him with the true nature of his pact. Though I knew not yet where Sawyers' firepits were, I planned to follow Whappools Brook south until I saw smoke but I had reckoned without the fences for the grove is not open like the chase; it is coppiced timber and each part is owned by a jealous lord. It was still dark when I climbed the stile at Manister's Barn and stepped down into that place. I carried some food and a pottle of water and, though I could see no paths, I pushed through the brush that pressed me in the dark. This first part of the grove is called Prior's; the trees are hazel and hornbeam and at that time they were cut shoulder-high amongst the chestnut. Keeping the dawn behind me, I walked west towards the brook until I came to a ditch. The ditch was lined with spikes and topped by a fence the height of a man. Unable to go forward I followed the trough up a slope where first wild birch, then ash had found a foothold. The ground here was steep and I had to grapple roots to clamber to the copse that crowned the slope. It was on this ridge that the Devil came to me once again.

This second time the Devil took the guise of a flea. I had scarcely reached the top when I got an itch under my arm. For a while I thought nothing of it but then I felt a nip so I stopped and gave myself a scratch. When I pulled out my left hand I found a mite perched on my knuckle; I knew it was Satan for he had seven red eyes.

I said, "Ah Imp, why do you come to me, now?"

The Devil said, "I have stuck to you all along for I feared you might give me the slip." The Devil crouched low. "Now, mind your choice: which is it to be, your soul or that of your child?" I cupped my other palm over my belly.

I said, "My child is not yet quickened; you must wait." The Devil shook his head.

He said, "You are lying. Besides, I must know now for it is Holy Week and I'm a soul short."

I looked at him scuttling there and was minded to give him a good swat, but instead I sought to buy time.

I said, "Wait long enough and you may have us both."

"You would give me *both* your own soul and that of your child?" At first the Devil gave a little skip but then he sensed a trick. "Why would you agree to that?"

I said, "My child and I are of one flesh and would not be apart. Heaven would mean nothing to me if I was not with her, indeed it would be a type of Hell." Now the Devil was gleeful.

"So be it but this pact must be signed in blood. Where would you have me bite you?" I knew I had outreached myself then and would have squished him but fleas are quick so I lifted my skirt and pointed.

I said, "Bite my arse. I care not for it is already numb with cold." So the Devil sucked my blood from a pimple, then he jumped to the ground and was gone.

On the ridge I knelt in sorrow for I had deceived myself. I was a fool for no one gyps the Devil; moreover, I had broken my oath to my child and caught us both in a bind. I said a prayer to my mother for I minded her time on the marsh with Robert. How, I wondered, had the Devil appeared to her: was it as a fox, a flea or an angel, even? So I faced the dawn; in far-off Winchmore a cock crowed but I knew I could not return there for I meant to find Edward to have it out with him, so I raised myself up and carried on.

Beyond that ridge was a ravine where a cabin sat in the woods. The cabin was roughly hewn: its roof was of brash and its chimney of stone. From the slope I watched a man wheel a barrow from the wood-store to the hearth; I knew he was not Edward for he was aged and lacked my husband's keen stride. When the man entered the cabin, I climbed down to slip by but I had reckoned without the dog. The dog was big and black and it leapt up at me.

"Who goes there?" The woodsman stood in the doorway. He called the mutt to heel and looked first at me then at my meagre bundle.

I said, "Know you the way to Sawyers' kiln?"

At this he softened then invited me in. Inside, the cabin smelt of sap. The man pulled up a stool and poured us both a warming posset. His name was Marlow and he knew Winchmore well.

He said, "You're Ned Sawyer's wife; I have seen you at church. Your man won't come here for the coppices are closely watched."

I cupped a hand over my belly and said, "My husband promised that the kilns would sustain us."

At this, Marlow rose to lift an urn from the hearth. He scooped a handful of dust from the jar and held it before me. The dust was black but in its mass were grains of white and silver, too. He let the powder drop through his fingers into his cup.

He said, "This is bone char; I make it, just as Sawyers do. Bone char is a cure ground from stags' horn burnt in oak. You may drink it down for it wards off ill." He passed his cup so that I might drink.

I said, "Can it cure all?"

"All but a broken heart."

"So Edward must face the beak for making this?" The old man drained his cup, dust and all.

He said, "Not for this. Your husband has had dealings with diviners from London. Theirs is a dark art of which I dare not speak – you being with child and all."

Later, when I had eaten some potage stew, Marlow counselled me to return home. He said the forest was full of shades: strange dog-men that would steal my soul and that of my child. I could have answered that I had carried the Devil halfway from Winchmore but instead I asked the way to Whappools Brook.

The bridge over the brook was but a few poles of timber lashed with a rope. When I crossed the ice my doubts multiplied for I knew that wherever I went the Devil was waiting for me now. The trees on the far side were alder: cut waist high close to the bank. I knew the kilns must be on dryer ground so I followed the path until I came to a flame-red hedge. This hedge was dogwood and marked the bounds of Wroth's holding. This being the Lord's Grove, which is Burghley's parish, Wroth's holding was small: no more than thirty rood. I quickly left it behind and came to a coppice of willow. Here I heard voices and came upon a group splitting poles by a cart; they were seven hewers and they stopped their chat when I came near. This time I made no mention of Edward's name, instead I asked the foreman the way to Estry's oaks.

The foreman said, "Who's asking?"

"I am Beth… Cronwell from Winchmore."

"Well, Beth Cronwell from Winchmore, Master Estry would know what business you have in the grove?"

"I seek mistletoe to make a love charm." The men guffawed but their foreman was not fooled.

"A love charm in Holy Week?" He looked askance and said, "Estry's oaks are out of bounds. Besides there are pits dug round here."

"Pits?"

"Aye, firepits that are hidden under snow and you'd likely fall in one." He pointed to my left. "Pass forty paces yonder and you will find the Bleeding Tree. The Bleeding Tree marks the centre of this place we call the Lord's Grove. Make your offerings there, then return home before night comes."

At first I made down the path but I soon turned off for I smelt smoke and was sure Edward was close. Following the smoke to a dyke, I climbed over and found myself in a rood of oaks: some of these were saplings, straight and new, while others were full-grown with limbs that twisted like a carpenter's screw. Walking amongst these older trees, I saw stacks of timber stripped of bark, which told me this was Estry's patch for at that time the woodward ran a tannery and paid peelers by the score. I knew then that I was close to Sawyers' pit; all I needed was to find Edward and learn the secret of his craft.

The first kiln was but a hole dug in the clay. Finding it cold, I walked on until I came to a clearing where smoke rose in a wide circle from the earth. The soil was hot here and I stood a while amongst the clods to thaw my toes. I stepped back when I caught a whiff of sulphur for I minded the Devil's brimstone breath and feared that a cauldron lay underneath my feet. To be safe I moved beyond the clearing and stood behind a trunk to watch what moved through the forest. All day I waited there but no one came: not Edward, not Master Estry's men, not the Devil himself – only smoke rose from the smouldering ground. By evening the silence had become wearisome for there was nothing in that place, only stillness and I could hear the beating of my own heart. So it was that, with the light fading and no refuge found, I faced a night alone in the forest. Too late I minded the warnings to return home. After a while I fell asleep against a tree.

Past midnight I was awoken by a wail. The moon shone into the clearing and cast shadows amongst the looming trees.

I was bitterly cold. The cry sounded again; it came from a single breath and started low and rose before falling away to a whimper. It was the call of a wolf and it came from behind me where I had left the path. Fearful that the beast had picked up my scent I thought to take flight and was barely on my feet when the cry came again but this time from far ahead of me. That is when a voice first spoke to me in my head; the voice was my mother's.

Grace said, "Now you must choose between the flesh and the spirit." I took a step back but then fear gripped me and I took to my heels. I knew not how far I ran that night. I ran through a drift of snow; I ran through a thicket of thorns; I ran over a pile of stumps and on until the ground gave way and I fell into a pit.

The blow from the fall knocked me out cold and for a while I lay in ash and bone. When I came to Grace's words were once more in my head. "You must choose between the flesh and the spirit." This time I answered her.

I said, "I have promised our souls already so what hope is there?"

Grace said, "You must give up all hope. Become as nothing but keep faith in your heart, then you may live."

By morning I was failing. I knew I must find a refuge, if not for myself then for my child, yet the kiln was deep and its sides were sheer. For a while I sat on my haunches, then – fearful that this cinder pit would be our grave – I stood again and hammered with my fists. This time a shard broke from the wall. Reaching through the crust, I found that new roots were pushing forth underground. This gave me heart so I prised away more, then gained a foothold and scaled the hole.

The way back was hard for I had taken a knock and had cramps in my belly. I was passing along the path shown by Estry's men when I spotted blood in the snow. At first I thought I was on the trail of a wounded bird but then I saw the blood came from me. Feeling the flow from my womb I knew then I must rest, or else I would lose my child, so I thought to find the Bleeding Tree.

The tree was an ancient yew. Its branches were like spires and the bark was blasted with age. Sitting against the roots that coiled into the frozen ground, I pressed my hand against the sap that oozed from the tree's side. The sap smelt sweet like rotting flesh.

I said, "Is this the Bleeding Tree?"

Grace said, "It is the Tree of Life."

I said, "Then how come it reeks of death?"

I pulled my hand free of the amber glue. The resin gave off a powerful scent like myrrh and mandrake root; it made me want to sleep for evermore so I dropped my head back against the sticky bark.

When I awoke, my child was lying at my feet. Seeing we two were still joined as one, I picked her up and pressed her to my heart to keep some warmth in her. I had hardly put her to my breast when I heard the padding of paws. The beast loped out of the mist. The wolf was black; he had red eyes and a shaggy mane. He dug his snout deep into my belly; then, he sniffed at the bloody snow. I covered my child against my breast but the Devil would not be denied.

He said, "You are like your mother before you."

I said, "What deal did you strike with Grace?"

"I struck no deal for my demand is always the same: 'give me your soul or that of your child'."

I said, "So I was spared." At this the Devil's lip curled back; he bared his fangs.

"Who says?"

"Why else would you come to me now? A soul cannot be given twice." At this the Devil pushed his maw so close I could smell his brimstone breath.

He said, "If you were spared it is because I ordained it. Now you are a begetter of souls and each time you bear a child I will return to claim what's mine." With that he snapped his jaws shut and wrenched my firstborn from my grasp.

* * *

For a while nothing stirred in the cell, then Goodcole put down his quill. "At last we have come to it," he said.

"Come to what?" Sawyer answered.

"We have come to the root of all, which is sin. Now I will speak plainly: because your uncle deemed himself so high and because your aunt stooped so low you have rejected the Church. Know you, to be at one with God you must atone, otherwise your soul belongs to the Devil? As your story says, your sin repeats your mother's sin, which repeats her mother's before that and so on all the way back to the Garden." For a while there was silence in the cell.

"So I was guilty even before I was born?" she said.

"Precisely, as it says in Psalm 51, you were conceived in sin and shapen in iniquity. Like all women you are unclean so all that issues from you is unclean. Only when you purify yourself through Mother Church can you atone." Goodcole stood up and pushed the stool he had been sitting on over to her. "We have at least made a start today. After Sunday service I will draw up a draft and, when I have checked the facts, I will return so that you may put your mark to your confession." So saying, he packed up his things and thumped three times on the door.

The chapel was situated under the guardhouse close to a spiral staircase that formed the main conduit between floors. Because there was no direct entrance from the stairwell, Goodcole was forced to walk a roundabout route along two corridors; these led past the refectory and the Stone Hold. Fretting that he would be late for the first meeting of Holy Week he reached the chapel door before second bell. He had barely time to prop open the door and rest his lantern before the scrape of chains announced the arrival of the first convicts. For a while he busied himself wiping grime off the lectern, then he opened Cranmer's Book of Common Prayer and appraised his congregation. In Newgate's cramped chapel more than twenty prisoners stood with heads bowed; all were what passed for men, though some were callow boys – most wore leg irons. Goodcole raised his voice. When he spoke he measured out his words in morsels. These he fed phrase by phrase to those who stood hungry for the Word,

"Brethren,

We stand here in godly discipline to…

Mind how notorious sinners are first…

Put to penance, then punished in this world.

We do this so that your souls may be saved."

Goodcole surveyed the ranks of felons. Each time he named a sin his eye flitted along the rows until it came to rest on a bowed head; in this he was like a shepherd watching over his flock. His litany now took the form of a call and response.

"Cursed are the covetous – adulterers and fornicators."

There was a grunt from a sharp-beaked fellow at the end of

the line. Goodcole fixed him with a stare and waited for him to respond with the others.

"*Amen.*"

"Cursed are slanderers, drunkards, extortioners."

"*Amen.*"

"Cursed is he that slays the soul of innocent blood."

"*A—*"

"For, as it is written in the book of Deuteronomy, 'Now is the axe put unto the root, so that… every tree that bringeth not forth good fruit… is hewn down and cast into the fire'."

"*Amen.*"

When the service was over, Goodcole watched the inmates lift their leg irons free of the sawdust-strewn floor. He waited for his charges to file out, then stepped forward to accost the last in line. This last man was a head taller than the rest and was deep in conversation with the sharp-beaked fellow almost half his height. Goodcole stepped between them; he pointed to the smudge of ash on the man's forehead – the wound was already blistering. "What is this Popish mark?" he asked. The prisoner was William Deicrowe about whom Goodcole had overheard some talk.

Deicrowe spoke with the assured tone of one versed in both Scripture and the law. "Today is Palm Sunday: the day our Saviour rode into Jerusalem," he said.

Goodcole looked up at the prisoner who was new to the chapel. He detected a West Country dialect softened by years of education; moreover, he could almost smell the touch of a priest off him. "I'll have no Romish rites performed in this prison: neither in the Master's Side nor in the Stone Hold," Goodcole said.

"Reverend, would you deny a man his hosanna when Calvary follows so close behind?" Deicrowe reached down to pick up the chunk of wood that served as a doorstop; he inspected its pitted grain then tucked it under his arm. "This will help me to while away the hours ahead." So saying, he strode back to his quarters for he wore no chains.

Goodcole caught the door and watched him go. He should have called him back but to do so would be to lose face. Instead, he decided to bide his time and to find out more about this man.

An hour later the chaplain watched the last of the women carry their chains out of the chapel; their service had been a shorter version of that conducted for the men. When all had clinked down the corridor, he swept the sawdust into piles and brushed these into a barrel that stood in an alcove under a walled-in arch. He surveyed the cramped space. Once this chamber had been grander with more doorways but a new stairwell, installed after a fire many years before, had cut the space by half and now all the entrances were sealed off bar one. These days the chapel had a forgotten feel, like an ill-sited storeroom stuck at the end of a passageway; only a few convicts spent time here and most never visited at all.

He pricked up his ears. Beyond the grind of doors and shake of keys he listened for the distant sound of St Sepulchre's bell ringing from beyond the prison. A chorus of jeers rose and subsided from the Stone Hold and then his patience was rewarded: he caught the toll of the bell, sounding slow and steady from outside the City wall. Patience, Goodcole reminded himself, was the key to this job and the regular measure of the church bell was a reminder of the prize that awaited him if he could pass off his tenure successfully; yet part of him was still fearful and a quiver of doubt passed up his spine. He thought of the witch lying in her filth in the lowest pit of the prison and wondered too, about Master Dicker riding back through Tottenham past High Cross. Although this posting was a step up from Ludgate Gaol, its opportunity was fraught with peril. Above him shone the prospect of a parsonage in the City but below lurked a slipway into the abyss and, in this sinkhole, anything was possible.

The stone treads up to Goodcole's study were worn by the footfalls of those who had held his post before him. At the top he tried not to breathe in too deeply. Although he was used to it now, he could still taste the prison on his tongue. That taste was sour as bile and it divulged Newgate's purpose for the gaol was an iron drain used to sieve sewage; to use Warden Travers' phrase, it was 'a conduit to draw off the waste of the nation'. Unlike a debtors' gaol such as Ludgate, 'the Whit', as felons called it, was plumbed into the criminal court on Old Bailey, itself part of the City's wall. Over time the prison had shaped itself into a funnel with the indicted on the first level, the guilty on the next and those awaiting evacuation to the gallows in Limbo, as the lowest part was called. Picturing the prison as he climbed the stairs, Henry Goodcole was minded of an Italian book he had leafed through in the bookstalls of St Paul's. The book daringly described a journey through Hell to Paradise and, though his Latin had allowed him to grasp little of what was written within, he had gleaned enough to know that Hell was arranged on three levels: with the incontinent – those unable to resist their appetites – on the first, the violent in some middle ring and the malign on the lowest. Here, those who had lost their souls to evil dwelt for all eternity with the Devil himself.

The study was small and airless but it was a refuge of sorts. He hung his lamp on its hook and sat down at his writing desk. His hand brushed the leather binding of the new edition of the King's Bible, then moved to the well-worn cover of his beloved psalter. The book had a crushed look and would hardly lie flat for it was his companion for life and had been stuffed into countless bags over the years. Goodcole opened the book at Psalm 51. He removed the folded letter that served as a bookmark and smoothed out the single page marked by a woman's hand. By the glow of the tallow lantern he read:

Dearest Father,

In piety I write to tell of my first days in service to Alderman Bull. Truly this is a household of wonders and I am most grateful to be here. Presently I am under the tutelage of a maid named Lucy Remnant and though I mostly work downstairs in the pump room, on Wednesday I had occasion to fetch linens from the panelled corridor outside my lady's chamber. What a view I there witnessed for, through mullioned glass, I spied the river: the Thames was a bright bar of silver flashing in the April sun and before it lay all of London.

Be assured that though the hours be long and the work hard I do not neglect to read the psalms you send me. Each evening after my prayers I put aside a moment to recite each and make most heartfelt appeal to God the Father. May He preserve you in your important work.

In all obedient duty,
Your daughter,
Joan

Goodcole traced his firstborn's signature with his finger. Needing to respond, he lifted his bag down from the peg and unpacked paper, a set of quills, sand and ink. Noting how worn the quills were, he trimmed one with a blade and then leant forward to write.

My dearest Joan,

Thank you for your news. It pleases me to know that you now live in a healthier part of the City as part of the alderman's household. As you may know, of late, Master Bull has acted as a rare champion of our family, supporting my advancement to my present post. In our own ways we may both now act as his faithful servants.

In undertaking my work I have, like you, been much consoled by the psalms. Never forget that The Book of Psalms was our Lord Jesus's own prayer book during his trial and when we follow his ordeal on the cross there is no better instruction than to read the Word that is contained therein. With this in mind and this being the start of Holy Week, I will remind us both of these words from King David's Psalm 118.

*The stone which the builders refused is become the head
stone of the corner.
This is the Lord's doing; it is marvellous in our eyes.*

Please write again for nothing 'refreshes my heart' as
much as reading what comes from you.

With all affection,
Your father

Goodcole waited for the ink to dry; reading over his words, he
felt elation. In particular the couplet from the psalm took on
a new meaning within the context of his letter for, although
he was condemned to work in this rathole, his daughter
was now free of the prison. Joan was his firstborn child and
though he had a pair of twin boys besides, she was the apple
of his eye. It was not something he had planned for, not
something he could explain, just something he had felt from
the first moment he had held her. Lying there, swaddled in
his lap, a clot of her mother's blood still twisted in her hair,
she was a moment of pure joy and he would do anything
now – fourteen years later – to keep her away from this: the
court, his lodgings in Newgate Street and the desperate stink
of the prison. The knowledge that she was now living in a
healthier, more prosperous part of the City gave him hope.
At last, for all his frustrations and false starts, he was building
a better future. That Joan was now part of the alderman's
household was providence; it was the Lord's doing – proof of
a personal bond between him and his maker. He told himself
this, but a sliver of doubt remained for his world was full
of signs and what was given could easily be taken away. For

a moment Goodcole cradled the paradox of his belief: how could someone so pure result from a carnal act? The answer of course was beyond him – known only to God. 'Thy will be done, on earth as it is in heaven', he prayed.

At midday Goodcole took the long corridor to the Master's Side. The Master's Side was on the south side of the prison and was so called because it had once been the warden's chambers. These days its rooms were shabby and cold but they were at least bright, lit by high barred windows that let in the April sunshine. Steeling himself against a cold draught, Goodcole approached the guard who lounged against the door.

"I'm looking for William Deicrowe," he said.

The guard nodded but said nothing.

"Is he here?"

In answer the guard first opened the door and, after pulling the blankets off several sleeping felons, shook his head. Goodcole pressed a groat into the man's palm.

"Has he had visitors?"

Again the guard shook his head. Then, sensing that he should earn his coin, he pointed to a low trestle bed. "He whittles," he said.

"Whittles?" Goodcole stepped through the stale reek of grog and sifted through the dark wood chips that lay sprinkled on the blankets. He remembered the block of wood that Deicrowe had removed from the chapel. *So he carves*, he thought. He pinched one of the chips between finger and thumb. Carving was something he associated with sailors; he recalled the West Country accent softened by years of education and imagined Deicrowe grounding a skiff in a cove and helping a priest onto wet shingle. He nodded at the guard and took his leave.

Downstairs in the refectory the men were filing in for lunch. Goodcole inserted himself behind a pair of dark-eyed tinkers and held out a bowl for a ladleful of slop. He picked up a wooden spoon and turned to survey the hall. There, several rows beyond a quarrelsome clump of hoods, sat the hunched figure of Deicrowe. Goodcole chose a bench some distance away and sat down to observe. The papist was not alone: he was deep in conversation with the same sharp-beaked fellow he had stood beside in the chapel. Goodcole knew the man from Ludgate: his name was George Scald. Scald was a petty thief and a procurer with contacts outside the prison and could lay his hands on almost anything. Yet if Deicrowe was hoping to keep his secrets close, he had made a mistake because Scald was also a snitch, passing on prisoners' requests directly to the warden. Goodcole smoothed the slop around the rim of his bowl and looked again at the two men. The body language was of a deal being struck with each party alternately leaning forward to say their piece. Then Deicrowe did something entirely unexpected: tipping back his head so only the whites of his eyes showed, he reached into his mouth and pulled something out with a bloodied hand. Lit in the glow of the tallow Goodcole caught a glint as Deicrowe passed a gold molar to Scald. Goodcole watched Scald pocket the tooth. *Payment*, he thought, but was it for bringing something in or smuggling something out of the prison?

Back in the chapel Goodcole was fitting brighter candles when he heard the tramp of feet in the corridor outside. Noting the speed and weight of the footfall, he knew he had been summoned. He picked up his Book of Common Prayer and waited for the door to swing open. The guard was one of the sheriff's own and he wore the red and white livery of the

London Company. He barely glanced at Goodcole and issued his command without greeting.

"Warden Travers requires your presence. You must attend his chambers now."

Goodcole bit back his ire at the man's lack of respect. He snuffed out the candles and followed the guard's retreating back down the corridor.

At the top of the South Tower the chaplain regarded the oak door with its polished brass fittings. The door was ajar but he lifted and dropped the knocker even so.

The warden's chamber was taller than it was wide. A vellum map hung on the wall and a hand-knotted rug softened the floor, turning the flagstones into a crimson bed of blooms. Goodcole stepped forward until his toes touched the plush of the hand-knotted pile. He looked around but Warden Travers was nowhere to be seen. Waiting there, clutching his Book of Common Prayer, he felt that same sense of fright he remembered from seminary school during his twentieth year. He looked at the oak table and chairs that rested on the Persian rug.

"Ordinary... Goodcole?" The voice came from above.

The chaplain looked up to the gallery where all was bathed in light. He swivelled round and flinched; the warden was standing above him. "Yes, Your Honour, I am the ordinary. I was appointed this Lent."

The warden's voice was shrill and unbending. "On whose authority were you appointed?"

"On the authority of the board of governors. I gained a personal recommendation from Alderman Bull. I was ordinary at Ludgate for five years before."

The warden descended the narrow staircase.

When he stepped down onto his level Goodcole saw that he was a small man clothed in sky-blue silks with a white lace ruff fastened around his neck.

The warden motioned to a chair and sat down behind his table. He leant forward and peered at the chaplain. "I've heard the dean opposed your appointment. You are a *lay* preacher, are you not?"

"I am a man of God – though not yet ordained."

The warden leant back in his chair; he narrowed his eyes. "As I say, a *lay* preacher and you believe you can exorcise this witch?"

"I am working on a conversion. Soon she will be back in the fold of the Church."

"You are *working on* it. Well, how long will it take, man?"

"Your Honour, the witch has confessed already. Conversion is merely the next step."

Warden Travers stood up abruptly; he dug his hands into his pockets. "The next step – what is this, the way to Jerusalem? That shrew either obeys or she does not. If she does not we will press her."

"Press her?"

"With weights until she bursts."

Goodcole recoiled. "In all humility, sir. I beg you not to. The woman is contrite and a full confession is all but signed." He held the prayer book in front of him as a shield and this made Travers pause.

The warden stuck out his chin then fondled the lace of his ruff. He spoke now with deliberation. "Ordinary Goodcole, you look to me like a man who is out of his depth. But you are new here and due some consideration: I will give you until tomorrow. If after Monday's dogwatch she has not put her mark to your words, we will settle this matter by other means."

Goodcole bowed. He was about to leave when the warden tapped a filed finger on the tabletop.

"One thing more, I believe you had words with the thief William Deicrowe this morning."

"At prayers. Yes, I did."

Warden Travers focused all his energy on the prison chaplain; his eyes were now narrow slits. "Leave him alone. He's being watched. If you learn anything, then tell the sergeant-at-arms. Do you understand?"

"Perfectly."

Goodcole descended the stairs and walked smartly down the corridor. His meeting with the warden had put him on his mettle. Once more he was impressed by how swift the pace of this prison was compared to Ludgate. There, one gate down along the City wall, debtors languished for years or were released on a whim. Here, the strict timetable of the court held sway. The weekly assizes, linked to the indictments of the City and Middlesex Sessions, were the pump that first sucked prisoners into the prison and then spat them out at the other end. There was something else, too; something ill-suited to a house of correction: a distinct commercial pressure. The chaplain suspected that the prison was being run as a business and not just by the prisoners who fuelled an illicit still in the Stone Hold or the guards who took bribes, but by the sheriff, who, if John Dicker was to be believed, now sat on the board of the London Company in St Sithes Lane. He thought back to the warden high up in the tower above his exotic carpet and map of the world. From where he was standing it was possible to look past the cathedral of St Paul's to that gateway of trade, the river. Who knows, from that height it might even be possible to see the tangle of masts that jostled beyond London Bridge.

Two guards in red and white livery were escorting a prisoner from the Master's Side. Goodcole flattened himself against the damp stonework so they could move past him to the stairs. He thought of the warden's warning about the condemned Catholic who this Sunday had somehow found a priest to give him his last rites in the prison. "He's being watched," the warden had said. In itself, this was not surprising because the prison was full of snitches and spies but why was he being watched? Was it to entrap others or for some other purpose altogether?

Inside his study the bell for the end of the afternoon watch told Goodcole that he did not have much time. Dicker was due back from Tottenham before sunset. The alderman's agent would verify details from the church register gleaned from Edmonton parish and Goodcole needed to be ready to compare notes. He wondered how best to proceed with Sawyer; his method required acceptance and establishing guilt was an important part of that. Acceptance of sin together with a promise of forgiveness by the Almighty was often enough to tip the condemned into signing a confession. After all, when death is certain there is little point fighting it and Goodcole's mantra 'a good death redeems a bad life' had achieved a number of successes in the past. By the time they reached the scaffold some prisoners even looked on him as a friend for he was, as he told them, there to ease their path from this world into the next. Sawyer, though, was not like this. She was actively looking forward to meeting her Maker and appeared to be humouring him at best; moreover, whilst transcribing the stories, Goodcole had picked up her disdain for the act of writing. In her case the tricky bit was not getting her to confess but rather persuading her to put her mark against his. This mattered because a signed confession provided a resolution. It provided a resolution since every offence, whether it was a child stealing a bag of flour or Francis Robinson faking the Great Seal of England, was a challenge to the rightful authority of the realm. Thus the king's justice was nothing less than the resolution of God's order on this earth and it was essential for the condemned to publicly acknowledge their wrongdoing before their peers.

Sifting through his papers, Goodcole collected his thoughts. Soon he would be ready to confront the Winchmore Witch with the true nature and scope of her sin. Now he thought again of the Italian book with its three levels of Hell. Which level would he place Elizabeth Sawyer on? Was she already damned or was there, as she believed, still a way through to Paradise? The old crone was certainly sluttish. Her degraded body showed that; besides she had a prior conviction for theft for which she had served time in Clerkenwell. At her trial her accusers claimed that she had a scathing tongue; in evidence they cited the curse Sawyer had laid on a neighbour who later died. The question remained however, was this woman truly malign? By malign Goodcole meant 'beyond hope', that is 'irrecoverably given over to evil'. Certainly there were moments in her story that looked towards redemption: a pious childhood, guilt at the loss of her first child and a powerful evocation of the Devil as a malevolent presence in her life. In particular the image of the Devil as a shapeshifting wolf reminded Goodcole of the Black Dog of Newgate, which was part of the folklore of the prison in which he now worked. Goodcole leafed through his papers, noting where he had underlined Sawyer's words. There was a deal in her account that didn't add up. She characterised the Church as a bad mother that excluded the unbaptised from the churchyard and yet tolerated idols in Potter's Field. Such details surprised him because the reformed Church of England forbade both these practices, which harkened back to the darkness of Rome. Goodcole remembered Dicker's warning to him outside the cell and part of him now regretted scribing Sawyer's stories at all. Her words were not just unreliable – they had a way of getting under his skin where they festered like thorns. So, wary of being drawn deeper into her world, he tried to widen his perspective. The witch, he decided, was bitter. Like other wives in the prison, she scorned the men who held sway over her – men who, to use her country phrase, were 'as flawed as old Adam'.

Goodcole leant back in his chair and stretched. What was perhaps most troubling about Sawyer was the way she misappropriated Scripture. He checked back through his transcript to her description of her mother Grace giving birth to her brother Robert by the Lea and was struck by her statement that the river 'took his life and gave it to him at the same time'. On one level the phrase was a meaningless contradiction but on another it retained a raw sacrificial power resonant of both the Old and New Testaments. It suggested that by forfeiting his life on this earth, Robert had somehow gained a toehold in the hereafter. Whilst this twisting of the Word repulsed the cleric in Goodcole, it fascinated him as a writer. It was revealing because it showed that although Sawyer's language had been shaped by a lifetime of hearing the Bible read to her in church, her understanding remained that of an ignorant country girl. A thought struck him and so he pulled out chalk and slate and scribbled down an image from each of the stories he had transcribed. The first one was set at the mill on the River Lea and so he wrote 'water'. The next seemed mostly concerned with Roman rites in Potter's Field and so he wrote 'clay' and the last was concerned with the witch's move to the Lord's Grove and so he wrote 'forest'. Pondering their collective meaning he scrambled up their order in his mind: 'forest, water, clay'. He then opened his King's Bible and read the first words from Genesis:

> *In the beginning God created the heaven and the earth.*
> *And the earth was without form, and void; and darkness*
> *was upon the face of the deep. And the spirit of God*
> *moved upon the face of the waters.*
> *And God said let there be light: and there was light.*
> *And God saw the light and it was good: and God divided*
> *the light from the darkness.*

Now when he looked back at the slate he realised something that should have been obvious from the start. The content of the woman's stories, as well as the order in which she had told them, mirrored the stages of creation: from the first day came the darkness of the primordial waters, from the second the separation of earth from the seas and from the third the fruiting trees. Goodcole leafed through the pages of his transcription. He checked each tale against the others and then worked his way back from the last page to the first. A further idea occurred to him: the witch's ramblings were less a confession of guilt and more three stories about motherhood. The first was told from a child's point of view, the second from a country girl on the cusp of womanhood and the third from an expectant mother fearful for her brood. Therefore, motherhood would be his theme during his next cross-examination of the witch and so, as he often did in such cases, Henry Goodcole, ordinary of Newgate, confessor to the poor and dispossessed, began to map out his line of enquiry. This evening, armed with dates of baptisms and burials from the parish register provided by Dicker, he would confront the prisoner with her twisting of Scripture and prevail on her to sign a statement confessing her guilt. The statement would be unequivocal: written in plain English it would detail the key failing that had corrupted a once pious child into the wretch who now languished below. Picking out his sharpest quill, he drew out a sheet of blank paper and wrote out the following in flowing script:

I, Elizabeth Sawyer, spinster from the parish of Edmonton in the county of Middlesex, do on the 15th day of April in the year of our Lord 1621 confess to making a pact with the Devil in which I foolishly delivered up my soul and that of my firstborn child. I did this in order that I might better survive the famine that followed the failure of the harvest in the first year of my marriage. This pact was sealed with blood, which I willingly offered up to him. I did this in order that my family might prosper and that I would be revenged on those neighbours that wish me ill and do thwart us every day.

In confessing my wrongdoing I acknowledge my fallen nature as a wife and a woman, who – impure as Eve – was tempted by the Great Deceiver into choosing between my own soul and that of my child when, as those

versed in Scripture must know, all souls rightly belong to
God and may through the offices of His Church on earth
rest with Him in perpetuity.

So, accepting the error of my ways, I hereby renounce
Satan and all his works and humbly acknowledge the
power of Almighty God and his representative the king
whose forgiveness I crave.

Signed,

....

Then, carried away by his own eloquence, he turned over the
page and wrote the following on the reverse:

As witnessed by,
Henry Goodcole – *ordinary of Newgate Prison*

The prison chaplain waited for his signature to dry and looked
with satisfaction at his new job title. It was the first time he had
seen it written down in black and white. The strike of a single
bell reminded him that the dogwatch had begun and that it
was time to be with Dicker in his lodgings in Newgate Street.
Leaving the draft confession on his desk, he closed a vent on
the lantern to lower the flame and locked his study door.

Outside the prison Newgate Street was crowded. A
procession of pilgrims, one seated on an ass, waved reeds
on their way through to St Paul's while, from the opposite
direction, a band of soldiers pushed through towards the
Saracen's Head Tavern beyond the city gate. Goodcole stepped
over the manure and looked up towards Christ's Hospital

where the last rays of sunlight warmed the brickwork and slipped into the alley that led to his lodgings. Having noted the horse tied up in the backyard, he was not surprised to find Dicker sitting in his parlour with his boots kicked off by his side. Goodcole greeted him and called to his wife to bring more ale and pie. "Welcome back. I trust the ride was a swift one?"

Dicker leant back in his chair and looked at him through weary eyes. Grime from the road was ingrained in his forehead up to a line where the brim of his hat had shielded his freckled skin. "Cambridge Way was busier than ever. Lines of wagons bound for the port. It is not surprising given the number of ships that are due to sail."

Goodcole's wife Anne appeared with a pie of humbles and a jug of ale. She leant forward to proffer the tray and the light caught on the amber bead that hung around her neck. Dicker nodded his appreciation, but the woman turned away.

"She says little," Goodcole said of his spouse. He poured out the ale and pushed a beaker to his guest, who looked around at the cramped lodgings.

"So you have settled in here and I'm hearing good things about your daughter. Joan has made a fine start in Alderman Bull's household, I'm told."

Goodcole beamed. "Aye, she's a good girl: diligent in mind and spirit." He signalled to his wife to leave them, then leant forward. "So, you bring news from Edmonton. Was Reverend Thickpenny helpful?"

"Reverend Thickpenny was most obliging. He is as keen as we are that this vexing case is laid to rest."

"And you made a copy of the entries for Cronwell and Sawyer in the parish register?"

"I did and after that I travelled to Winchmore where the family works and lives." Goodcole remembered the name from the last of the woman's stories.

"I believe the village of Winchmore stands on a coppiced slope known as 'Lord's Grove' – how found you things there?"

"It is a poor place and most run-down. The village is of two camps: those who are for Sawyers and those who are against them."

"And what do those who are against the woman say?"

"They fear her. As I warned you, she is not to be trifled with." The prison chaplain leaned closer to the alderman's agent.

"Yes, but *why* do they fear her?"

"They say she is a dissembler."

"She lies?"

"More than that. She is able to twist the truth so as to change it."

Goodcole leant back to consider Dicker's words. "She can twist the truth so as to change it. That is dark magic, indeed."

"It is storyteller's magic. For the story is not just a story, it is a spell and once told it has the power to change everything."

"To turn black into white?"

"Aye, and back again if the witch so desires." The two men lapsed into silence.

Goodcole thought of the folder in his study. It contained page after page of Elizabeth Sawyer's dictated words. Now he wondered whether any of what she had told him was true. He looked up and caught Dicker's eye. For a moment he felt that same shiver of doubt that had assailed him in the warden's chambers, then he took a grip of himself. Asserting his role as paterfamilias he called through to his wife who was scrubbing the floor in the pantry. "Wife, Master Dicker will lodge with us tonight. Make up a bed and provide fresh linens." He waved away his colleague's protests. "You must stay for you are saddle-sore and will get no rest at the Saracen's Head," he said.

Outside the great bell of St Paul's began to toll. Above them each peel resounded. Dicker listened for a while then reached over to Goodcole. "Come, take communion with me," he said. "Afterwards, I will show you my notes from the parish and we will discuss tomorrow's business."

Goodcole hesitated. "I had planned on returning to the gaol to obtain a confession this very night but perhaps you are right. Holy Week comes but once a year and we should fortify ourselves. Besides, it will do us no harm to be seen by the dean."

The sun had already set when the two men joined the throng on Newgate Street. Keen to make up for lost time, they pressed into the crowd only to find their way blocked by traders wheeling barrows back from the Shambles. Faced with an unending flow of wares, the two men backtracked as far as Warwick Lane where they turned left. Here their hopes of finding a quick way through were dashed when they found themselves caught between two rival groups of apprentices.

"It is the book-boys of Paternoster Row," Dicker said. He swerved around a youth waving a placard.

"Each time one sets up a hoarding, the others tear it down," Goodcole replied. He spotted Stephen Butler whose father ran a printing press in Ave Maria Lane; the boy wielded a blunt stave of wood. The two men picked their way through the roaring boys but were no sooner clear of them than the bells fell silent. As the last echo died Goodcole looked up at the cathedral. On top of the hill it glowered like a fortress, the windows giving no clue to the lights that burned within.

"We are late," he said when they reached the steps. They entered the cathedral from the north and, stepping over beggars who lay camped on the steps, moved along the transept to the centre of the edifice. Here, dwarfed within the vaulted nave, they stopped, their way barred by the teeming crowd. "We have missed both the homily and the exhortation," Goodcole hissed. He stepped back and trod on an old soldier who sat slumped in the shadows. The man let out a shout and Goodcole slipped him a coin to silence him only to find him grasping his hem for more.

Dicker pulled his colleague into the crowd that pressed forward towards the churchwardens. "Come, we may yet partake of bread and wine," he said. So the two colleagues fought for space amongst the faithful. Finally, after much pushing, they emerged to the blaze of tallow which backlit the dean.

The dean was now standing uncomfortably close. His face was impassive as he blessed the sacraments that were laid out in front of him on the white linen tablecloth.

The blood of our Lord Jesus Christ, which was shed for thee, preserve thy body and soul into everlasting life…

Goodcole savoured the wine on his lips. The sacrament restored his calm. He took succour and relished the rush of relief that accompanied the forgiveness of his past sins. Opening his eyes, he felt an intense sense of brotherhood for those who jostled around him; then, he broke away to the sweep of the nave.

After the rite was over the two men left the cathedral by the west end. Once outside Goodcole reached down to pick up a reed from the cathedral steps. It was folded into the shape of a cross and had been thrown there by pilgrims celebrating Palm Sunday. He thought of the tall man who had spoken of hosannas in the chapel and turned to Dicker. "What know you about the thief William Deicrowe?" he said.

His colleague was surprised by the sudden question. He looked warily about him. "Enough to counsel you to leave him well alone," Dicker answered.

"The man came to morning prayers today. He is an insolent fellow with a superior tone. I don't want him mixing with my congregation."

Dicker shrugged. "Then you will have your wish. He is due to be confined this very night."

"Good. Know you his background?"

Dicker turned a deaf ear to his colleague's request. Pulling up his collar against the chill of the April night, he quickened his step and shot a look at Goodcole. "Is not one difficult case enough for you?" he said.

"I sense there is more to him than meets the eye. He has a Jesuitical air which I abhor."

Dicker stopped in his tracks. He looked back at the cathedral and then turned to his colleague. "As you know it is unusual to hang people in Holy Week, yet William Deicrowe will go to the gallows this Tuesday and Elizabeth Sawyer will follow on Maundy Thursday. That the court wants to swiftly rid us of both speaks for itself."

Goodcole was surprised to learn of this first execution. Now he understood Deicrowe's reference to Calvary and yet he was unclear why this hanging took precedence over Sawyer's. Surely hers was the more pressing case.

"Are their two lives connected?" he asked.

Dicker just grimaced. "No two souls could be more different," he said, dropping the topic. So they walked on in silence, but Goodcole's thoughts remained on the prisoner. He pictured him praying alone in Limbo with a holy relic in his hands. The calmness of the man's demeanour bothered him; besides, he still could not explain his appearance at chapel that morning with the sign of the cross burnt on his forehead. He thought hard: according to his slim knowledge of Romish rites a smudge on the temple was reserved for Ash Wednesday at the start of Lent, not for Palm Sunday at its end.

Later, sharing a jug of fortified wine back at his lodgings in Newgate Street, Goodcole determined to steer the conversation back to the thief. He refilled the agent's glass and tried another tack. "I understand why the court wants to rid us of a scold like Mother Sawyer who broke with the Church, but why punish an educated man with a background in Scripture and law – could he be guilty of more than just receiving stolen goods?"

At this Dicker exhaled. The alcohol had softened his mood now and, warmed by the open fire, he felt more relaxed. "May I?" he asked.

Goodcole looked doubtfully at the black herb that his guest had pinched between his fingers and then at the clay pipe that he held in his other hand. He had heard tell that this was a noxious weed but he was keen to learn more about Deicrowe so he nodded his assent then pressed on with another question. "Think you this man guilty of receiving stolen goods, or is there something darker afoot?"

Dicker lit a taper from the hearth. He touched its flame to the bowl of his pipe and sucked hard. The tobacco glowed brightly before emitting a choking cloud.

Goodcole watched with horror. "Friend, that is the Devil's fire you're playing with there." For a while there was silence as the two men were enveloped in blue smoke. When it cleared, Anne Goodcole was standing in the doorway with a bucket of water at the ready. Goodcole waved his wife away. "Our guest is not on fire. He is merely *fumigating*, that's all."

John Dicker was struggling to breathe. "'Tis the new Spanish strain… grown by the company and… brought back to us across the ocean," he said.

Goodcole waved away the smoke and cast his line again. "Tell me, I must know: is Deicrowe guilty of receiving more than stolen goods? I have been warned off talking to him and yet it is my duty to pay him a visit."

Dicker had regained his composure, now. Taking smaller puffs he struck a philosophical note. "In Newgate nothing is truly as it seems. A man may be guilty of receiving even when the goods are *not* stolen," he said.

Goodcole pressed on. "I've heard he is a fence for 'gold, frankincense and myrrh'. Can that be true?"

Dicker stretched out. He knew his colleague was fishing and, mellow with the weed, was happy to play along. "I have heard that story, too. Though a fence may be different things… depending on which side you stand."

"How do you mean?"

"I mean the same fence holds some people in whilst

keeping others out. Is that not its point?"

"I suppose it is, but in Deicrowe's case *the law…*"

Dicker raised his hands in mock horror. He sucked in before exhaling out of the side of his mouth. "The law? Now that's another question altogether. Besides, to which law do you refer: to man or God's?"

"In this case I mean the court of law whose authority comes ultimately from God," Goodcole said.

"Then it is even more complicated for in court 'a fence' may plead guilty even when he's innocent."

"How so?"

"His offence may be his only defence." John Dicker had played with words for long enough and decided to put the matter to rest. "You told me that the prisoner took possession of gold, frankincense and myrrh, did you not? Well if I told you that the gold took the form of an engraved chalice used for celebrating the Roman mass, the frankincense took the form of altar sticks used in a private chapel and the myrrh was actually embalming oil used in a knight's crypt, would you still say this man is guilty of theft?"

"He is a heretic. He should recant or die."

"Aye, but if he took possession of those goods to shield his master the knight from prosecution, he would at least be innocent of theft and a dutiful servant to boot."

"If he is a servant of the Bishop of Rome, we would be well rid of him."

"Precisely, which is why William Deicrowe goes to the gallows this Tuesday." Dicker tapped out the pipe and left it on the hearth to cool. He then reached over to his saddlebag and removed a sheaf of notes from a linen binder. He smoothed down the paper with a freckled fist. "Now, we have work to do for tomorrow will be a busy day and our reputation rests on its outcome," he declared.

Day 3

At sunrise Goodcole packed his bag and returned to the prison. Unlocking the door to his study, he found the little room darker and more airless than ever. The lantern had burned out overnight and he had first to scrape out the wax and light a new piece of tallow before he could settle down to write. This done, he regarded his desk. The paper, quills and ink were where he had left them but something was missing. For a while he was at a loss to know what it was but then he remembered the confession that he had written out the previous afternoon. He had left the draft on a stack of blank paper and weighted down each corner by a silver groat. Now the coins were still in place but there was no sign of the confession itself. He checked the stone floor in case a draught had lifted the document from its resting place but there were only cobwebs and woodlice. He looked again at the sheaf of white paper on his desk. A blot had bled onto the topmost page and yet the source of the blemish, the confession itself, had vanished. Goodcole sat back down again. In itself the loss of the confession was unimportant – he could write out another without delay – but the idea that someone had access to his inner sanctum was as troubling as the notion that they felt free to help themselves to his papers. Clearly the thief was not after money, otherwise he would have scooped up the coins and yet it was unclear why anyone would want to take the confession itself. Goodcole was aware of the new-found fame of Mother Sawyer. He had read cheap ballads about her in bookstores in Fleet Street but there was little in his draft that could compete with what was already out there, besides it was unsigned by her. Worryingly his draft did contain his own signature and this might be put to a number of uses: authorisation of illicit acts within the prison, blackmail and forgery with an eye to publish outside, all came to mind. In this Goodcole was mindful of the case of Francis Robinson, whose conversion and confession he had managed to secure three years before when he was seconded in from Ludgate. Robinson was a clerk who had counterfeited the king's seal and used it to dupe gullible publicans around the City. Goodcole soon dismissed the idea; the two cases were hardly comparable. In truth, even as ordinary, he wielded little authority in the gaol and his signature would be of no interest to prisoners, most of whom could not even read. Nevertheless, someone had taken the draft. So, keen to understand the intent behind the sinful act, Goodcole looked again at his desk. On the face of it all else was where it should be: the King's Bible lay beside the psalter, then, stung by the notion that he might have endangered his beloved daughter, he lifted his psalter to check that Joan's letter was still in place. The book fell open at Psalm 51 and, to his great relief, the letter was there folded as he had left it. He chided himself when he remembered Dicker's words from the night before: 'in Newgate nothing is truly as it seems'. He determined to be more careful in future for a locked door was only secure if one possessed the sole key and yet who knew who possessed what in the Whit?

Down in Sawyer's cell Goodcole waited for the bolt to shoot home. Reassured that the guard was still on the other side, he turned and raised his lantern. The prisoner was sitting on a three-legged stool. She did not look up when he entered but carried on plaiting a twist of hair pulled from her own scalp. Goodcole observed her carefully then settled himself at his desk. He opened his leather bag and laid out paper, quills and ink, as was his custom. After a while he cleared his throat and, tired of being ignored, announced himself.

"Elizabeth Sawyer, I am returned this day to witness your final confession three days before you go to meet your Maker."

The old woman did not react; her fingers continued to separate and twine the silver strands of hair. Finally, when she had tied both ends of the braid and slipped it like a bangle over her wrist, she spoke. "I mind you from before," she said.

"And do you mind what you told me about your early years, maidenhood and marriage?"

Sawyer still did not look up. There was an edge of contempt in her voice. "Do *you* not, Master Goodcole – you went to such pains to write it all down?"

He leant forward; his tone was inquisitorial. "I know what you *told* me. Whether it is a true record of your sins and transgressions has yet to be seen."

Now the old woman looked at him through her one good eye. "What I have told you is true in all ways but one," she conceded.

"In what way have you lied?"

Her voice softened. "I have not lied but sometimes the order of things has got the better of me. You see it all happened such a long time ago."

Goodcole pulled out Dicker's transcription of the register from All Saints Church Edmonton. "The parish records show that you married Edward Sawyer on the fifth day of December in the year 1591 and that your firstborn son Robert was baptised on the first day of October in the following year. That means that your account of the Devil's visit to you on the eve of Lady Day in the spring of 1592 and the subsequent loss of that child is entirely false, does it not?"

"It was the Starving Time, when winter would not relent."

"And yet the record for that particular year shows that the harvest was a fine one. It was only in the latter years of that decade that dearth struck."

The old woman seemed taken aback. She said nothing for a while and sank into a reverie, then her focus returned and she peered across at the sheaf of papers on Goodcole's desk. "You keep a count of such things in your book?"

"We keep a count of all things," he said.

The old woman was rueful. "Aye, we are all the same: we keep a count of things but they slip from our grasp just the same. And you want me to put my mark under what you have written but you cannot do it."

"I cannot?" Goodcole was taken aback.

"Because you have lost your page. It is as I say, we keep a count of things but they slip through our grasp just the same – like water through clay," she said.

Now for the first time Goodcole felt the power of Elizabeth Sawyer's nature. He tried not to react because five years in Ludgate Prison had taught him to be sanguine and remain calm but the thought that Sawyer's reach somehow extended beyond the cell appalled him. He took a breath of stale Newgate air and willed his deductive mind to take control of the situation. In his experience inmates generally divided into three types: the bad, the sad and the mad and, while it was possible to strike a deal with the first and provide solace for the second, the last group could not be reasoned with. In his time as a prison chaplain Goodcole had witnessed only two cases of true possession. After the first he had learned to cut short his words with a prayer to the Almighty for he had received no training from the Church in exorcism and there was no point trying to converse with a demonic power.

Standing before her now, he reminded himself that Sawyer had already admitted to making a pact with the Devil. The complication seemed to be that she was not truly contrite, or specifically not contrite to him. Thinking back over her stories, he picked out a recurrent theme: in spite of her father's best efforts, Sawyer had never truly lived within the precepts of the Church. Faced with the field magic practised by her aunt, Sawyer's father had reached out to the girl's uncle, Francis Cronwell. Though educated, he was a poor choice of teacher for he was hardly orthodox and, typical of the mercantile class, held some very lax views on divine grace. According to him grace was not dependent on the Church at all. It was like water: free-flowing throughout Creation. The idea made Goodcole feel rather ill for he had always been fearful of formless things, so he put it out of his mind and decided, instead, to focus on the sin of pride. Recalling Sawyer's girlish saying that she was 'the first and last child', he decided that she was ruined before her catechism. Thus his problem was not that she was an unbeliever but quite the opposite: she had personalised her relationship with God so much that she didn't feel that she needed the Church at all. Faced with this fact Goodcole decided to take a break. He would discuss the matter with Dicker and then regroup and modify his approach. With this in mind he turned around and banged sharply on the cell door.

When Goodcole emerged into the light of the corridor, Dicker was there to meet him.

"Your goodwife Anne asked me to pass on Joan's letter." He pressed the folded paper into Goodcole's hands and glanced back at Sawyer's cell. "Progress?" he asked. Goodcole shook his head and Dicker continued. "It is as I thought: she is not penitent and has no intention of admitting to anything."

Goodcole bit back his response for though he valued Dicker's opinion, he sensed the agent saw the world as a series of transactions and lacked a chaplain's patience to probe the human soul.

Up in his study Goodcole showed his colleague the blank paper where the draft confession had been left. He pointed to the blot where his own signature had bled from the original to the succeeding page.

Dicker looked around him; he examined the lock on the door and then picked up the lantern with its new piece of tallow. "It is a strange fact that there are few places in this city that are less secure than this prison. You remember what I told you about removing your personal effects from the witch's cell?"

Goodcole wiped sweat off his brow. "You forbade me to leave so much as 'a hair from my head' in the room with her."

"Well, from now on I would extend that rule to Newgate, itself. If others have access to this room then we may assume that is the case elsewhere, too."

Goodcole took the lantern from his colleague's grasp and replaced it on its hook. "She knew about this theft," he said.

Dicker noted his colleague's frown. "My friend, you are playing that woman's game, by which I mean you are letting her into your head. Think about it, how could she have known? She was merely surmising – that's all. As they told me in the parish, that shrew has a way of reading people and sniffing out their weak spots. It is one of the reasons she is so loathed."

Goodcole packed up. He dropped the silver coins into his purse and placed his Bible and psalter into his bag. "You think she is playing me for a fool," he said.

"I think that she knows you need her mark on your paper. To her you are like the court clerk she observed during her trial: you must keep a fair record of everything and she is using that fact to gain leverage over you."

"She believes that I need this confession more than she does?"

"She doesn't believe that she needs it at all. A woman like that knows all by heart. To her the act of writing is itself a sign of weakness. She is like the country women you see at market – she has you weighed up before you even ask the price of her wares."

Goodcole grimaced. "You know, she has absolutely no inclination to accept the Church as an intermediary in her faith."

Dicker shot him an impatient glance. "Tell her she has had her chance and that others will deal with her from now on."

"Others like the warden's men?"

"Aye, tell her that. But do not delay, we have until tonight, remember? I have to meet company shareholders at the Guildhall at noon and will see you when I return." With that the agent hurried off.

For a while Goodcole stood at the top of the stairs and mulled over Dicker's advice. Although he understood the tactic of walking away, his colleague was wrong to liken him to a man striking a bargain at a country fair. After all he was not attempting to buy something from Sawyer, nor did he want to haggle with her. His role as chaplain was to persuade her to atone of her own volition and to be successful he had to show her that the Church was her only hope. Whatever its inaccuracies, her third story told that in the first year of her marriage she had been tricked into making a false choice between her own soul and that of her firstborn. The choice was false because the Devil had no right to demand such a thing. Put simply, all souls belonged to God and the only way to God was through the Church – that was what atonement meant. 'Do you believe that you may yet find salvation?' he had asked her at their first meeting; 'that is my discovery', she had replied. He would return to her now and broach the subject of her children. Surely if she would not renounce evil for herself, she would do it for them. Looking at Dicker's transcription of the register, he saw that five of her eleven baptised infants were still alive and working in her parish. To be sure of their names he placed the copy into his bag, then he picked up his lantern and steeled himself for another confrontation.

Down in Limbo the witch had not moved from her stool. Settling himself with care, Goodcole spoke to the darkness. "Though time is tight, there is still a chance of salvation," he said.

The old woman appeared unimpressed. "Salvation is not within your gift," she replied.

Goodcole opened up his bag and spread out Dicker's notes. "If you will not seek salvation for your own soul, seek it for Francis, Elizabeth, William, Edward... and John. There is still time for them," he said. A cold silence followed the roll-call of the woman's living children.

Sawyer spoke quietly. "Do you think that I would trust you, a stranger, with the souls of my own flesh and blood?"

"I am your last chance. I am their last chance," Goodcole said.

"I am done with this world. Soon, they will be too," she answered. The finality of her statement left him at a loss.

"Done with this world?" he repeated.

"In this world the poor always lose for it is as it says in the Black Book: unto every one that *hath* shall be given; but from him that *hath not* shall be taken away even that which he hath."

Goodcole shook his head. "No, you misunderstand the meaning of Scripture. Those words come from the Parable of the Bad Servant. We are all servants in one way or another."

"Aye, 'tis true. So tell me, who do you serve?" she asked.

Somehow, he felt compelled to answer her. "I serve God."

"'Tis not true. You serve the alderman."

Goodcole rose. He moved to rebuke her but caught himself just in time. "The alderman?" he said, feigning ignorance.

"Aye, you are like Mistress Hayes from my parish. You pretend to serve God while really you slave for the alderman and all his worldly wealth."

For a moment Goodcole wondered to whom he was being compared but then he remembered the woman's second tale. "Ah yes, your stories – designed to distract and dissemble," he said.

"If you don't believe me, you may ask your companion who rode to Winchmore. Mistress Hayes still lives in the Glebe. There, she pretends to be humble while stealing from the poor – there is no greater fakery than that."

This time Goodcole lost his temper; he stepped over to the woman, grabbed her by the shoulders and shook her. "How dare you impugn me? I do not steal from the poor."

She was unbowed and waited for him to release her. "Oh, but you do and, like her, you believe that knowing a few letters places you closer to God than me."

He stood over her; his breath was ragged now and sweat covered him. "If I am closer to God it is because I am His servant, whereas you are a thief, a liar and a conjuror of spells."

Elizabeth Sawyer regarded him coldly. "It is as I say: you serve the alderman," she said.

Goodcole stepped away from her then for he knew that what she said was true.

On Monday St Sepulchre's bell called the faithful to confess outside the wall. Above London its toll mingled with the chimes from the churches within the City: with those from St Bartholomew the Less, St Anne, St Antholin, St Lawrence Jewry and more besides. Together the bells set up an uneven counterpoint, which carried on a southerly breeze to All Saints' Edmonton, eight miles to the north, where, at the nexus of three counties, nineteen-year-old Elizabeth Cronwell had married Edward Sawyer almost thirty years before.

Deep in the bowels of Newgate Goodcole caught only faint echoes, although he did feel a shiver of the great bell of St Paul's as it rumbled through London clay. Intent on completing his morning round, Goodcole had moved on to his other difficult case and was now a door down from Sawyer outside the adjoining cell where, since the small hours of Monday morning, William Deicrowe had been kept in solitary confinement. Not for the first time Goodcole cursed the lack of respect afforded to the post of ordinary. Had he been briefed properly he could have prepared a line of enquiry that encouraged the prisoner to repent. As it was they had clearly got off on the wrong foot and it would be hard now to gain his trust. Standing in the corridor, caught in the flicker of rush lights with their reek of burning lard, he reflected on how airless it was. Without warning a great grinding reverberated from above. It was as if a stone plinth was being forced into position higher in the prison. The tremor caused dust to fall from the ceiling and brought home the fact that they were all entombed in the earth. Outside Deicrowe's cell Goodcole signalled to the guard to hold off opening the door. He listened to the low monotone of the man praying within.

"Paternoster, *qui es in cœlis, sanctificatur nomen tuum…*"

The Latin words were meant to provide comfort but they provoked revulsion in Goodcole because they were the Roman version of the Lord's Prayer. He forced himself to listen to more.

"*Et ne nos inducas in tentationem: sed libera nos a malo…*"

Goodcole pictured Deicrowe kneeling at the altar of a private chapel somewhere in Cornwall or Devon. Behind the altar a priest dressed in white and gold was blessing blood from a freshly slaughtered pig that had been poured into an ornate chalice. The priest had a swarthy caste to him and was probably Spanish or French. He looked up at the silver crucifix that hung in the apse, then down at the supplicant before him and told him to drink 'the blood of Christ'. Goodcole shook himself free of the nightmare and, holding the lantern high, signalled for the guard to unbolt the door. When he entered, Deicrowe was still on his knees. Goodcole ordered him to stand.

"Answer me one question," he said without preamble.

Deicrowe rose. He held his left hand in front of his face and shielded himself from the glare of the light. "You want to know why I attended morning prayers yesterday?" he guessed.

"Why yesterday when never before?" Goodcole replied.

"I wanted to share my last Sabbath with my fellows: not the braggarts on the Master's Side but with ordinary folk like those in your chapel," Deicrowe said.

Goodcole looked at the tall figure that stooped in the darkness. Again he noted the West Country accent and the quiet self-assurance that an education provided. The man's composure was maddening. Goodcole knew he must calm down yet the goading by Sawyer followed by the paternoster had raised his hackles. "Know you, *you are in error*? You and your master will burn in Hell for idolatry."

William Deicrowe straightened his back. "We are all in error, sir. My fealties are a matter of debt: my brother and I owe our lives to our master Lord Arundel. But for His Lordship's charity, we would have perished in the famine that killed our village. We are his faithful servants, that is all."

Goodcole mopped his brow. "What village was this?" he asked.

"The village I was born into sits high up on Bodmin Moor where ancient stones are aligned to the sun."

The mention of somewhere so far removed as the Duchy piqued Goodcole's interest. He reminded himself to follow his usual method and sat down on a stool. "Tell me about that time," he said. He motioned for Deicrowe to settle back on the low trestle bed but the condemned man remained standing.

"Very well. I will describe for you my last memory of my childhood home but first allow me to ask you one question: have you ever lived through a time of dearth?"

Goodcole looked at him doubtfully. "Like most, I have gone hungry," he said.

Deicrowe shook his head. "Hunger and famine are two different things. Hunger is going short and feeding on scraps but famine is a stripping away of all hope. Famine kills slowly. It shows you your own death before it happens."

At this Goodcole snorted. "How so?" he said.

"Before famine comes for you, it takes your family one by one. There is another thing." Deicrowe had begun to pace now. "It is well known that before each one succumbs, he sees a black dog."

"A black dog? That is mere hearsay," Goodcole retorted.

"The dog is a harbinger of death. A man sees many signs besides for one's need is like a fever by the end."

"Tell me about your childhood in Bodmin," Goodcole said.

"Bodmin is a windswept place for like all of Cornwall it has the ocean on three sides. The village I grew up in is called Minions. I have but one memory of my mother's home. I recall lying on a horsehair mattress on my trestle bed – I must have been three or four years of age. I mind the sight of my mother and brother Nicholas clumped at the hearth and I mind the cold that came up through the floor. Though Nicholas was swathed in a blanket, I could hear the smack of his lips on my mother's breast. That sound was hopeless. It was like a dog licking a stone. It competed with the wind down the chimney and the numbing cold. The sucking sound went on all day and all night. It was hopeless because my mother was already dead. It went on until Lord Arundel's men broke down the door."

"Lord Arundel?" Goodcole said.

"The Arundels of Lanherne. It is who we have served since."

"And what of your brother, now?"

"My brother is departed."

Goodcole's manner softened. "You are the last of your brood, so you sought solace in my chapel?" He stood up and raised the lantern to examine the puckered burn on the prisoner's forehead. He understood now why Deicrowe had sought refuge for the bloods in the Master's Side would have allowed him little peace. "You stand here branded a heretic. Recant now and you may be forgiven."

"I cannot recant my faith."

"Your 'faith' in the Bishop of Rome is little better than a pact with the Devil. Trust me, I have had experience with one such as you. Francis Robinson was a papist, yet he died well having embraced the Protestant faith in his final hours." But Deicrowe folded his arms; he looked him in the eye.

"My faith is who I am – without it I am nothing," he said.

Goodcole took a step back; he lowered his voice. "There is another way: recite Psalm 51 to me now and I will quash your death sentence."

In the half-light William Deicrowe blinked. "You have the authority to do such a thing?"

"According to ecclesiastical law any man who recites the psalm may plead benefit of clergy and go free."

Deicrowe allowed himself a bitter smile. "Reverend, do you come to tempt me? Would it profit me to trade a few more days on this wretched earth for an eternity in Heaven? My course is set. Let me be."

Goodcole squatted down on his haunches and thrust his chin close to Deicrowe so the steam from his breath blew into the other man's face. "Listen now and heed my warning. Let me tell you how it will be. Tomorrow at four bells you will be driven beyond our gates to Smithfield – that same place where Queen Mary and her cardinals burned our brethren. The crowd will be waiting for you and many will follow your progress along the Oxford Road. At Tyburn I will mount the cart and intercede on your behalf. Believe me when I tell you that the crowd will expect penitence. Nay, they will demand it. You must declare your allegiance to God and the king or face the wrath of all."

"I have no speech prepared," Deicrowe said.

"Then I will craft one for you, now," Goodcole said.

"Leave me now to pray. Tomorrow I will speak openly and without rancour," he said.

"Will you repeat the oath of allegiance to the king?"

"If the crowd will let me, then I will do it."

"If the crowd sense true remorse, then they will allow it," Goodcole said.

After he had left the cell, Goodcole resolved to find out more about the prisoner so, instead of returning to his lodgings for lunch, he climbed the four flights of steps to the record office where the court calendar was kept. The record office was located in the South Tower of the gatehouse and was run by

an associate of the chaplain, one Martin Stamp. Goodcole had
known Stamp since his first days in Ludgate. As a boy the clerk
had run messages between the prison and the Old Bailey before
taking a position in the new library funded by Alderman Bull.
Now, like Goodcole, Stamp had been moved to Newgate to
speed up the processing of prisoners. The record office was one
of the few places where Goodcole felt at ease in the prison.
Perhaps it was the sense of calm that prevailed in an archive
where everything had a rightful place; perhaps it was the smell
given off by dried paper and aging vellum, or perhaps it was
simply the greeting of a friend who, like him, knew the pitfalls
of a career where patronage trumped ability.

Goodcole found the record office crowded. Seeing there
had been a delivery of felons from the assizes, he waited for
the captain to hand over his list and watched as the wives
traipsed past to be shackled. The woman closest to him
had flaming red hair. She was not yet twenty and, heavily
pregnant, stood with her hands on her waist – panting.
Goodcole tried to avoid her pungent smell. Taking a step
away, he regarded her with distaste and waited for the clerk
to reappear.

Martin Stamp tipped his hat in greeting; he wore a forlorn
air. "It does them no good, but still they try," he said.

Goodcole looked back at the woman who was moving off
to the guardhouse. "They try what?" he asked.

"They plead their bellies in the hope the court will be
lenient and spare them the rope."

"On account of the unborn child within their womb?"

"Aye, and it fouls up our bookkeeping for we have more
bodies going out than coming in the prison."

"Are they not spared, then?" Goodcole asked.

"They are spared until they give birth and then hanged as sentenced. It is not lenient because the children die here or live a life of neglect on the street."

Goodcole shrugged. He checked that no guards were nearby and then lowered his voice. "I'm interested in the trial records of one William Deicrowe," he said.

Stamp stiffened slightly. He lifted a ledger off a shelf and laid it on the counter. "He is due at Tyburn this time tomorrow," Stamp said. He leafed through the Calendar of Indictments and Depositions and, finding the page, ran his index finger down the margin. "Deicrowe, William: found guilty of grand larceny on the second day of this month. A note declares William and Nicholas Deicrowe to be known recusants in the employ of Lord and Lady Arundel of Lanherne. William Deicrowe was arrested in Bodmin in March and a warrant has been issued for his brother who is still at large."

Goodcole peered at the neat script. "Is there nothing else other than the value of the goods stolen?"

Stamp shook his head. "To merit a death sentence the value of the goods must be greater than a shilling. A more complete record is kept by Potts, the clerk at Old Bailey, but the facts of the case seem clear. Theft is theft, after all."

"Theft is theft," Goodcole repeated.

Stamp gave him a quizzical look; he replaced the book on the shelf and then leant over the counter. "Do not misunderstand me, sir. I make no judgement about those who pass through this place. Each of us must face our Maker soon enough and only He can truly judge."

At this Goodcole extended his hand. "Thank you, my friend," he said.

Outside the prison the chaplain felt a weight fall off his shoulders. He lengthened his stride down Newgate Street and inhaled a blast of fresh air; he could almost taste the tang of salt from the sea. Passing a group of sailors fresh from Tilbury docks, he found himself staring at an old salt's walnut skin and piercing blue eyes. What must it be like to sail across the wild yonder and set foot on heathen lands? Part of him – the boyish part – was still taken with the idea of discovery. Driving this desire was the notion of deliverance: the hope that somewhere over the ocean, lay the Promised Land, a place of milk and honey akin to Paradise. He remembered people and objects brought back on salty boards: a nut the size of a man's head, a savage princess with seashells draped around her neck and a giant fish's tooth carved with a map of an unknown continent. What would you name such a place: 'Virginia' after the queen or 'James Town' after the king? How much better to name it 'Zion' after the citadel in the psalms? But the preacher in him rebelled against such vanities. The truth was that Zion was a place in a man's heart and it could not be reached by seamanship, but by suffering. Only when you had scaled the mountain of your own pride could you approach God on this celestial peak. Anyway, this entire world was a place of exile.

He turned up Warwick Lane and sidestepped a child demanding alms. The boy was nimble and caught at his coat but Goodcole shooed him away with a curse. He followed the narrowing street up to Amen Corner and entered Ave Maria Lane at its junction with Paternoster Row. Here, opposite the Bishop's Palace, a colonnade of shops was bookended by taller buildings on either side. Goodcole read the gilded sign of William Butler & Son and glanced at the grey distemper of the shutters. The printer's workshop was locked up for Holy

Week and Goodcole bit back his disappointment at finding it closed.

His conversation with Deicrowe had reminded him of the printers. It was now almost three years since he had written his account of Francis Robinson's conversion and he was impatient to publish again. Most of all he missed the smell of the ink, the wetted paper and trays of metal type because the machine of the press gave him a sense of power. A busy print workshop was like an alchemist's forge; in it a succession of base elements were brought together with great force to create something fine: knowledge.

Goodcole tightened his kerchief against the brisk wind. Perhaps it was a mercy that Butler had locked up his shop for, though the writer in him was chafing at the bit, publication was fraught with risks and in many ways everything was against the venture: Sawyer was uncooperative, he was new in his post and he lacked funds to pay. Besides, if weighed poorly, his words could land him in hot water either with the London Company or the dean.

He was about to turn on his heel when a movement in an upper window gave him pause. What if, behind closed doors, the press was running, anyway? It would not be the first time Butler had broken the Sabbath or disregarded a holy day to run out a first edition. For a moment Goodcole was caught in a quandary: his professional self was impatient to extend his reach as a writer, but his god-fearing side rebelled against the notion. Surely Holy Week was sacrosanct, or did the rightness of his cause justify him in making an exception?

The bell from St Martin's Ludgate broke into his thoughts. Time was getting on and he realised that he could not now call home for lunch. He imagined Anne pursing her lips in silent reproach. Retracing his steps down the cobbled slope, Goodcole avoided the boozy warmth of the Mermaid Inn and quickened his pace past a brewer's cart that was swapping empty barrels for full ones. All those years back in Barking he had given Anne his word and he had kept it, hadn't he? 'Given it and kept it' – it sounded like a line from a country riddle: 'when do you keep the thing you give away?' Yes, he had given his word to provide for a better life and in return she had promised to honour and obey, which she had done until now – until, that is, he had started with the witch.

So Goodcole's thoughts turned to Sawyer: he pictured her twining her hair down in her cell and whiling away the hours as pressure mounted on him. The dogwatch would end at eight o'clock in the evening and, although this gave him three hours, he sensed that he had barely scratched the surface with this woman. If anything Sawyer's attitude seemed to have hardened. She had no interest in the Church yet still believed in salvation, which put him in a difficult position. For a moment walking down Newgate Street, he was tempted to follow Dicker's advice and turn her over to the warden's men but he quickly dismissed the idea. He had never given up on a prisoner yet and to concede this early would prove himself unworthy of his vocation. Besides, the woman had already explained how she had been led astray. He decided to simplify her statement using a few phrases from her last story. If she would not put her name to her own words, then the Devil could take her.

Goodcole had barely passed under Newgate's portcullis when a guard ordered him to attend Warden Travers' chambers. The man was the same that had summoned him from the chapel and his manner was as curt as ever.

Inside the topmost tower Goodcole found the warden sitting behind his table.

Travers waited for him to close the door and placed a small black carving on the table in front of him. "What can you tell me about this mommet? I'm told it comes from your chapel."

Goodcole picked up the small black figure. He examined all five inches of its length and returned it to the table. The texture of the wood had a slight sheen like the shell of a scarab beetle. "It looks like a chess piece. Perhaps, it is the black queen."

"An interesting idea and yet the pose is wrong. The way the hands are outstretched suggests something crude and cultish."

"A Madonna?"

"Very likely. The man who handed it in, one George Scald, swears that the prisoner Deicrowe picked it from the chapel floor. He says you were present when this happened."

"Then he is lying."

"Is he?" The warden seemed to take pleasure in Goodcole's discomfort. He spun the carving carelessly over the tabletop as if rolling a die and looked back at him. "You first suggested this is a playing counter, then agreed it could be a popish totem. One thing is sure: when this maquette was intercepted it was on its way out of the prison. Are you aware that the thief's brother Nicholas Deicrowe is still at large?"

Goodcole shook his head. Having only just learned this from Stamp, it was safer to play dumb.

Warden Travers' mouth twitched. "I would suggest to you that whatever this effigy represents and whoever it is for, its function is the same. It gives succour to those who seek to make this nation state a vassal of the 'Holy' Roman Empire." He tossed the figure through the air and watched with amusement as Goodcole fumbled a catch. "Burn it," he said. As the warden stood up his buckled boots sank deeper into the hand-knotted carpet. "Now, returning to our other troublesome tick, has the Winchmore Witch confessed?"

"She has confessed but is yet to sign her mark."

The warden's face tensed with annoyance. Wetting his finger on his tongue he drew a cross of saliva on the polished surface of the table.

Goodcole looked at the smear and was briefly reminded of the burn on William Deicrowe's forehead.

"Bring it to me by eight."

Down in his study Goodcole drew a fresh sheet of paper off the pile and wrote out another confession for Sawyer to sign. This draft made no reference to the witch's first child or the exact date of 'the Starving Time'.

When he reached Limbo Goodcole found that Sawyer was ready to talk. He unpacked his quills and ink and had no sooner written '16 April 1621' at the top of his page than she shifted her weight away from her painful ulcer and leant forward on her stool.

"What bird did you pluck to make your pen?" she breathed.

Goodcole held his best quill to the light of the lantern. "This feather is taken from a goose," he said.

"We roast a goose at Michaelmas. It is best stuffed with sage and skeggs."

"Skeggs?"

"The berries from the bramble. To avoid the Devil's curse you must pick them no later than one week before the feast. Their skins turn your fingers the colour of that ink." She pointed at the glass well on the table.

"This comes from the ocean deep. It is milked from a sea creature called the squid."

"A squid." The old woman laughed at the strange-sounding word. "And there was I thinking it was made from the soot of a candle."

Sensing a softening in her tone, Goodcole tried to humour the old woman. "You are right; sometimes ink is made from burned wicks. Printers use a tint called lamp black which they mix with varnish and egg white."

After a long pause Sawyer spoke.

> *"First the spark,*
> *Then the dark*
> *That makes the mark,*
> *That sets us free."*

Believing that the woman was opening up to him, Goodcole leant forward to look at her more directly. "What riddle is this?" he asked.

"It is what foresters say about bone char," Elizabeth Sawyer said.

Goodcole raised an eyebrow and rested his chin on his hands. "What then is 'the mark', for char is a cure, is it not?"

"Char turns your tongue black. Only when you swallow it do you feel free."

Goodcole took out the confession from his bag and smoothed it flat on the table. "Sign your mark here and you shall be truly free." He pointed to the base of the page where he had left a space for her to sign.

"So," she said.

He fixed her within his gaze. "There can be no salvation except through the offices of the Church. Here, I will read it to you:

I, Elizabeth Sawyer, spinster from the parish of Edmonton in the county of Middlesex, do on the 16th day of April in the year of our Lord 1621 confess to making a pact with the Devil. I did this so that my family might better survive the famine that beset my parish during the early years of my marriage.

Accepting the error of my ways, I hereby renounce Satan and all his works and humbly acknowledge the power of the Established Church and the king, whose forgiveness I crave.

Signed,

....

As witnessed by,
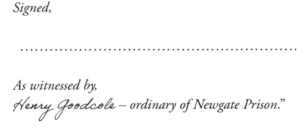*Henry Goodcole* – ordinary of Newgate Prison."

Silence greeted the reading of the confession. For a while that silence held as both chaplain and prisoner breathed in the same stale air, then Sawyer spoke.

"I will not put my mark on your paper."

"That is a pity. To do so would show a contrite heart and prepare the way for atonement."

"Aye, to you men of the law, maybe, but not to God. I have made my peace with Him and I need no man to speak on my behalf."

Up in the chapel Goodcole looked at the spot where the doorstop had once lain. He thought of the mommet that the warden had thrown at him and recalled that the little figure still lay in his bag. He should have disposed of it already but there had been no fit time for, in a place like Newgate, you could not simply drop a likeness into a fire; such an action might be perceived as an act of magic in itself. He looked again at where the doorstop had festered and wondered why Deicrowe had carved the figure in the first place. Was it just to while away the hours or did the totem have a more sinister purpose? The way the Madonna held her arms out at her sides recalled Sawyer's description of the idol in Potter's Field. For a moment he wondered whether there was a connection but then he dismissed the thought. Dicker had said that 'no two souls could be more different'. More likely the mommet, which had been intercepted on its way out of the prison, was a coded message of encouragement to his brother. Perhaps it bore a resemblance to some popish relic in the Arundel's chapel in Cornwall. Perhaps it signalled a final farewell before Nicholas boarded a ship for the New World.

Goodcole sighed. He had made a frustrating start to Holy Week and was acutely aware that his time to secure a confession from both Sawyer and Deicrowe was running out. The pressure from the warden was galling for Travers was interested in worldly matters and cared not a jot for Sawyer or Deicrowe's soul. Then again he knew that Travers was under pressure from the top. He had to please the board of governors and a signature, even if it was just the smudge of a thumb, kept the board – that is Alderman Bull, the dean of St Paul's, Sir Edwin Sandys from the London Company and Lord Chief Justice Hunt – off his back.

To cheer himself up, as he often did in moments of adversity, Goodcole pulled Joan's latest letter from his breast pocket. The letter was the same that Dicker had passed to him outside Sawyer's cell and it bore the alderman's mark showing it had been delivered from his house in Walbrook Ward. Breaking the seal, he carefully unfolded the single page and, checking his hands for grime, flattened it out on the surface of the lectern. He drew in his breath and read:

"Dearest Father,

I write again to 'refresh your heart' and share our latest news. Here Mistress Bull is now confined as the alderman awaits the delivery of his first child. At this we are excited and prayerful in equal measure. My companion, Lucy Remnant, is knowledgeable about the month's lying-in that must follow the birth and has advised that we will be kept busy until Ascension providing clean linens and serving my lady before she is churched.

Be assured that I will visit when I am able. In the meantime please say a prayer for all of us, most especially for Mistress Bull and her unborn. I will write again when I have more to tell.

In all obedient duty,
Your daughter,
Joan."

Goodcole intoned a prayer from the lectern in the empty chapel. He folded the letter and was about to place it in his psalter when he noticed a single auburn hair caught on the edge of the page. The hair was the length of his forearm and it shone with the unmistakeable lustre of his daughter's locks. Moving the lantern closer he disentangled the wisp as one might a stray thread of silk and wound its length around his thumb, producing a single curl. This he secured by turning the end in on itself. Aware that his own breath might blow his keepsake into the grime and corruption of the gaol, the chaplain slipped it between the pages of his psalter. Here it would remain pressed like a dried flower – a reminder of his favourite child.

He had barely packed his bag when he heard the bell strike. The eight chimes, which signalled the end of the dogwatch, confirmed what he already knew: he had failed to meet Warden Travers' deadline.

Outside the warden's chambers in the South Tower Goodcole was about to lift the knocker when the door opened and John Dicker appeared before him.

Dicker was ashen-faced; he pointed to Goodcole's bag. "Do you have it?" he hissed.

Goodcole lifted the confession out of his folder only to have it snatched from his hands.

Dicker glanced at the draft and breathed a sigh of relief. "Good, it is signed," he said.

"No, she would not put her mark to it," he corrected.

"But it is *signed*." The agent pointed to the flourish of Goodcole's own scrawl at the end. "As long as it has your name on it I can put in her mark now." With these words he produced a silverpoint and scratched a cross roughly into the paper. Then he turned on his heel and, holding the document aloft, returned to Warden Travers' chambers.

Finding the door shut in his face, Goodcole stood at the top of the stairs and reflected on the agent's abrupt change in manner. Since his move to the prison Dicker had proved himself to be a dependable ally. In the past week alone he had undertaken a demanding journey and shown himself a brother in Christ by taking communion with him and so it came as a surprise that he had lost his scruples, now. After all, why bother riding to Edmonton to check facts if you were prepared to lie on your return? Recalling that the agent had just come back from a meeting of the London Virginia Company at the Guildhall – a meeting that Warden Travers had attended – Goodcole surmised that pressure was being put on his associate. Faced with the closed door of the warden's chambers, he now opted to turn to an older friend: Martin Stamp in the record office.

Down in the record office Goodcole found Stamp perusing one of his inventories.

"What can I do for you?" the clerk asked.

"Perhaps nothing. It depends on how long your records go back."

Stamp turned and pulled a weighty tome from a shelf behind him. "Most of the archive was lost in the fire that destroyed the chapel but this calendar lists entries as far back as the thirtieth year of our late queen's reign: that is 1588 – the year of the Spanish," he said.

Goodcole bit his lip. "I'm interested in entries from the parish of Enfield," he said.

The clerk opened the leather cover; his finger ran through the introductory page then scanned the list of indictments. He turned to a section midway through the book. "I have here cases brought before the Middlesex Sessions but I need a name. Have you no details?"

Goodcole lowered his voice. "Look for Sawyer, Cronwell or... Mead," he said, thinking of the witch's cousins.

Again Stamp's beady eye scanned the entries. Presently the clerk's index finger came to rest. "There's no mention of a Sawyer or Cronwell, but I have here a long list of women indicted for riotous affray in a place called Potter's Field in the year 1589."

"Potter's Field?"

"Aye, Potter's Field. Apparently it sits on the bounds between Enfield and Edmonton parish... and yes, it notes a Margaret *Mead* and her sister Eve, the latter great with child."

Goodcole peered at the book then wiped his brow with his woollen cap. "Is there no more?" he asked.

The clerk seemed to take satisfaction in what he had already found. "The calendar merely provides a summary of each offence. Return tomorrow and I will find the full deposition – if it survives," he said.

When he had completed his duties for the day, Goodcole sat for a while in his study. The prison was quiet now and, with all the inmates locked into their quarters, an uneasy stillness had settled on the place. Though ready to return to his lodgings he had time to complete his favoured final act of the day: to reply to his daughter.

My dearest Joan,

Thank you for your news with its promise of a firstborn child. What joy new life brings but how easily we forfeit all. Tonight in the chapel I said a prayer for the entire household and I will continue to hold the alderman,

Mistress Bull and their child in my thoughts in the coming days.

Duty comes first so I understand that you may not visit before Ascension. Purification is indeed a blessing and Psalm 51 shows that though we are 'shapen in iniquity' and 'conceived in sin' yet God may still create 'a clean heart' and 'renew a right spirit' in each of us.

This week we should be mindful of how our Saviour suffered. The psalmist's words speak for all when he implores the Lord: 'cast me not away from thy presence… restore unto me the joy of thy salvation and uphold me with thy free spirit'.

Write again when there is more to tell for nothing 'refreshes my heart' as reading what comes from you my sweet one.

With all affection,
Your father

Goodcole had barely put down his quill when there was a bang on his study door. It was Dicker.

"Thank you for today," the agent said.

Goodcole squinted at his colleague. "What exactly are you thanking me for?" he asked.

Dicker stepped quickly into the study. "May I speak plainly?" he asked.

"I'm sure it can wait until morning." Goodcole ignored the interruption and continued to pack his bag.

"In this case I'm afraid it can't for it concerns the man who goes west, tomorrow."

"You mean William Deicrowe who will be hanged at Tyburn?"

"You once asked me if there was a connection between him and the Winchmore Witch. I should have divulged all but you broached the subject in the street which was not wise."

Goodcole looked the agent squarely in the eye. "I sense that your trip to Edmonton was a cover for some greater endeavour. You should have told me that Deicrowe and his brother were both lifelong servants of Lord and Lady Arundel," he said.

Dicker looked unembarrassed. "Would that have helped you gain a confession? You stick to your brief and I will stick to mine," he said.

"And what is your brief, exactly?"

"My brief is to execute the alderman's will to the letter. I am his agent."

Goodcole stood up and faced his colleague. "What then is mine?"

"Your brief is to prepare the condemned. You allow them to keep faith. You are their *only* friend." Dicker said the words solicitously. "Besides, we are on the same side. Whether it be Sawyer or Deicrowe we fight sorcery and sedition," he said.

Goodcole was tired. It had been a long day and he had little to show for it. He glanced at his lantern and saw that the tallow had burned down and the wick was adrift in a pool of wax. He stood up to leave, but Dicker blocked his path to the door. The agent sensed he was riled and was intent on conciliation.

"Friend, walk with me to London Bridge tomorrow. There is something there I must show you," he said.

"Something – will you not tell me now?"

"I want you to see it with your own eyes," he said.

"You know I must be back in the prison by first light to prepare Deicrowe. Cannot it wait for another day?"

"No, by tomorrow evening our ship will have sailed. Come, I'll meet you early at your lodgings. We will catch sunrise over the Thames and you will be back here to prepare Deicrowe before four bells."

Day 4

The sky was still dark when early the next morning the two men walked from Newgate Street towards Eleanor's Cross. A pungent smell of manure was blowing in from Dung Wharf and the creak of barrows and carts suggested a city preparing for a new day. They had reached Cheapside when John Dicker pointed down Paternoster Row.

"I believe you use a printer hereabouts," he said.

"Yes, William Butler runs a press in Ave Maria Lane," Goodcole replied.

Dicker was enthusiastic. "I mind his name from the frontispiece of your pamphlet, *The Happy Conversion of Francis Robinson*."

"You have read it?"

"I have, as has Alderman Bull. It is what swayed him to support your nomination as ordinary."

Goodcole had mixed feelings about Dicker's praise: part of him felt gratified but he also felt guilt. While Robinson, who had suffered an excruciating death, had been spared eternal damnation, the same would not be true of Deicrowe. Right now, Goodcole knew that he should be down on the lowest level of the prison holding a vigil with the condemned heretic; instead he was off to greet the dawn with someone he hardly knew. "It may be a while before I publish again," he said guardedly.

His companion was having none of it and clapped him on the back. "Don't be despondent, man. You have a gift." Dicker drew in his breath. "*The Happy Conversion of Francis Robinson, Gentleman, who for Counterfeiting the Great Seal of England was Hanged, Drawn and Quartered*," he continued. "The title is a story in itself and contains all one could hope for: intrigue, blood, guts and redemption in one purchase."

Goodcole looked east towards the Mercer's Hall where a group of tradesmen stood clumped around a brazier. Inwardly he doubted whether Dicker had read more than the frontispiece of his pamphlet for while his publications sold on the promise of salacious detail, inside they contained little, bearing witness instead to the atonement of the soul in question. The suggestion that Alderman Bull had personally read Robinson's confession was interesting in itself for the clerk's treason had involved the affairs of the London Company. Not for the first time Goodcole wondered about the reasons for his own appointment. He worried, too, whether he could trust Dicker. There was something in the agent's manner that did not sit well with his stated role as the alderman's servant. Since that tricky moment outside the warden's chambers the man had lost his sobriety. Put simply, he was enjoying himself too much. The two men were drawing near to the thoroughfare of Poultry when they had to sidestep a string of horses accompanied by grooms. The horses were mostly greys and their burnished flanks shimmered as they swept by. Goodcole noted the triple crowns emblazoned on their azure quarter sheets and concluded that the boys worked for the Worshipful Company of Drapers. He marvelled at the wealth in the City; so many of the old guilds now boasted halls modeled in the latest foreign style.

"Hurry up, man." Dicker had reached Stocks Market and was pointing down Lombard Street. "Come let us pass by the alderman's house in Walbrook Ward. It is most imposing and stands but a stone's throw away."

They moved towards an arbour of trees that rose black against the brightening sky. The houses they passed now were grander for, instead of timber-frame, many were built in the new style. In these, rugged stonework at street level turned to fine brickwork above: here facades were cut through with round-arched windows, each flanked by a pair of pilasters. Goodcole looked up beyond the balustrade of a balcony. Lamps behind mullioned glass made the interior glitter like a jewel casket and he spotted servants moving back and forth in the glow. The building was finer than any he had seen. It looked like it had been transported from some Italian city state, perhaps Genoa, of which Goodcole had once seen a print. The palace spoke of all that London aspired to: trade, banking and the rule of law.

Continuing on their way they passed St Mary Woolchurch and found Bearbinder Lane, which marked the start of Walbrook Ward. From here it was a short walk to Alderman Bull's main London residence. When they reached it, Goodcole stood and gawped.

The building was a barn of a place and impressive by its size alone. Plastered with wattle and daub the alderman's residence was typical of the merchants' houses built in King Edward's time. With its top-heavy construction the house resembled an over-proofed loaf, which was slowly sagging after being taken out of the oven. Goodcole caught the faint glow of a light on the middle floor. He thought of Joan keeping vigil by her mistress's bed. He said a silent prayer for the household and then broke free of its tilting beams and sagging floors.

Dicker pointed to an arch through which the silhouettes of trees stood out in the dim light. "More remarkable even than the house is the garden. Alderman Bull keeps a full orchard around the back."

Goodcole turned away. He had a bad feeling about the place and wanted only to see his daughter. He pointed down the fall of St Lawrence's Hill where a turner's horse struck sparks on the stones. "Come, the bridge is close and we have no time to tarry."

The two men found their way onto Thames Street and threaded through the murk of low-lying mist to the river. The traffic was heavier here and at New Fish Street a train of wagons waited at a standstill, their horses eating out of nosebags, their drivers anxious about the boys who sidled in-between. "It is the malt," Goodcole said eying the bulging sacks of barley that were stacked on boards within the carts.

"Aye the brewers and bakers are desperate for it, but the Enfield men have held back for a keener price."

"And meanwhile the sparrows have their fill," Goodcole agreed. They watched as a boy ran a blade through hessian and filled a bucket with cascading grain.

Passing the tower of St Magnus the Martyr, they noticed the first streak of daylight to the east and so they joined the crowd that pressed through an arch onto the span of London Bridge.

The bridge itself was like a congested street for an encrustation of houses, shops and stalls had attached themselves like barnacles to its crumbling length. Pushed into a display of leatherwear Dicker struggled to regain his footing; meanwhile, Goodcole fended off a basket of flapping squabs only to fall into the hands of a girl selling posies.

She placed a ball of primroses into his hand. "These will protect you, sir."

"Protect me?"

"Against evil on the week Judas betrayed our Lord."

Goodcole pressed a silver coin into her palm and pushed past but he fumbled and dropped the blooms onto the road where they were crushed under the wheel of a cart.

Dicker caught his arm and guided him forwards through the melee.

They were passing under the North Tower now and Goodcole looked up to find the antique lettering, which spelled out 'Jhesus' in its blackened stone. He barely glanced at the cluster of human heads that tilted high in the wind against the brightening sky; those heads were from Tyburn and the Tower and they were skewered on poles. Having reached the apex of its span, the two men now stood at the bridge's centre. They gripped the granite balustrade and looked west into space and then peered over the parapet to where a cog was raising its mast having passed under the bridge from the seaward side.

"The river smells worse than ever," Goodcole held his nose against the reek of it all.

"Aye, but soon that tide will turn and all that stink will be washed clean out to sea."

"Is that what you brought me here to witness?" Goodcole joked.

His companion pointed down at the cog, which was now steering towards Queen's Hithe. Heavily laden it travelled low in ripples that reflected back the first light of dawn. Dicker widened his stance then rested his elbow on the granite wall. "I brought you here to share a truth, my friend," he said.

"And what truth is that?"

"That you and I are standing on a gateway."

"A gateway?"

"A gateway to trade for we live at the dawning of a golden age." Dicker said the words with relish. He looked up and briefly gestured to the traitors' heads that were silhouetted above the North Tower. For the most part the skulls were picked clean but a few shreds of hair still blew in the wind. "That, my friend is the past. But this is the future." So saying, he pushed Goodcole to the seaward side of the bridge where the first rays of the sun were igniting Stepney Marsh.

Goodcole looked east to the Isle of Dogs where the Lea joined the Thames, then he watched in awe as the City's walls turned gold. Dicker drew his attention to a ship that rose on the flooding tide at Somer's Quay. Now it, too, shone like a gold bar.

"Behold the *Bonaventure*," Dicker said.

Goodcole was dazzled. He winced against the glare and saw greens and purples behind his eyelids. When he opened his eyes again he was careful to look down at the water, only then did he look at the ship. The *Bonaventure* was a three-masted carrack that was built like a barrel to withstand the ocean's waves. That it had moored up to take on provisions from Billingsgate – fresh water, salted pork, peas and beans – was unsurprising.

Beside him Dicker was leaning forward with the fervour of a convert. "It is the company's ship and it sails today for Virginia," he said.

Goodcole could not match his enthusiasm. "Aye, and we are the company's men, after all." He said the words wearily, but Dicker would not be put off.

"That is what I wanted to show you: you see, this vessel will carry felons from our shores. The company will set them to work in the plantations and bring back riches in their stead."

A bell sounded from St Magnus the Martyr and it reminded Goodcole that he had a hanging to attend to. "That is hardly news. The company has been shipping out men of dubious character for years. I thought you brought me here to explain the link between Deicrowe and the Winchmore Witch," he said.

Dicker could not tear his eyes away from the *Bonaventure*. He waved away his colleague's protest. "Don't spare them another thought – they belong to the past. Instead, turn and face the future. Put your writing at the service of the company."

"To do what exactly?"

"To recruit for the New Jerusalem that lies over the ocean."

After his return to Newgate Goodcole walked out into the press-yard where the lurch was being prepared. Here he found Deicrowe amongst the cobs that would pull him to Tyburn.

"There's still time," Goodcole said.

"Precious little," Deicrowe replied.

"Have you thought what you will say to the crowd?"

"I will beg theirs and the king's forgiveness."

Goodcole knew penitence when he saw it and he sensed that Deicrowe was holding back. "Simply being sorry is not enough – you have to be in awe," he said.

Deicrowe held Goodcole's gaze. "I am not in awe. I am just truly sorry," he said.

"Then you must pray – *in English*," Goodcole added, mindful of the paternoster he had heard the day before.

"I will say, 'forgive them Father for they know not what they do'. It will be my paschal prayer."

Goodcole glared at him. It was as he suspected for under that humility lurked a Jesuitical arrogance; the man still thought he was going to Paradise. He pointed to the rope that was looped around the lurch's box rail. "Try saying that and you'll feel the burn of hemp before you finish your sentence."

"I have finished my sentence and soon I shall be free," Deicrowe replied.

Goodcole stepped away. He saw from the crust of spittle that the prisoner's mouth was dry but observed that, though Deicrowe was afraid, he was still set on martyrdom. He knew from long experience that true remorse involved a type of terror and terror caused rupture – rupture with the self and its loyalties and desires. No one faced that truth unless they absolutely had to and Deicrowe still believed he had a get-out. He watched the undersheriff take receipt of the living body and waited for the farrier to put the cobs into harness.

The lurch was a four-wheeled cart with high sides and a dropdown back. From a distance it looked battered but Goodcole soon realised that what he took for peeling paint was the shrivelled remains of fruit and offal hurled by Londoners. The lurch was, after all, a mobile pillory on which the mob vented its spleen and this fact explained its sour smell for the boards were rancid with stale juice and urine from the deceased. Goodcole was relieved to see that the yeoman of the guard was still Captain Paul Simeon. He remembered

Simeon, a Huguenot, from Robinson's execution three years before and knew him as a man with a cool head. Simeon was a veteran of campaigns in the Low Countries and the Palatinate. He walked with a pronounced limp, still carrying a ball of shot in his right knee.

The old soldier greeted Goodcole and asked him in guttural tones whether he would make the journey to Tyburn, then he spelled out their running order. "One rides upfront as bellvether, then you, followed by the lurch and myself bringing up the rear. The hangman's boy vill ride on the cart with the driver and I vill be there at the back to keep back the crowd."

Goodcole nodded. He was not unduly concerned about the journey and didn't expect uproar, as during the Robinson affair, when a mob had attempted to drag the prisoner onto the cobbles midway up the Oxford Road. Part of him, though, worried about Thursday's execution. That would be a different matter for the ballads and broadsides were already circulating and a huge crowd would turn out for the witch. He looked up past the blackened battlements at the clouds scudding through the April sky. Their easterly course promised that the day would remain clear. He watched the hangman's boy checking his ropes.

At a sign from the driver the lad bid Deicrowe step up. When he had done so, he positioned the prisoner with his back to the horses so that he was looking out of the rear of the cart. The boy wound a light gauge cord around Deicrowe's torso and, pulling it tight into the crook of his elbows, he secured it to a ring in the floor of the cart with a hitch.

Goodcole stepped forward. "Flex your hands," he ordered. Deicrowe wiggled his fingers and raised his hands to his chest. "It is so you can pray on the scaffold," Goodcole said.

Ink84 Bookshop
84 Highbury Park
London
N5 2XE
Telephone
info@ink84bookshop.co.uk
ink84bookshop.co.uk

VAT Number

The Wonderful Discovery of Eli   £8.99

Subtotal.   £8.99

Total.   £8.99

Payment

Card: £8.99

Thank you for your custom.

---- VAT SUMMARY ----

Vat @ 20%.   £0.00

Date   14-Oct-2022 19:37:42
Receipt 98,069

When the halter man permitted it, the boy lashed Deicrowe's wrists to the rails on his left and right side. The boy then signalled the driver who in turn raised a hand to the captain of the guard.

Simeon called the little party to order. "Ve vill proceed at the bell. My orders are to make haste to Tyburn." He turned to the driver. "No stops – the varden wants this over by midday."

The old Newgate bell hung on an iron pole by the portcullis that led west out of the press-yard. Cracked by one of the fires that had consumed the stable block during Mayor Whittington's restoration it now hung disused – a silent witness to the suffering of another age. When Goodcole heard the knell rung on a hand bell by a gaoler, he walked into the stable, led out his mount and swung up stiffly into the saddle. He took his place in front of the lurch and pulled his kerchief up over his mouth. The whole party then waited for St Sepulchre's bell to sound. The great toll was not long coming and at its echo Simeon gave the order. The winding up of the portcullis sent a flock of pigeons wheeling off into the April sky, then Goodcole flicked his reins and, sensing that his horse was sluggish, dug his heels into its flank causing it to prance off underneath the iron grill. Thus their party passed beyond the prison and the City in a single sweep and from thence turned away from St Sepulchre's to Pie Corner and the spread of Smithfield.

Entered from its southern end Smithfield was a great mart divided into paddocks and stalls. Goodcole breathed in the heavy scent of stock and looked past the pens of steaming beasts to the turf in the centre where the well-trodden mud was crowned by a col of scorched earth. Here, amidst scattered sheaves of hay, a central post marked the place called the Elms where the Protestant martyrs had been burnt during the reign of Queen Mary. He looked to his right to the church of St Bartholomew the Less and imagined the grandstand from which her Spanish counsellors had watched the spectacle. Behind him he could hear the breath of the horses pulling the lurch. He wanted Deicrowe to see what he was seeing, to understand the abomination of what had happened here: when seven men of conscience had died in a single day, but Deicrowe was tied backwards and would only be able to view the stake when the lurch had reached the northern end – halfway around its circuit of the market.

Goodcole glanced to his left and was surprised to see a barrel upended by the post. A barrel of pitch suggested that another execution was imminent and he cast his mind back, wondering whether Potts from the Old Bailey had mentioned such a case. These days, burnings were rare. He recalled that ten years before the dissenter Bartholomew Legate had died here and tried to count the number of women that had been scorched since. He remembered Alice Clark whose execution he had heard described but could not come up with a tally. To be burnt a woman had to be guilty of treason or murder not witchcraft. Goodcole agreed that flaming was preferable to drawing and quartering. After all, cutting open a woman's belly in public might encourage the very lust that the Church sought to prevent.

They had reached the northern end of Smithfield now and here, in an area larger than that laid out for sheep and cattle, everything was given over to the horse trade. At first Goodcole wondered how their party might fit through. He looked at the stalls and paddocks where a hodgepodge of ponies stood penned and marvelled at the maze of new fences that had been constructed since his last visit. *Keep close to the bellwether*, he thought, reflecting that Simeon had been right to arrange their group into a tight unit. The traders were all around them now, leaning on fences or pressing in from either side. The guard in front slowed the pace, picking his way between a barrowful of fodder and two jeering yokels. For a moment the wheels of the lurch slithered, then there was a shout from the hangman's boy and all came to a juddering stop. Goodcole looked back to Simeon then at the white form that lay twitching in the mud. A line scored into the frostbitten ground marked the point where the dog had gone under the lurch's wheels. *A white bull terrier*, Goodcole thought. To kill a dog was a bad omen; it suggested a calamity to come. A quote from Revelation popped up in his head but he stifled it and urged his horse forward. Simeon had his harquebusier drawn. He pointed his sword onwards and Goodcole dug in his heels to force his cob back into life. Thus they completed their circuit of Smithfield by passing over Turnmill Brook, which fed the rows of troughs put out for livestock of all types.

The crowd that lined Hosier Street was well acquainted with the gallows run. Having heard St Sepulchre sounding the death knell they had waited for the lurch to complete its round of the market before greeting its arrival with a chorus of jeers. When Goodcole glanced behind, he saw that Deicrowe had widened his stance; it was perhaps a reaction to the bumpy ground or the accident with the dog. Drawn backwards into space his figure was stooped, locked in a pose of one craning to hear.

A dart flew in from Goodcole's right. He sensed the object as a shadow in the corner of his eye and then he heard an impact. The dart was thrown from the crowd of onlookers who stood outside The Three Tuns Inn. It was a steel-tipped cooper's wedge used for driving hoops onto barrels and it hit Deicrowe above his left ear where it punctured his skull.

When Goodcole looked back he saw his charge genuflect then loll to his right. Dark blood spouted from the hole in his head and ran in rivulets down his right side onto the boards below. Goodcole tried to react. His first thought was to dismount to staunch the flow for he knew they should keep Deicrowe alive at least until he reached the gallows, but Simeon's sword caught the light and it was pointed resolutely forward and so they sped on towards the River Fleet and Holborn.

For the rest of the journey Goodcole tried not to look back. He reasoned that the quicker they reached their destination the sooner he could treat Deicrowe but he knew, too, that his strength must be ebbing away for no man could bleed like that and remain conscious for long. So, when they passed first Ely Place and then the Inns of Court, Goodcole weighed up the new situation and wondered how he might present Deicrowe to the crowd at the end of their journey. Since a confession was now out of the question, Goodcole could say whatever he wanted. This however left the matter of Deicrowe's bloodied appearance for the execution was not meant to be a lynching but a public hanging and it was important for the king's justice to be served. So, jigging along in their cavalcade, he thought how he might clothe him in a borrowed smock and perhaps use a hat to cover his broken head, if only to take the bad look off things.

They were drawing close to the new spire of St Giles in the Fields. Here they passed an Easter procession of nuns walking from Uxbridge to the City. The leaders carried lamps to remind onlookers of the Parable of the Wise and Foolish Virgins while the rear of their party was made up of mules packed with provisions for the trip. Goodcole guessed they had set off early from Twyford and that they would soon strike camp. Since St Giles had a walled convent that functioned as a hospital, a stop here would allow their party two days to reach St Paul's in time for the Passion. The nuns seemed hardly to see Deicrowe as they bustled by. Goodcole listened to them sing and felt a pang of envy for they enjoyed true fellowship while he worked alone.

Beyond St Giles, below the slopes of Chyld's Hill amongst the water meadows and marsh, the Tyburn bubbled up from subterranean wells and flowed south to Mary's Church. Before it reached the King's enclosure at Hyde it crossed underneath the Oxford Road where it watered the Triple Tree.

The construction of the Tyburn Tree was unlike anything else in England. Its geometry was that of a triangular prism upended in the earth. It was the geometry of death and was recognisable as three interlinked doorways that led out of this life. Set into the ground in the year of Elizabeth Sawyer's birth, the Tree functioned as a gamekeeper's fence warning all who passed by that lawbreakers would end their days despoiled and displayed here on the king's highway.

That Tuesday the water in the stream was high. It overbrimmed the ford where the women soaped their clothes and sped through the culverts spattering the cattle that trampled the muddy banks in the village. Sitting up in his saddle, Goodcole didn't give the stream a second thought – so intent was he on reaching the grim outline of the Triple Tree and performing his role as the ordinary of Newgate.

On arriving at Tyburn House, he thought the turnout poor: a scattering of around a hundred people with hawkers and peddlers drifting between the clumps. Only when they reached Oswald's Stone, an ancient dolmen that stood to the south-east of the gibbet, did Goodcole realise that many of those who had watched on the Oxford Road were following, giving their party a ragged tail that grew longer with every step. Now, when he turned, he saw that the multitude behind stretched back for half a mile or more. The mood of the crowd was subdued. Aside from the odd catcall or greeting most walked as you would at a funeral, following the stricken figure of Deicrowe as he was drawn to the gallows as a hooked fish is pulled into land. Beneath the triangular beam a lone figure awaited their arrival. The hangman wore a kerchief and doublet buttoned up against the wind and leather breeches that were tied below the knee. He nodded to the boy and signalled their party to circle.

Their circuit around the Triple Tree was completed in three stages during which the riders held their position before and after the lurch. Each time the cart drew level with a side of the gallows, it stopped and waited. Goodcole knew the count was fourscore and ten, but he let others call it. The orders now came from the hangman who signalled to the boy to dismount and pick up his drum and move them on.

Goodcole sat back in his saddle. He looked down the turnpike to the fields of Bayswater, then around at the farm and its outbuildings that made up the village. The low pulse of the drum walked them on a few paces until they were on the westernmost side of the triangle looking south. From this vantage point Goodcole could see the spires of Westminster and, beyond them, the City where the great tower of St Paul's rose like a castle on a hill. Then he looked closer to hand and watched the people flowing in from the Oxford Road. Most of all he wondered at their silence for he had never seen a London crowd so subdued. He worried about the state of the prisoner: what if he could not be revived? He tried to put the question out of his mind for he had been pitched into a bad situation and Deicrowe's case had been poorly handled from the start. Insufficiently briefed he had made his own enquiries only to be warned off by first the warden and then Dicker. Last night the latter had promised to level with him, while today he had used a time-wasting trip to London Bridge as a ruse to co-opt him into the dealings of the London Company. Goodcole bit his lip at the thought of it. Dicker had a nerve. Up and down the land the stock company was a byword for corruption, having squandered investors' money for ten years or more and now it was at it again – keen to throw good money after bad.

The horse in front swished away a fly with its tail and, to the beat of the drum, moved forward to the third side of the tree. Goodcole followed and looked over the heads of the crowd to Tyburn House where Potts, the clerk from the Old Bailey, and Judge Topping who had sentenced Deicrowe, had emerged into the cold April light. The two members of the judiciary could not have looked more different: Potts was a small man, neat and contained in every way, whereas Topping cut a shambling figure. His winter coat barely contained his girth and his uncertain gait suggested that he had enjoyed an early lunch, a feast that would be resumed once Deicrowe had been dispatched.

At the final smack of the drum Goodcole dismounted. He tethered his mount close to the trough and, adjusting his bag on his shoulder, watched as Simeon and his guard took up their positions to the left and right of him. The lurch was moving again now: backing in between the uprights until the prisoner was aligned underneath the beam. After the hangman signalled the driver to stop, the boy unfastened the cord that attached Deicrowe to the lurch and, like a shore-hand throwing a line to a ship, tossed the rope up to the hangman who sat astride the beam. Goodcole walked in for a closer view. Only now, when he approached the cart from the back, did he appreciate the fatality of the head wound. Suspended in three places Deicrowe hung over the end of the lurch like a marionette waiting to be jerked into life. Goodcole stood underneath him and took in the limp body, the contorted wrists and broken head. Deicrowe's hair was dark now, matted with the last oozings of blood.

"What's this ordinary, have you brought us damaged goods?"

Goodcole turned to face Topping who had arrived through the crowd; beside him Potts was brandishing a sheaf of papers. Goodcole pointed to the cooper's wedge, which was now stuck to the boards, then to the spilled brains that lay all around like fish scraps. "I'm afraid the life has flowed out of him," he said.

Potts cut in. "Most irregular. For justice to be served the condemned must answer to the charge."

Goodcole turned to the clerk. "He is the first I have lost." He had barely said the words when, tugged by the hangman attaching the noose, Deicrowe straightened and looked down at him through lifeless eyes. In those eyes – as tarnished as a dead fish – Goodcole saw the finality of death because it was done now and there was no way back: Deicrowe's soul was lost and, sundered from its Maker, was in torment.

Goodcole turned to Topping. "M'Lud, let me prepare the prisoner so you may speak from the cart." Goodcole swallowed. He climbed onto the lurch beside the driver and made his way to the back. Then he addressed the boy who was loosening Deicrowe's bonds. "Before he is hoisted, I want him to wear these." He unbuttoned his coat and stretched his woollen cap over the caved-in skull. For a while he and the boy struggled to stuff the lifeless arms into the still warm coat. They managed, although Deicrowe's thumb remained stubbornly caught in the left sleeve. Behind them as they worked, they heard the clipped tones of Potts as he read out the charge.

"William Deicrowe of Lanherne, a common thief indicted and found guilty of stealing silver, spices and oil from his master's house in Tottenham Wood – the value of the theft being five pound and four pence for which crime he is sentenced to death."

Above him Goodcole sensed the hangman adjusting the slack. He could hear the hemp cord stretch as it took Deicrowe's weight. Then he turned to face the crowd.

"Let *him* speak," someone shouted.

"Aye, for you have silenced him," another accused.

Goodcole looked out over the upturned faces. He saw grizzled old-timers, mothers with babies, even the odd gentleman distracted from the road.

"I have been this man's visitor in Newgate where I am now chaplain. I will speak in his stead."

"You, what do you know? Let *him* speak," the voices called again.

Goodcole stepped up onto the driver's seat of the lurch. "I spent the morning with this man and together we said a paschal prayer. He is most heartily sorry for what he has done and prays that... all wrongdoers against God and the king may be punished. His words are, 'forgive them Father for they know not what they do'." A mildewed apple flew through the air. It was quickly followed by a turnip, which bounced off an upright of the gibbet. Goodcole watched Simeon drive the crowd back.

"Wrap it up, man," Potts said behind him.

Stepping down from his perch, Goodcole turned to Judge Topping. "M'Lud are we ready to proceed?"

The judge responded with a flourish. "Let the king's justice be... served," he said.

They moved a safe distance between the crowd and the Triple Tree. Goodcole heard the drum roll before the crack of the whip sent the lurch speeding forward. He heard the rope go taut before the crowd sighed – like the drawing back of the sea. A couple of feet clear of the ground, now stretched between land and sky, Deicrowe swung free. He moved like a pendulum slowly back and forth. There was no struggle, no St Vitus's dance, no life at all. Dressed in ill-fitting clothes he looked like a stretched version of Goodcole himself and as he creaked his leaden swing told the chaplain that he had failed. There was no denying it: his first outing as ordinary of Newgate had gone badly awry.

Potts was at his elbow now. The clerk screwed up his nose. "A poor show," he said.

Goodcole, too, sensed the anger simmering in the crowd. Knowing they would need their escort to escape, he moved over to the horses where Simeon stood. He reached back to the hitching rail, untied his horse and cast a last despairing look back at the dangling corpse.

It was a travesty that Deicrowe had been hanged, not for his beliefs, but on a false charge. In his opinion the story of the Arundels should have been told to the crowd because it provided a timely warning how underlings become ensnared in their masters' schemes. Instead, as Dicker had made clear, it suited powerful men to portray this servant of Rome as a petty criminal; that way his true loyalties could be ignored. Goodcole knew that in doing this the court had perpetrated a type of theft. It was theft because it denied the true course of Deicrowe's life and stripped him of who he was. Lest he point the finger solely at others, Goodcole knew that he had been complicit too because, prompted by an obsequious desire to succeed, he had gone along with this lie. Now, when Goodcole looked back at the figure twisting in the April sunshine, he saw an effigy of himself. It was a warning that things could still go badly wrong for he was caught between powerful interests and there was no easier place to incriminate a person than in a prison. He knew that while he struggled to find a way between the machinations of the London Company and the dean he would have to watch his back.

On re-entering the gatehouse, Goodcole spoke the Word from Revelation:

> *"Blessed are they that do His commandments, that they may have the right to the tree of life, and may enter in through the gates of His city... for without are dogs, and sorcerers, and whosoever loveth and maketh a lie."*

He intoned the verse like a prayer and told himself that this was how it was and how it always would be, world without end. Then he looked through the iron grill to the earthly City where one day he hoped to minister to a parish of his own. He was about to greet the guards when John Dicker appeared out of an archway.

"What's this Goodcole, no coat?" Dicker touched his shoulder with a solicitous air. "I hear it went well," he said.

"Hardly. There was almost a riot."

"But all's well. I'm told Deicrowe dropped, silent as a stone." Dicker looked at him brightly.

"He could say nothing so the crowd grew angry, if it wasn't for Simeon…"

Dicker laughed. Again he squeezed his shoulder. "There's no pleasing the London mob. Get in and get out, that's the rule."

"I must get on. Today has been made more irksome by our trip to London Bridge this morning. Unless of course you are prepared to divulge the connection between Deicrowe and the Winchmore Witch?"

Dicker winced and glanced at the guards. "Not *here*, tomorrow," he said.

"Aye, always tomorrow," Goodcole barked. He stepped away from the untrustworthy Dicker and turned into the record office to find companionship.

Finding the counter unattended, the chaplain coughed loudly. When Martin Stamp appeared, he was carrying a bundle of scrolls in the crook of his arm. His face lit up when he saw Goodcole.

"My friend, I hoped you would come," he said. Goodcole peered at the rolls that the clerk dropped on the counter. The first two were made of paper but the third was vellum with a wax seal attached. Having unfurled each, Stamp weighted the corners with plumbs taken from a set of market scales. He made room for his friend to join him on his side of the counter then addressed himself to the first document. "Yesterday, you asked me to find out more about the events in Potter's Field the year after the Spanish ships came to our shores. This is the original indictment, which describes the offence committed by Enfield women on 31 July in 1589. It reads: 'on the said day about ten a.m. at Joan Potter's in the parish of Enfield and county of Middlesex, Alicia Ward wife of Thomas Ward butcher, Margery Hunsdon wife of William Hunsdon yeoman, Katherine Elborne wife of John Elborne labourer, Margaret Mead, spinster, Eve Cubley wife of Francis Cubley tanner…' it lists twenty-seven women in all '…assembled themselves riotously and in warlike manner, being armed with swords, daggers, staves, knives and other weapons, and then and there maliciously injured and plucked up a fence belonging to Alice Hayes, widow, to the grave injury of the said Alice Hayes'."

Goodcole pored over the document. His head had been so scrambled by the rush of the morning that he had almost forgotten about his request. He looked at the flowing script of the court clerk and then at the long list of women. Sawyer would have been seventeen at the time and although she was not mentioned in the indictment, both her cousins Meg and Eve were. He imagined a group of thirty women armed with swords, scythes, daggers and hoes; they must have made a hardy band and put him in mind of the Peasant's Revolt. "It sounds like they fought a pitched battle," he said.

Stamp shook his head. "No, don't be misled by the court clerk's words for affray. It seems that all these women did was to pull down a fence which infringed upon their common land." He moved onto the second document. "This records the punishment handed down by Justices Wroth, Middlemore and Machel: each of the women received a whipping and six months' imprisonment."

"And what of this third document?" Goodcole peered at the vellum scroll.

"That shouldn't be here at all. It is addressed to the Cecil family and will be returned to them forthwith." Stamp's soft fingers glided over the shape of the cat pressed into the molten wax. "This is an appeal to Lord Burghley who controlled the manor across the brook from Potter's Field in Edmonton. It begs him to overturn the sentences. It complains that those who stole the land, namely Justices Wroth, Middlemore and Machel, have 'sat in invidious judgement' over the women who defended their birthright." Stamp picked up a sheet of paper that lay curled within the vellum. Unlike the scroll this scrap was stained and smudged by many hands. He held it up to the light. "This tells how many of the women gave birth here in Newgate. It counts at least ten mothers brought to bed."

Goodcole shuddered. "Did any survive?"

"It seems unlikely. There was plague in the prison that year," Stamp replied.

Down in the chapel Goodcole prepared for evening prayers. It being Holy Tuesday he had thought up a short homily titled 'make ready for judgement'. It was partly inspired by the group of nuns whom he had passed at St Giles for he was struck by the contrast between the two parties: the desolate Deicrowe heading west and these fair sisters heading east borne up by the prospect of the soon-to-be-risen Christ.

Theirs, he reminded himself, was a simple fellowship based on prayer and vigilance; of course such fidelity came easier within the sanctity of a convent than the degradation of a prison. In Newgate he was still shocked by how often prisoners were moved: most changed cell every few days with the result that it was hard to keep track of people. The practice was made more extreme by the warden's insistence on using ship's watches to punctuate the day. The timings of these watches were taken from an hourglass in the guardhouse and they changed every thirty minutes. Even at Easter, when the liturgical calendar held sway, the relentless rhythm continued. Perhaps the aim was to prevent fellowship for this constant shifting of prisoners meant most spent their days cheek by jowl with strangers who knew little and cared less about their plight. So, as Goodcole watched the men file into the chapel, it came as no surprise that he recognised fewer than half. He said prayers, delivered his homily and sent them on their way and then he scraped out the wax from the candleholders and spread fresh sawdust for the women.

Soon enough he heard the clink of chains from the corridor. When they arrived, he recalled two of the wives from Monday's delivery from the assizes, though, to his relief, the red-headed woman was not present. He let the women file into rows and waited for them to settle before addressing them from the lectern. As ever he measured out his words in morsels, feeding them phrase by phrase to those who stood hungry for the Word.

"Sistren,

We stand here in godly discipline to…

Mind how notorious sinners are first…

Put to penance, then punished in this world…"

The chaplain surveyed the bowed heads. He saw tousled hair on bare shoulders and looked lower to where hemp shifts covered bruised torsos and limbs. In the flickering light he saw more than he wanted to see: one of the women was bleeding; a thin trickle of blood seeped through leg irons onto the sawdust-strewn floor. Goodcole remembered the primordial waters referred to in Genesis. He shifted his stance for although he was used to ministering to women one-on-one, he was ill at ease when sharing such a small space with so many perspiring bodies. Those bodies were leaky and unclean; their fluids were as changeable as the tides and like them, under the spell of the moon, they could overbrim the stoutest of harbour walls. He tried to put these thoughts out of his mind. He stood behind his lectern and stuck to his order of service, which required their response.

"Cursed are the covetous: adulterers and fornicators."

"Aye, cursed are the covetous."

"Cursed are slanderers, drunkards, extortioners."

"Damn them."

"Cursed is he that slays the soul of innocent blood." When he uttered these words, one of the women let out a wail, while another, who was heavily pregnant, leaned forward to comfort her.

After the service Goodcole swept up the sawdust and snuffed out the candles. Again he glanced down to where the doorstop had once lain and recalled the dark pile of woodchips on Deicrowe's bed in the Master's Side. He had stowed the mommet away for safekeeping but what if it was discovered? He would have a hard time explaining that to the dean.

Up in his study Goodcole got down on his hands and knees and, holding the lantern ahead of him like a miner's lamp, searched the farthest recesses between the floor and end wall. He was both sweating and breathless when he found the swaddled totem amidst the woodlice. Goodcole stood up and dusted himself down. He shot a glance at the door and, reassured that he was alone, unwrapped the linen strip that he had wound round Deicrowe's carving. Goodcole then stood the idol in the glow of the lantern and, caught between revulsion and fascination, inspected its shape. He observed its lifelike pose: the way the Madonna stood with her palms open, as if blessing the ground on which she stood. He observed, too, her swelling belly, a sign of the waters within and this thought made him shudder with disgust. God is watching you; he sees into your heart. *You should have burned this fetish when you were able*, his conscience told him. But he had not burned it and now he was afraid to for burning a likeness brought its own consequences – didn't it? Goodcole thought first of Sawyer in her cell, then of the perspiring bodies in the chapel. He dug his thumbnail into the statue's stomach and, appalled by what he was holding, dropped the little figure onto his table. Though he could not put it into words he knew deep down that there was some link between this cultish figure, the women in the chapel and the events in Potter's Field recounted by Stamp. He was about to panic when a flash of insight came to his rescue. Dicker was not the right person to ask; he had cast in his lot with the London Company and so would tell him nothing, whereas the witch, who enjoyed taunting him, might yet reveal the key to the whole business. He replaced the mommet in its hiding place and packed his Bible and psalter into his bag.

Down in Limbo Goodcole found Sawyer crouched on all fours. He lifted the lantern so the light shone over first the arch of her spine, then the flagstones of the floor.

"What are you doing?" he asked her.

"I'm scraping up drops of wax," she replied.

"Why?"

"'Tis something to do. For three days and four nights I have lain in this pit with only you and the rats for company."

"Aye, the rats have the run of the place," he said. In the darkness around him he detected a fetid smell, which brought to mind the mudflats at Barking at low tide.

"Know you, the rats come straight from the river?"

"The river, how could you possibly know?"

"I mind the smell off their fur. When the rains are heavy and the river is high, the rats take shelter in the City wall. 'Tis my guess they can run right round."

Goodcole placed the lantern on its hook and unpacked his bag. Widening his stance he held up the king's Bible. "Mind you what this is?" he said.

Sawyer was rolling a ball of wax in her palm; it was about the size of a pea. She looked up at the leather-bound volume and wiped a bead of spittle from her lower lip. For a moment she seemed to shrink back into herself. "It is the Black Book. It holds the Word of God within," she said.

Goodcole sensed her reverence. He knew the Bible gave him power and so he leaned forward. "It contains those same tales that you have heard recounted your whole life: those read to you first by Gunn, then Thickpenny," he said.

Sawyer was squatting on the ground; she pulled up her knees in anticipation. Her pose was that of a young girl waiting for a bedtime story. "Will you read to me now?" she asked.

"What would you have me read?" he replied.

Sawyer thought for a moment and pulled the blanket around her. "Read to me about 'the camel'. Mistress Hayes once described that beast as a goat with a pointed back."

Goodcole opened the Bible. "I doubt she ever saw one. The camel is a desert-dweller that frequents Barbary and the Holy Land." He thought of the Three Wise Men travelling from the east and turned to Matthew's Gospel, but Sawyer interrupted him.

"The camel may shrink itself to the size of a flea to pass through the eye of a needle." Again she was like a little girl.

Goodcole scratched his head. "No, you misunderstand." He turned to Mark and finding the passage he cleared his throat. "Our Saviour taught that '*it is easier for a camel to pass through the eye of a needle than for a rich man to enter the Kingdom of God*' which is to say that those who take reward in this life shall forfeit salvation in the next." There was a moment of pure silence during which Sawyer first drew in her breath and then exhaled.

"Do you believe that?" she asked.

"It is the Word of God," he said.

She leant forward. "Then, 'tis as I thought. If this life is sour, the next is sweet and the other way round." She peered up at the silk ribbon that Goodcole used to mark his page and seemed to take heart. "Read me more," she said.

Goodcole sensed his advantage. "In a moment I will read to you but first recount to me the events in Potter's Field the year of the Spanish."

There was a bad tempered grunt from the floor. "I have already told you," she said.

At this Goodcole closed the Bible and opened up a linen binder full of notes. "You have only told me what happened that Lammas-time. Describe to me what happened next: the events that led to the breaking of the fence."

"Aye, I tried already but you stopped me. 'Waste not your time with curses' you said."

"That was because you were abusing the Church, which is your only hope."

"I was about to tell of the burning of the shrine, which was the real crime."

Goodcole stretched his hands out at his sides. Without realising it, he was echoing the pose of the Madonna blessing the ground at her feet. "Very well, tell me about the burning of the shrine." He trimmed his quill with a blade and prepared to write.

* * *

"It was the seventeenth of November, which is St Hugh's Day. All summer we heard stories of the Spanish ships: that they had landed in the west; that they would sail up the Thames; that their soldiers would creep up the Lea and come for us in our beds. By November – thank the Almighty – the danger seemed past. Storms had blown the fleet north. We heard from drovers on the marshes that great hulks were breaking up on the sands beyond Ely and that the pride of the Pope's army was drowned, or seeking shelter. St Hugh's is always a great feast, especially in those days when harvests were good. That year relief at our deliverance mixed with glee for it was thirty years to the day since Bess became queen.

The procession was the same as at Rogation, which is the 'beating of the bounds' that I have told you about. It was a proud moment when folk vied to prove their worth. First came Curate Thickpenny walking with Churchwarden Wyld. Behind them trudged Reverend Gunn, flanked by a choir of five and after these orderly types chased a crowd of ruffians with staves in their hands. Many times Churchwarden Wyld had to act as constable because half the men were full-drunk and the others bent on mischief. It was a surprise to me that no one died that day but they may as well have for there was a greater hurt done.

When the procession reached the end of Bungie Lane it stopped under the Judas Tree. First Reverend Gunn stood with his back to the fence, then the choir spread out on either side and sang, "Sing unto the Lord with thanksgiving." Next our minister turned to Churchwarden Wyld who stepped forward with his axe. Wyld split the stile with one blow and the crowd surged forward. The men climbed the slope and, afraid at first, gathered below the clump of yews on the ridge. Here they awaited the minister. Reverend Gunn was slow to reach them for Thickpenny had to support him amongst the hummocks and the tufts. After a deal of effort he made his way to the hollow where the water spilled from the earth. Gunn commanded them to be silent then. He looked at the idol below the spring. He pointed to the offerings laid on the slope and then our minister stepped over an urn and ground his heel down into it. He made a show of this to prove all was crushed and only dust remained. Then he raised his voice and said, "Who's on the Lord's side?" The crowd answered as one so he ordered them to burn the idol and break up the graves. And this they did: they made a bone fire and kicked and stamped until there was nothing left. So when Meg, Eve and I came there early the next day, we found only bits because the whole slope was defiled. We three watched others sift through the ash and knelt and cried because those we loved had been brought to nothing."

* * *

Goodcole held up his hand for Sawyer to stop. "These 'others' who sifted the ash for remains were they known to you?"

"Some were, but most were not. They were strangers to the parish. I heard later they were Arundel's men. They took what was left of the idol back to M'Lud's house in Tottenham Wood."

"So this relic was not consumed by the flames?"

"The statue was carved from bog oak that had lain in the marsh since time out of mind. It was more stone than wood."

Goodcole noted down what she had told him. Then he put his papers in order and replaced them in his bag. "Now, what passage would you have me read?" he asked.

"Read how the meek shall inherit the earth," she said.

Once up in his study Goodcole counted his blessings. A frustrating morning had given way to an afternoon in which he had made progress, not only winning Sawyer's confidence but also uncovering the link between her and Deicrowe. That the court had found a way now, thirty-two years on, to rid itself of both suggested some extremely tardy housekeeping on its part. He replaced the tallow and looked with renewed interest at Sawyer's second story. Leafing through the pages he skimmed through the lines of his own sloping script until he found her description of Potter's Field. Here he read the words: 'the soil there is the richest in the parish and yet, up until that year, it had neither been cropped nor put out to pasture'. Given what she had just told him, those words hinted why a group of more than twenty women had banded together to pull down the fence of a rich widow. As was his way, Goodcole tried to put himself in the minds of the guilty and so he imagined the aftermath of the St Hugh's Day procession in Elizabeth's parish when, three decades before, the Church had finally acted to break up the shrine. All winter, shock at the destruction at Potter's must have festered but it was only the following spring, after Lady Day in March, when paddocks were built and Wroth's cattle put out to pasture that the women had acted.

The arrival of those cattle was a cruel blow for each time they walked to church the women would have witnessed M'Lud's prize herd trampling on those they had loved and lost. Goodcole recalled Sawyer's disdain for her old teacher Alice Hayes and he remembered her stinging gibe that he, like her, 'pretended to be humble while stealing off the poor'. Now he understood why her feelings ran so deep: how insulting it must have been when a woman who held herself up as a pillar of the community took advantage of Wroth's greed and set her cattle on the graves too.

He thought back to the date found by Stamp: the offence had occurred on 31 July, which showed that the women had held back. To protect themselves against the full force of the law they had selected a group of young wives, most of them pregnant. These women who included Sawyer's cousins Margaret and Eve, had gone forward with instructions to break down one single fence – that belonging to their old teacher. It was a calculated act and they must have known that by making it they risked the death penalty but they simply had to do something.

Goodcole wondered about Sawyer's role in the protest: had she taken part or fled across the bounds to the forest in

Edmonton? Then he reversed his viewpoint and considered the disorder from the authorities' point of view. The fate of the shrine would have been common knowledge, as would have been the Arundels' interest in it. More importantly, the fact that the poorest women could now make common cause with such a well-connected Catholic family would have rung alarm bells. There would have been constables' reports and spies posted to the Arundels' house in Tottenham Wood. Given what Sawyer had just told him, Goodcole felt sure that Deicrowe had helped remove the statue. He pictured William and Nicholas working quickly, first wrapping the statue in sacking and then wheeling it in a barrow to their cart while Sawyer and her cousins looked on. Surely it was no coincidence that two people who had stood on the same turf thirty-two years earlier should spend their final days next to each other in Limbo? The question was not so much 'why?' as 'why now?'.

Outside the prison night had closed in when Goodcole returned to his lodgings. Anne gave him a warming posset to drink and served up a plate of flounders. Goodcole looked at the four empty chairs that were pulled in close to the board at which he sat. The place was so pristine that he could not tell whether the others had eaten already.

"Are the twins in bed?" he asked.

Anne ignored his question. She moved around to Joan's empty place and, pressing her palms together in an attitude of prayer, looped a string holding a single translucent bead onto the back of her chair.

Goodcole took the hint and extended grace into a prayer for the safety of his household, making sure to mention his favourite by name. Then he stood up and examined the charm. The bead was made of amber. It glowed in the light of the candle: a single teardrop of sap that had bled onto the forest floor an aeon ago. He looked up at his wife. "Is it the charm that you wore during childbirth?" he asked.

She shot him a fierce look. "I did not lie with you so that our children might be laid low by a country crone," she said.

"You were but a child yourself when you first lay with me," he replied. Goodcole dismissed her then and put her words out of his mind. He pushed a slither of flounder to the side of his bowl, speared it with a pricker and guided it into his mouth. The fish tasted of the mudflats. It had been caught in the age-old way by baiting a hawthorn prickle and waiting out the rise and fall of the tide. He thought of the ships coming and going in the estuary and of the plans afoot in St Sithes Row.

Dipping the bread into the liquor of the bowl he made a decision. He was sure now: tomorrow he would return to Butler & Son to broach printing a pamphlet on Sawyer. If they could agree terms he would then register his publication in the book at Stationer's Hall. While the prospect of a well-worded pamphlet would keep the alderman happy for now, its contents would allow Goodcole to justify his actions to the dean if relations turned sour with the London Company. It was a strategy that had served him well in the past for, amidst all the lies and innuendo of the Robinson affair, his report had allowed him to present a clear account of the facts. In this case, however, the facts would require deft handling because they showed that the Church had been slow to exert its will on the witch's parish. Thus for his pamphlet Goodcole decided to omit all reference to the specific locale in which Sawyer grew up. He would dwell instead on the sly figure of the Devil who promised to empower the poor against the just cause of the Church.

Day 5

Henry Goodcole watched William Butler stir the ink. He leaned in closer to breathe in the heady fumes, then looked around at the low-beamed room. To his left a rack of shelves held papers of different grades; to his right a charcoal stove dried the air. Turning back, he traced the bubbles that turned in the earthenware jar below him and saw his reflection broken into ripples of black.

"Do you use soot from the wick of a lamp?" he enquired.

Butler lifted the jar with both hands and placed it on the outer edge of the stove to warm. "For this I have mixed in nutgalls to vitriol. Later I will add gum arabic as a fixer and a drop of brandy to stop putrefaction."

Goodcole, who had an aversion to hard liquor, screwed up his nose. "This is quill ink, is it not? Am I right that it is yet too early to make ink for the press?"

Butler motioned to his son to take over stirring and wiped down his hands on a rag. "I take it from your visit that you intend to publish?" he asked.

"I am interested in the science of your craft, that is all."

The printer raised an eyebrow and tucked the rag in his apron. "The press is a different beast altogether. It uses a mix of oils and each printer swears by his own blend so we must guard our secrets for these things are like magic and may not be divulged." Butler was only half serious and soon relented. "Come round the back and I'll show you how it's done." He ushered Goodcole into a cramped yard where barrels of woodchips lay soaking under a lean-to.

Out in the April sunshine Goodcole's eye was drawn up to the tenements above Butler's workshop. By the tower of St Martin's a maid was stringing out washing. He brought his gaze back down to earth and studied first the barrels of pulp then the pockmarked face of his printer.

Butler reached in his hand and skimmed frothy scum off the bark. "We cut the hawthorn early this year. When it has given up its sap, we will boil it black and leave it to cure in the sun."

Goodcole leant forward and sniffed at the mixture. "At the dye-works they add urine to make it bite," he remarked.

Butler was noncommittal. "We add many things: we grind up bones. I've heard that some even add in the blood of a firstborn child." Butler winked mischievously, but as ever Goodcole remained serious.

"It is a solemn art you perform here for all learning depends on it. Where would the book trade be without your services?" he said.

"We would be reading only Latin."

"Aye, and doffing our caps to the King of Spain."

The printer smiled back at him and Goodcole noticed he had lost another tooth. Butler touched his finger to his nose and pointed up the rickety stairs that led from the backyard up to the first floor. "I have just installed the new press. It was shipped from Holland – will you take a look?" he asked.

On the first floor, the square bulk of the press blotted out the light. It looked outsized in the timber-frame house, like a siege engine stored below decks in a ship. Goodcole observed the braces that buttressed between beam and joist; then, he walked over to the windows where a compositor's rack held a frame of metal type. For a moment he tried to read the gunmetal text but all was back to front. He looked down at the trestle where a heap of wetted paper drained into a tray and prodded a virgin page. Feeling it cold and damp, he turned back to the press.

"She is a beast," he said.

At this Butler murmured in satisfaction. "You're in time to see us pull the first proofs." The printer stepped behind the bulk of the press and called downstairs to his son who arrived with a tray of black varnish. Sliding out the type-stone from the carriage Butler waited as his son applied the sticky shellac with a pair of leather pads, rocking them to and fro on characters that were locked around a carved block of wood. Butler then lifted a sheet of still-wet paper onto the frame and slid the carriage back into the press in a single move. Checking that they were standing clear, he grasped the lever and rocked back hard on his heel so the full weight compressed between beam and floor joists. Goodcole witnessed the timbers groan and watched Butler repeat the move.

The sheet they took from the press was no longer white; it bore the imprint of sudden and incomparable weight. At its centre the chaplain was surprised to see a woodcut of a country girl. He read the text: 'Maids for the New Life of Virginia: a call to English women, young, chaste and honest to serve God and Country in Nova Britannia'. Goodcole turned to Butler. "Is there no escaping the London Company?" he asked.

Maids for the New Life of Virginia:

A call to English women, young, chaste and honest
to serve God and Country in Nova Britannia

Public notice by authority of Sir John Ferrar
in St Sithes Lane, Billingsgate

Printed by William Butler & Son, Ave Maria lane, London, 1621

The printer gave him a curious look then cast his professional eye over the first impression. "They pay more than you," he said. "Besides, with this press we are better suited to bigger print runs. We won this order off our rival Nicholas Okes for now we may print four pages to his one."

"Aye, but this is Robinson's idea: they want breeders for the colony."

Butler hardly heard him now. He ran his thumbnail over the proof and addressed his son. "Add a smear more bear fat, then we will work through the heap."

While the two men worked the press, Goodcole put his rancour aside and weighed up his options. Butler knew that he wanted to publish; the problem was the price, or more precisely the payment because presently Goodcole had only four shillings to his name. He thought back to the pamphlet that Dicker claimed to have read. *The Happy Conversion of Francis Robinson* had been a modest success and had brought him to the attention to the board of governors. Before reading it, the dean had opposed giving the post to a lay preacher such as himself, but an eleventh hour conversion of a Catholic was hard to resist and in the end he had wavered his veto. Goodcole thought for a while, then, surrounded by the thump and grind of the press, an idea came to him: the dean should provide funds. After all, the publishing business had its centre in St Paul's Churchyard; why not suggest that the dean, or at least his office, act as backer for someone with a proven record of success?

No sooner had the solution suggested itself than Goodcole's native caution cut in. Several difficulties suggested themselves: firstly, the timeline was tight; if he was to profit from the notoriety of the Sawyer case any publication would have to be agreed today to be on the shelves for the following week; secondly, his intention to publish during Holy Week – a time of fasting and reflection – might cast him in a bad light. Weighing up both, Goodcole concluded that while the first problem was practical, the second was more about perception; after all, the court had decided to execute Sawyer on Maundy Thursday. The secret was to tie his pamphlet to the Easter theme of redemption and forgiveness. If he succeeded in doing that, he might well win the dean's support, improving his chances of preferment in the process.

When Butler and his son had reached the end of the heap, they snagged each page in their drying wrack and hoisted the entire run to head height on a pulley.

Goodcole looked up admiringly at the crowd of country girls that turned in the breeze; they seemed like giant playing cards beckoning him – as fresh as the young Anne when he had first met her. He reflected on the printing process and was minded of Sawyer's riddle: first the spark of an idea, then the ink that made the mark that set the reader free. He turned to the sweating Butler. "I have in my head a frontispiece like your poster here: the same but aged. Could you find me a woodblock of an old crone: someone bent double with a stick?"

Butler wiped his brow with a towel. "Not a problem," he said. He pointed down the stairs. "Come down and we can discuss terms."

Back in the shop, surrounded by the smell of quill ink, Goodcole and Butler haggled over folios, typefaces and costs. Because he had given this new pamphlet so little thought Goodcole settled for more or less the same format that he had used for Robinson and agreed to drop in a down payment later in the day.

"You need to register your title in the book in Stationer's Hall," Butler said when the two had shaken hands. He regarded Goodcole warmly and paused.

"Is there something else?" Goodcole asked.

Butler reached into a cabinet of drawers and then placed a single page on the counter. "I wanted to ask you about this," he said.

Goodcole looked down at the manuscript. His first thought was that it had dropped out of his bag but then something made him look closer. He read the text and stepped back in indignation. The document purported to be a pardon absolving Elizabeth Sawyer of all wrongdoing. Although the wording was different, it was clearly modeled on the first draft that had been stolen from his study. The writing was almost identical to his; only the letter 's' was exaggerated, invading the line below. "Who brought this in?" he asked.

Butler had been watching his reaction. He seemed relieved. "A gentleman. He claimed authority from the dean and offered to pay for one hundred copies in advance. Of course, I have no dealings with the dean so I wondered."

"Could you not tell that I would never write such a thing?"

"Aye, the words are not your style but the end looks sound enough." So saying the printer flipped the page over and Goodcole stared at his signature. There was no doubting that this part was the work of his hand; he could tell by the flourish at the end where the quill had spattered ink when he turned it between forefinger and thumb. "What grade of paper do you usually write on?" Butler asked.

Goodcole picked up the page. "This is heavier than I am used to," he said.

Butler folded the page in half and picked at the edge with his thumbnail. "There," he said pointing at the fold. "As we say in the print trade, 'wherever there is an original, there is also a copy waiting to be made'. This manuscript is unusual for it is both. The first page is a forgery while the reverse, which contains your name, is genuine. Those that pasted them together knew what they were doing. They would first use a thin size to fix the writing, then rewet the paper to bond the two sheets together."

"The 'gentleman' who brought this to you spoke how exactly?" Goodcole had no sooner asked the question than he thought of George Scald, a man expert at moving things in and out of the prison.

"The man who brought this in was well spoken. He said he was acting for the Chapter of St Paul's."

Dismissing Scald from his mind, Goodcole now cast about for other suspects but could find none that fitted the description. "He was acting, certainly. Sure, the City is full of changelings. It would be my guess that his aim was to discredit the Church," he said.

Butler raised an eyebrow. "A Puritan, perhaps?" he said.

"Aye, dissenters for what better way to show us in a bad light than to say we tolerate witchcraft?"

After he had left Butler & Son, Goodcole walked the short distance up Ave Maria Lane to Stationer's Hall. The hall was a fine building marked out by its herringbone brick and tall Tudor chimneys. Entering up its curving stone steps, Goodcole greeted the sergeant and made his way up the oak staircase to the library. Here, all texts printed in the king's realm had to be noted down prior to production. A small queue had formed in front of the registrar and Goodcole took his place behind a raffish character in riding boots and a cloak. Enthralled, yet fearful of his surroundings, Goodcole looked around at the cabinets and dark panelling. The room was like the sacred space of a scriptorium and it reminded him that he was now part of the eminent guild of writers. This not only meant that he was a success and someone to be reckoned with in this world but it aligned him with the Church. He basked in the glow of the thought as the man in front stepped forward to speak to the registrar.

"Name?"

"I am... William Rowley, sir." The man savoured his name as if it was a fine wine.

"Title of publication?"

"*All's Lost by Lust*: 'tis a tragicomedy to be played in the Phoenix, Drury Lane."

"It is a play?"

"It is a play in every sense, sir. Seriously funny, yet uncannily grave." The registrar shot him a weary look.

"Printer?"

"Nicholas Okes…"

"I have the address."

Goodcole listened to the exchange and steadied his nerve. With the scratch of a pen the title of his next publication would be fixed for eternity. For a brief moment he was tempted to play safe but then gall fired in his veins and he decided to stick with his original choice.

"Name?"

"Henry Goodcole."

"Title of publication?"

"*The Wonderful Discovery of Elizabeth Sawyer, a witch late of Edmonton, her conviction and condemnation and death... together with the relation of the Devil's access to her and their conference together.*" The registrar looked up.

"Must your titles be so long? They leave no space on the line." He tetchily scratched in the entry in full. "Do you have a printer, sir?"

"William Butler & Son." The registrar waved him away.

"I have the address," he said.

On his way back to the prison Goodcole mulled over his choice of title; it was in some ways a risk because 'the wonderful discovery' could be interpreted in different ways. Goodcole's first intent had been to communicate the way divine providence had uncovered Sawyer's evil desires but he was open to other interpretations, too. Although she was a hard nut to crack, he had struck up an accord with her and was not completely against the woman. Illiterate and slovenly, she was also spirited and had a perceptive eye for detail. She had, too, benefitted from his ministrations: her new understanding of the power of the meek proved the point. Goodcole had no sooner congratulated himself than doubt clouded his thoughts and a new question raised its head: what if Elizabeth Sawyer believed *she* was meek all along? Worse, what if she mistook the Saviour's comments about the rich man who struggled to enter the Kingdom of Heaven as some way of getting back at her betters? The thought put a chill through him for this was the way dissenters saw the world; drawing on notions of Passover in the Old Testament and Easter in the New, they foretold how, to right a great wrong, the innocents would rise up and topple the strong. Such talk was seditious because it aimed at nothing less than deposing the king and sweeping away the rule of the Church. Goodcole stopped by Amen Corner. He was about to turn on his heel when he checked himself. His title was already in the registrar's book so there was now no way of changing it. He stared at the shopfronts and tried to steady himself. Surely a vindictive scold like that could not believe that *she* was meek and pure of heart? But five years in Ludgate had taught him that people were good at self-deception and saw faults in others long before they examined their own hearts. Besides, the true meaning of the word 'meek' would be lost on Sawyer. Goodcole cursed his own stupidity for words could prove fickle and he should have chosen a title that was clear, not clever. Now, when he turned it over in his mind, *The Wonderful Discovery of Elizabeth Sawyer* smacked of something malign: a revelation of dark powers, worthy of a witch.

The forenoon watch was half over when Goodcole made it back to the chapel. He trimmed his lamp and, standing at the lectern, opened the king's Bible at John 13. The passage was a favourite of his and he had discussed it many times with his daughter Joan. It described how Jesus had washed his disciples' feet after breaking bread with them at the Last Supper. The pathos of the story came from the fact that, although Jesus knew that His followers had betrayed Him, He was still able to lower Himself before them. This was the true meaning of 'meek' for in acting with selfless courage, Jesus had overcome pride, the sin that separates us one from another and leads to our spiritual death. Knowing he would need to simplify the story for the felons, Goodcole skimmed through the chapter and made a mental note of certain key phrases. He repeated to himself:

"Jesus knew his hour had come…
He knew he was come from God and went to God.
He poureth water into a basin and began to wash his disciples' feet and to wipe them…
'I have given you an example… do as I have done to you.'."

The simplicity of the King's English calmed him. It told him that faith was on his side and reassured him that all his doubts would dissolve before the miracle of Easter. That miracle was now only four days away.

When the wives filed in, Goodcole sensed their bitter mood. On his rounds in the Stone Hold he had watched them sew the shift that Sawyer would wear to the scaffold. He recalled the deft movements as each threaded the bone needle through the cloth; he minded how the garment was passed down the line, one woman stitching the sleeves, another the hem and he remembered, too, the simmering anger that had made him move on. Wasn't Sawyer a mother who had suffered and wouldn't her children soon be orphans? Counting the wives into the chapel, Goodcole noticed that all but two were heavily pregnant. This only confirmed what he already knew: a higher proportion of expectant wives attended morning prayers than any other group in the prison; moreover, the way these women worshipped set them apart for they prayed with a fervour that others lacked. Standing behind his lectern, he looked around him at the truncated space of the chapel. Now that he had installed brighter candles, there was less shadow in the place. He glanced over at the walled-in arch behind his barrel of sawdust and wondered what its original purpose had been. If it had formed the entrance to a side chapel dedicated to the Holy Mother, it might explain why illiterate women still sought solace here, especially before childbirth.

At midday Goodcole set off to visit the dean's chambers in St Paul's. Although he had no appointment or knowledge of the dean's movements that day, he sensed that it was a time to be bold. His plan was to rid himself of Deicrowe's mommet on the way and then seek funds for his pamphlet in the Chapter House. Instead of following the direct route that he and Dicker had taken on Sunday, Goodcole took a roundabout path to the cathedral. Stepping outside the City, he walked briskly past the Old Bailey and turned west down the hill. Here, where the wall projected out to meet the River Fleet, he knew a spot perfect for disposing Deicrowe's carving. The drain was located at the end of a cul-de-sac where it sat in shadow at the base of the old Roman foundations. Once used by the dye-house that was built downstream of Fleet Bridge, the channel had long since fallen into disrepair. These days it was the resting place for rubbish that Londoners vainly hoped would wash away from their houses into the Thames. Goodcole stepped gingerly over the slimy cobbles and moved crablike down the slope until he stood over the rusted iron grill. Here he shielded his nose from the filth that had gathered below and cast an eye at the traffic crossing Fleet Bridge; then, checking he was alone, he reached into his bag to grasp the muslin-covered mommet. He had hoped to accomplish the drop in one movement but the bars of the grill were set too close together. Trying again, he unwound the swaddling and tried to ease the carving through the gap yet the little figure would not slip through. Goodcole thought of the Madonna's pose – the outspread arms and tilt of the swollen tummy – then he heard footsteps. Panicking, he stood up abruptly, stuffed the mommet back into his bag and set off towards Ludgate.

The Chapter House of St Paul's was built into the cloister south-west of the nave of the cathedral. Goodcole walked past the crowd of seminarians outside St Peter's College and, ignoring the scholars' curious looks, stepped into the sacred space of the cloister. Here where all was calm, he took a moment to savour the protection offered by Mother Church and then followed a cassocked figure who had passed beyond. The Chapter House was an octagonal building supported by buttresses that rose above the height of its eight gothic windows. Like St Paul's itself, which had lost its spire some sixty years before, it looked incomplete, as if its ambition to reach skywards had been thwarted. Entering through the south-facing door, Goodcole felt his confidence melt away; he steeled himself for rejection and then marvelled. Entering there was like walking into a great lantern. Light from all sides filtered through glass with prismatic panes staining the floor blue and rose. He regarded the long table with chairs set on either side and was about to peer skywards when a voice from above stopped him dead.

"Who are you?"

"I am seeking an audience with the dean." There was a pause in which the interrogator descended from the clerestory. Goodcole looked up to where a frocked figure was swooping like a gull.

"*Who* are you... exactly?"

"I am Henry Goodcole, recently appointed ordinary of Newgate."

The man sniffed distastefully; his nose had already detected the fetid smell of the prison. "You are the… ordinary and you think you can walk in here and see the very reverend dean?"

Goodcole bit the inside of his lip. He had half expected this for wherever there was power and influence there was always a gatekeeper. Gatekeepers were worker bees who, though lowly in themselves, used their position to deny access to the hive. They were highly aggressive but their venom was light. Goodcole decided to counter. "I have come here to consult with the dean about a matter of import: the case of a witch who has put a curse on Mother Church and all who work for her."

Blood drained from the verger's face. He was about to say something when a deeper voice intervened.

"The dean cannot see you now because he has a meeting. Come to the deanery in an hour's time and he will hear your concerns." The speaker was the dean, himself.

"So you have an appointment after all," Goodcole purred once he had stepped outside. Since he had an hour to kill, he opted to reward himself by perusing the bookstalls in the churchyard. It didn't take long to skirt around the east end to the yard under St Paul's Cross. He avoided the crowd that had gathered to hear the sermon from a travelling preacher and moved, instead, to the encampment of tents clustered around the footings of the cathedral. Goodcole was drawn to the glow of hot coals from braziers and caught a whiff of stewed pork and roasted chestnuts, too. For a habitué such as himself the pleasure of such a market came from its combination of the familiar with the strange. Joining the throng that milled under the tarpaulins he moved through the fug of spicy Ipocras to where the real merchandise was kept – inside the cathedral itself.

Goodcole entered the building from the northern transept and moved past an array of maps to a stall he often frequented which specialised in psalters. Standing in the echoing hall, he looked at the hand-tooled leather covers and promised himself that one day, when he ran his own parish, he would treat himself to a new edition to replace his threadbare original. He was about to ask the price when a glint within the cavernous space caught his eye. A man and his wife were unpacking their wares and each time they reached down a flash of light reflected up to their faces or to the underside of their board. Goodcole decided to investigate and, walking towards them, continued to observe glints from the packing case until he spotted the inkwells placed above. The inkwells and inkhorns came in all shapes and forms: some were stoneware disks, others were cubes of blue Murano glass and still others were cast out of silver. These silver wells were the most ornate he had ever seen and were fashioned with claw feet and a fierce head to mimic the shape of a hissing cat. It was these that had caught the light from the candles burning above. Goodcole was repelled by the cats, which reminded him of the gargoyles that still adorned the corners of some church towers so he moved deeper into the cathedral to a stall run by Nicholas Okes. In the dim light he spied a row of recent pamphlets and, drawing closer, was disappointed to find that his own on Francis Robinson was not amongst them. His eye settled instead on a biblical title, which quoted the Old Testament. The frontispiece announced in bold type 'Ester hath hanged

Haman'. He looked at the boy behind the stall and recognised him as one of the lads who had been fighting on Sunday. He pointed to the odd title.

"What's this?" he asked.

"'Tis an answer to this," the boy pointed at an adjacent pamphlet called 'The Arraignment of Women'.

Goodcole picked up the first title to discover the author. Glancing down the frontispiece, he read the declaration, 'Ester hath hanged Haman: written by Ester Sowernam, neither maid, wife nor widow, yet really all and therefore experienced to defend all'.

"This is written by a *woman*?" Goodcole was amazed.

"Aye, it is on its third edition," the boy said cheerfully. Goodcole looked closer. He dipped into the text at random and read the following paragraph:

'If a man abuse a maid and get her with child, no matter is made of it – but as a trick of youth; but it is made so heinous an offence in the maid that she is disparaged and utterly undone by it'. He took a step back. Shock, shame and anger passed over him in quick succession.

"Do you print… this *rubbish*?" he said.

The boy remained carefree. "We print what sells," he said with a smile.

The toll of a bell reminded Goodcole that he had a meeting to attend. Dropping the pamphlet as if it carried contagion, he stalked off through the myriad of stalls. Now he couldn't wait to get out of the place for, smarting at what he read, he saw the market through different eyes. Once upon a time there were only manuscripts created by monks, then a single book was printed. That book was the translated Word of God and it was sacred. After this, a select few had followed with edifying treatises but now it was a free-for-all. After all, what kind of world was it where women were allowed to print *their* thoughts and opinions? *We have made for ourselves a Babel* he concluded and pushed through to the echoing nave of St Paul's Walk.

The deanery was a heavy brick structure located within the cathedral precinct close to the junction between Creed and Carter Lane. Goodcole was no sooner through the studded door than he was called over by a clerk with a list. The man took a note of his name, occupation and query and pointed to a bench. Goodcole looked around at the other waiting figures and noticed with disappointment that most were tradesmen not clerics. Sitting there, he felt the same unease he had known since seminary school. He studied the black-and-white tiles, worn down by many feet and looked up at the crumbling beams above him. Part of him regretted coming, the other part was fearful that he would leave with nothing.

When called he entered a room that was so white it made his eyes sting. Once these walls had contained murals, probably a Last Judgement. The dean was sitting on a high-backed chair with his secretary tucked behind a desk in the corner. Goodcole walked stolidly to the middle of the room and waited; he tried to still his beating heart and took slow measured breaths. The dean shot him a glance. Goodcole noticed how sunken cheekbones contrasted with an aquiline nose, which projected like a beak. The churchman spoke into the stillness in a dry voice that was very clear. Removed from the cavernous echo of the cathedral his words felt unnervingly close.

"My assistant tells me that you come seeking funds. This is a surprise – you must know that I opposed your appointment."

Goodcole widened his stance. "Except for my pamphlet you would have stopped it," he said.

"Yes, I believed you to be no match for the warden. Unsurprisingly, Alderman Bull wanted you in post."

Goodcole bowed deeply. "I wish to serve, that is all."

The dean studied him carefully; he was suspicious of fawning gestures. "Aye, but serve whom, that is the question. Alderman Bull is about trade. Tell me Goodcole, what do you understand by the term?"

"Trade is the exchange of goods, either by barter or coin. We are all much the richer for it."

"Yes, you are right, at least with regard to a country market, but in the City trade is about people."

"I see: traders and merchants, like Alderman Bull, himself."

"No, I mean that trade in this port turns on the exchange of people. They are the new commodity to be bought and sold overseas. I say 'new', but it was ever thus for London was founded by Latins. They didn't come here for the climate – they came to enslave."

Goodcole felt like he was back at school; he was in danger of losing the dean's thread. "I don't understand, you said people are the 'new commodity'," he said.

"New *for us*. Five years ago we were sending wastrels and knaves to Virginia, this year, we are sending women." It seemed that the dean had little time for the London Company; this at least was good news. Goodcole thought of the proofs that Butler had pulled from his press.

"I have seen the posters asking for volunteers," he said.

"Know you the price of one such unsullied maid?"

"The price?"

"One hundred and fifty pounds of tobacco leaf. That is what each settler must pay to have one for a wife."

Goodcole stood awkwardly. He was keen to steer the topic back onto the subject of publication but he had little choice but to follow the dean's lead.

"And have the women no say in the matter?" he said.

"They have a say, but there are many ways to cajole or force them to go. You may say it is their duty, or invent some scandal about them at home."

"You don't believe that it is their duty to go where sent?"

"We all have a duty, Goodcole. Most of all, we have a duty to serve God – even the king must do that. But Alderman Bull is not interested in duty. He has invested funds and is only interested in bodies. We, on the other hand, are interested in souls and souls need watching over."

At last we are coming to it, Goodcole thought. "What do you want me to do?"

"I want you to furnish me with names. You are friendly with Stamp in the record office, send me daily reports on the prisoners and their spiritual health."

"You want updates on *all* the prisoners who pass through Newgate?"

"I want daily reports on the women who attend chapel – in particular, those that are with child. There is something foul afoot there and it stems from that witch."

Goodcole bowed again. When he looked up he saw that the dean had moved on and his secretary was briefing him on his next case. He cleared his throat.

"And will you furnish me with funds to publish?" he asked. The dean seemed surprised that he was still there. He narrowed his eyes.

"Publish?"

"Publish a pamphlet excoriating the witch."

The timbre of the dean's voice did not change but he tilted his head as if probing an unusual conundrum. "Tell me now, why would I wish to fund a publication about a sour old countrywoman?"

"To quench the rumours. You yourself have said there is something foul afoot. I'm told there is a lively trade in the taverns of ballads telling how she may turn day into night, white to black and good to evil."

The dean looked at him with a new appreciation. Goodcole was like a novice who had tried to outwit him with a daring chess move.

"Very good, I see what you are up to: you are forging a link with the Robinson affair, but the two cases are of a different order. Robinson was guilty of high treason and his case was known throughout the country. This woman cursed a neighbour in Winchmore where she killed a few cattle. To write about her might increase her fame."

On leaving the deanery, Goodcole reflected on the injustice of being low-born. All his life he had worked hard; though he came from a modest home in Clerkenwell, he had first won a scholarship and then earned a place in seminary school. Since that time, despite all the knock-backs, he had, through diligence and dedication, succeeded at a thankless job and had even published a series of erudite pamphlets. Yet now, when he sought support to help the unwashed, those above him treated him like some sort of a joke. For goodness sake, the beggars on the steps of the cathedral probably earned more than him; perhaps he would be better seeking alms off them. Aye, and they'd probably give him something, too. In his experience those who had most were the meanest people on earth.

Goodcole stopped off at his lodgings before returning to the prison. Noting the newly delivered letter from Joan on the chest in the hall, he barely greeted his wife. Determined to find something of worth that could augment his four groats and make up William Butler's deposit he first searched through Anne's housekeeping jar in the kitchen and then, in desperation, checked the lining of his summer coat. Finding both empty, he was about to leave in high dudgeon when his eye settled on the amber charm. It was still looped around the back of Joan's chair where Anne had left it the previous night. On impulse he scooped up the charm and reached for the door. He had a hand on the latch when she appeared beside him. He had thought she was pressing food into his hands but she pointed to his closed fist, which still contained her charm. He tried to shake her off and opened the door but she clung on. Anne Goodcole was a head shorter than her husband but she forced open his left hand as if her life depended on it.

"Damn you, woman," Goodcole exclaimed. Releasing his grip he watched her kiss the amber bead and was about to break free when she pulled a purse from between her breasts.

"Is it for her?" She spoke in a fierce whisper. Goodcole was so taken aback that at first he did not respond; he knew she was talking about Sawyer.

"It is so I might publish my account of her last days," he said at last.

"May this give you the last word," she replied. The coin that she pressed into his hand was a silver crown. It was more money than he had ever seen her touch and he knew then that she must have guarded it all their married life.

He looked down at the stamp of the king prancing on his horse then turned the coin between finger and thumb; on the reverse he read the Latin on the rim: 'let no one separate what God has joined'. Anne was watching him and he returned her gaze with gratitude – he had underestimated her.

When Goodcole had placed this deposit with Butler he returned without delay to the prison. Entering the gatehouse, he gave his usual nod to the guard on duty, only to be stopped and pulled aside.

"Open your bag," the guard said flatly. Goodcole was baffled. He shrugged his shoulders and had already flicked open the buckle of his bag when he remembered the half-wrapped mommet inside. Since his meeting with the dean he had been so preoccupied that the hateful thing had completely slipped his mind.

"There's nothing in my bag."

The guard shot him a jaded look. "Empty it, now."

Goodcole pulled out a folder of notes and a roll that contained his quills and vial of ink. A flap of muslin was now protruding from the bag and Goodcole had no choice but to lift out the half-bandaged figure.

The guard's manner stiffened; he turned and called into the guardhouse from where his sergeant appeared. The man was short and red-faced; he had been playing dice and was annoyed at being disturbed. He cast his eye over the mannequin with distaste. "Why are you bringing *this* into the prison?" he asked.

Goodcole felt the blood draining from his face. Somewhere in the back of his mind he sensed that Deicrowe was laughing at him from a great distance. "For goodness sake, man. It's a child's toy: I have bought it for my daughter – that's all."

The sergeant looked at him with contempt. "Take it away," he said.

When he had completed his round of the Master's Side, Goodcole paid a visit to the record office. It had been a day of surprises, most of them unpleasant and he still faced the tricky job of preparing Sawyer for her execution. Yet the dean's comments had made him uneasy; he thought back to his ruminations in the chapel at morning prayers and wondered if he was missing something.

Stamp ushered Goodcole into a back room where he poured out ale. He listened to the description of the search without surprise. As ever he was calm and accepting for his long experience of the penal system had taught him not to judge things by appearances. "The warden is running checks on all that comes in and all that goes out," he explained.

Goodcole detected a glimmer of pity in the clerk's eye. "Why now?" he asked.

"'Tis on account of the rumour going round."

"Rumour?"

"That Sawyer and the Black Dog are one. The warden is worried there will be a riot." Martin Stamp shrugged. "As you know, prisons are full of idle talk but my friend you have a problem for, in confined quarters such as these, a rumour is like a fire – once it takes hold, it spreads until it consumes everything."

Goodcole took in his friend's concern. Up to now he had dismissed the Black Dog tale as a revenge fantasy cooked up in the heated heads of felons but now Newgate's folklore was starting to impinge on his work. He decided to press on with his original enquiry. "Tell me about the fire that destroyed the chapel," he said.

"That was well before my time," Stamp replied.

"Aye, but you must know why or how it occurred."

Stamp took a slurp of ale and then placed his tankard down firmly on the table. He seemed to be mulling over whether to share a confidence. For the first time Goodcole noticed the toll that years of service had taken on the clerk: what was left of his friend's hair was turning from grey to fluffy white around his ears. Stamp lowered his voice. "Fires are a fact of prison life and many are started deliberately," he said.

"Why?"

"When a place is so rotten, fire is sometimes the only thing that can cleanse it. It is perhaps a surer method than walling in."

Goodcole looked startled. "Walling in – does that happen here?" he asked.

Stamp nodded. "It has happened," he said.

"But what of the prisoners?"

"What of them?" There was a long silence during which each man sluiced the dregs of their ale around their tankards.

Eventually, Goodcole found his voice. "Well, this rumour about the Black Dog speaks of evil days," he said.

Down in Limbo Goodcole found that the warden had posted an extra guard outside Sawyer's cell. Putting his best foot forward he tucked the heavy text of the king's Bible under his arm and instructed the sergeant-at-arms to open the door.

As before he found Sawyer crouched on all fours. He hooked his lantern to its stand and laid the Bible on the desk.

"What passage would you have me read?" he said. Sawyer was still scrabbling in the dirt so he simply sat and waited. After a deal of scraping and scratching, she came to heel. There was a period of silence during which both listened to reverberations from above and then she spoke.

"Enough words. I am glad I go to the gallows tomorrow," she said.

"Glad, why?"

"Because tomorrow is Maundy Thursday when the greatest will become least. There will be a great reckoning."

Goodcole was sure now that she wanted revenge. He decided to push on and broach the subject of her declaration at Tyburn. "We should agree on the words you will say to the crowd. You have had enough of this ragman's roll so let us together choose one of King David's psalms. On the scaffold I will whisper it to you so that you can proclaim it out to all."

For a while there was silence as she considered his offer. "Which psalm?" she asked.

Goodcole held his psalter up between two palms and then let it fall open on the writing desk. The book parted at the silk marker. "The book says Psalm 51," he said.

Slowly, painfully, Sawyer stood up. She spoke the words as if standing in the Glebe at the time of her catechism. Her body was old and broken but she sounded almost young for there was hope in her voice.

> *"Purge me with hyssop, and I shall be clean: wash me,*
> *and I shall be whiter than snow.*
> *Make me to hear joy and gladness; that the bones, which*
> *thou hast broken may rejoice.*

I mind it from when Mistress Hayes taught it to me," she said.

"And will you say it on the scaffold?" Goodcole asked.

"I will say it if you say it with me."

"I will give you the words."

"No, I will say it if you say it with me – together, out to the crowd," she said.

Goodcole leaned forward. "But I am not the one who must be contrite," he said.

At this her mouth puckered up and she fixed him with her one good eye. "Are you not?" she said.

The chaplain did not answer her. Instead, he placed the Bible in his bag and gathered up his notes. He raised the lamp, lifted his heavy text and left her in the darkness.

Up in the chapel Goodcole tried to ignore the rats scraping and skittering in the cavities between the walls. The place smelt as sour as ever. He wiped down the lectern and intoned the prayer of thanks for those who had made charitable bequests to Newgate since Whittington's time. It wasn't a long list but it contained some notable names: last but not least was Humphrey Weld, a mayor of London who had been a member of the Worshipful Company of Grocers and whose estate still provided the dole served up to prisoners in the refectory. He completed his prayers, had unhooked his lantern and was casting a last look around when he minded the dean's comment that 'something foul' was afoot in the chapel. Again he sniffed the air but detected nothing above Newgate's perpetually stale, dank odour of unwashed bodies. Then, in case he had missed something, he walked around the perimeter of the room. Goodcole looked up at the barrel-vaulted ceiling and down to where the flags abutted the walls.

He was on the point of turning when he noticed something strange. Midway along the end wall, touching the floor, was a stone with no mortar; yet the wall was the newest in the chapel, having been built by masons almost forty years before to make room for the new stairwell. Goodcole looked closer: the stone was an oblong block about one foot wide and half a foot high. He shone the lantern over the granulated surface then kicked at the stone's base but though he sent a shower of sawdust into the air, nothing moved. Perhaps he was mistaken. Perhaps this stone, though mortared in place, was merely inset more than the others. The strike of two bells broke into his thoughts and so he locked the chapel for the night and headed back to the refectory to observe the women. A comparison of their numbers there with their attendance in the chapel would form the basis of his first report to the dean.

The refectory was busy when he arrived. Goodcole edged past the line of women in the corridor and found a spot on the blind side of the door where he might remain unnoticed. He recalled Deicrowe sitting in close conversation with George Scald at the far end of the hall and it occurred to him that he had not seen Scald since; doubtless he was busy striking more deals and informing on those he incriminated. Goodcole even wondered whether Scald had been behind the theft of the draft confession from his study but he dismissed the thought. Such speculation could undo a man in Newgate for, as Dicker had once intimated, you could never be sure of what was really going on in a place like 'the Whit'.

Goodcole's thoughts were interrupted by the arrival of a large woman on the bench a few feet from him. She sat down heavily and dug her wooden spoon into her bowl of pulp. Then she turned her back and must have beckoned others because three of her friends followed and joined her on the bench. When they had settled in, the woman turned and stared directly at him. She was barely at arm's length and he could smell her suety breath. At first, Goodcole ignored her and lifted his eyes to the new arrivals who filtered to the other benches but after a while he returned her gaze. She was younger than him and had a face marked by the pox but her eyes were clear and determined.

"You not eating?" she said.

Goodcole looked calmly back. He glanced from one to another of the women and, realising that none attended chapel, decided to brazen out their stares.

"He's from the Master's Side," one of the others said.

"Come to ogle," the first woman agreed.

"A night creeper," another said.

"A *cock*-roach, so called." This last comment tipped the others into laughter. They cared little for Goodcole now who, as the butt of their joke, was trapped between the end of the bench and the door. The first woman slapped her spoon down on the table with a thwack.

"Let's send this 'creepy crawler' back with a message." Goodcole felt four pairs of eyes drilling into him. First the large woman flicked the spoon so its scoop hung off the edge of the table, then her left hand settled on the handle, holding it in place. "It's dark in the Stone Hold," she said. The other voices murmured agreement. "When the flame's out it's hard to tell who's who. And there's been a deal of coming and going at night." She raised her hand in mock alarm.

"The girls who go don't come back, see?" the second voice said.

"The young'uns," the others chorused. They looked back to the first woman who was clearly the group's leader.

"Aye, so now we're telling you, *enough's enough*." The hand came down suddenly; it beheaded the spoon, which fell into two pieces on the floor.

Goodcole steadied himself. He was about to ease himself off the bench when he noticed two men approaching: one wore the red and white livery of the London Company, the other was dressed for the road and carried a broad-brimmed hat under his arm. Dicker swatted the women away as if they were flies pestering his horse.

"Goodcole, I'm surprised to find you here. Is everything alright?" The chaplain watched the women bustle away; then, he looked up at his colleague.

"Things are what they are but I have no complaints. Are you here on pastoral business?"

Dicker ignored the gibe. "I'm here to see a mother and daughter on the orders of the alderman," he said.

Up in his study Goodcole reflected on a busy day's work. He concluded that, although Spy Wednesday had been fraught, it had passed off reasonably well. The visit to the dean had been a risky move but it had opened up a line of communication; the pamphlet was arranged with Butler and, not before time, he had made progress with Sawyer. He felt sure that the coming night would concentrate her mind and that a last visit at daybreak would allow him to tie up any loose ends ahead of her final journey to Tyburn.

Goodcole opened the vent on the lantern. He shuffled fresh paper, poured out ink and sharpened his quill; he was in a mood to write and wanted to sketch out a new approach that would cement his fortunes with the Church. While the dean had refused to fund his tract per se, he had set him a test: to deduce Sawyer's malign influence on the wives who attended chapel. To address this he would need to redraw her. First, he would replace the penitent mother of the confession with a character drawn from life, her caustic self, then, to explain how her reach somehow extended beyond her locked cell in Limbo, he would develop that persona into a force of nature who could summon up Satan at will. To do this Goodcole needed only to borrow from the witch's spiraling reputation both inside and outside the prison.

The result of this attempt to placate the powerful was a first draft, which took the form of an interrogation. In this account Goodcole's forensic questions set up Sawyer's pithy answers allowing him to develop a dramatic duel between the forces of good and evil. 'How then can you summon up Satan?' he wrote in his dialogue. 'The first time Satan came to me, he took the form of a dog-fox. He taught me the greeting *sanctificetur nomen tuum*, which means "hallowed be thy name" and comes from the Roman mass', he made Sawyer reply.

When he read through his script Goodcole congratulated himself. Now he had the formula by which his pamphlet could be three things at once. While this new version contained a germ of truth, starting with details from Sawyer's third story, it heightened this with dramatic elements taken from Deicrowe's time in the prison. The result of course was a concoction; perceptive readers would spot that a countrywoman like Sawyer could not know such a Latin phrase. The Latin words, therefore, must have a diabolic origin proving Sawyer's guilt; moreover, and this was the beauty of it, they would speak to the competing agendas of the alderman and the dean who, in their different ways, sought to counter the influence of the Catholic Church. This new conception of the pamphlet provided the solution to all his problems, or so he thought.

Goodcole stood up to let the blood back into his legs. The wave of euphoria had no sooner passed than it was replaced by a nagging void. How craven he was: trying to impress men who neither knew nor cared about the truth. He looked past the king's Bible and psalter to the dark spaces where spiders and woodlice scuttled and thought again of Deicrowe's mommet. In the last few hours the carving had been outside the walls, inside the deanery, roundabout the City and yet here it was back where it had started, propped against his study wall. He wanted to hurl the thing into the ditch on his way back home but he was tired now and needed to end the day on a good note. As was his habit he reached into his bag for Joan's latest letter, only to realise that he had left it on the chest in his lodgings. Disappointed, he decided to make do by rereading one of her earlier missives and had hold of his psalter when a deep sense of shame swept over him. At first he was at a loss to know its source, then, going over his day, he realised that the feeling harkened back to a moment at Okes' stall in St Paul's market; moreover, the later confrontation with the wives in the refectory confirmed that he was missing something important. This warned of dread to come: dread so fearful that it might engulf him, his family and the world outside, too. He remembered the title of the pamphlet he had picked up from Okes' stall: it was called 'Ester Hath Hanged Haman'. To check the facts he replaced the letter in his psalter and, opening the Bible, read back through the Old Testament.

The Book of Ester was one of the least known to him; it came between Nehemiah and Job. From its ten chapters he gleaned the following: Ester was a servant girl, an orphan Jew, who caught the eye of the king of Persia because of her beauty. When the king's most trusted servant, Haman, tried to destroy her people, she invited both to a banquet where she seduced the king into choosing between his desire for her and his respect for his servant. Needless to say the king chose her and Haman was strung up on the gallows he had created for the Jews.

At first Goodcole was reassured. The story of Ester seemed quite removed from the simple truth of his own life. It was really about God's covenant with the Hebers and had little relevance to his and Anne's story. Ester was a servant girl just as Anne had been a servant girl but there the similarity ended for, far from being a temptress, Anne had been an innocent and it had been Goodcole who had bedded her. He leant forward; instead of finding peace, he felt guilt – why was that? He thought back to the pamphlet on Okes' stall. He remembered the spiteful tone more than exact words but one phrase had stuck with him: 'if a man abuse a maid and get her with child, no matter is made of it'. How false that was – at least in his case. He had paid dearly for his folly with Anne; without it he would have been ordained and ministering in the City, so why the chastising guilt? The answer related to providence – God's covenant with his younger self – because, although the Almighty had punished him, He had also rewarded him with the sweetest thing in his life: Joan.

Goodcole cast his mind back to the time of the seduction. It had happened shortly before his twentieth birthday when he was lodged at the household seminary of William Eames. Eames was a graduate of Emmanuel where he was known as 'a born teacher of transcendent ability and exalted piety'. His seminary was situated in Barking: a small fishing town some nine miles east of London. Perhaps because he was a polymath with wide-ranging interests, Eames was sometimes too trusting when running his household. He was fond of quoting Peter: 'Love the brotherhood. Fear God. Honour the king,' he would say to his charges and while such advice inspired loyalty when he was present, it did little to remove temptation when he was away. So it was that during the witching month of May in Goodcole's twentieth year buds had burst forth and sap had spilled over. Because Eames was away at his alma mater in Cambridge, Goodcole's two housemates, Bowyer and Bates, were out gambling in the taverns. As the only true scholar in the group Goodcole was not party to these games; besides, he had no money. So while the others were out to all hours he had remained closeted amongst the books in the library that Eames kept on the ground floor of his house.

The longer Eames was away the more lax the seminary became and when the housekeeper, who ran another boarding establishment besides, stayed over in the town, the cook and other servants often did the same. At these times the household drifted like a ship without a crew. Left to his own devices Goodcole might have gone hungry unless a young servant girl, Anne Brite, hadn't taken it upon herself to bring in provisions for him. Just fourteen years of age Anne was practical and intelligent and she struck up a friendship with Goodcole – a relationship, which should never have progressed beyond lodger and maid.

That May, when the children of the town were out nettle-flogging and Bowyer and Bates were attending 'the garland dance', Goodcole remained at work. Surrounded by the don's collection of manuscripts and printed tomes he had taken to declaiming passages of the Word from a rare edition of Coverdale's translation of the New Testament.

"Suffer little children to come to me," he proclaimed in a grand voice one morning when there came a knock at the door.

"Oh, it's you. I thought for a moment that the master was back," Anne had said. At that moment Goodcole felt like he was the master. So, he invited her to stay to witness the array of almanacs he had laid out on the table before him.

"I dare not touch," Anne had said. He guessed from the smell of lye soap that she had been mopping up the vomit left by Bowyer in the hall after his return in the small hours.

"Let me be your guide," Goodcole replied. In his mind he had advanced from scholar to orator to teacher in a few neat bounds and he saw that Anne was curious. Surely these volumes were unlike any she had ever seen before; moreover, they were illuminated with beautiful pictures.

"Will you read to me now?" she had asked.

"Knowledge is for everyone," Goodcole had replied and so he had pulled up a seat. The effect of having a brown-eyed sparrow of a thing pressed so close was new to him. He felt the flutter of her breath on the page and saw the sweat rising off her nape and shoulders from her exertions in the hall. His voice was now an elevated thing; it seemed to hover above them giving flight to the vowels like music – music that was both solemn and joyful.

So it was that they had struck up an alliance: she would leave food out for him in the kitchen and, in return, he would read to her in the library. Together they moved beyond the Word, exploring texts as diverse as *Gerard's Herbal*, *Mellarius' Treatise on Bees* and John Chrysostom's *Book of Beasts*.

"What is that?" she had said when they came to a picture of a three-headed dog.

"It is called Cerberus," Goodcole explained. He had known then that she was a cherry, ripe for the picking.

He had bedded her one sunlit morning at the top of the house. He had asked her to show him the servants' quarters, which were now hardly used since the maids mostly boarded in town. He remembered telling her about a swarm of bees he had spied from the outside of the house and had watched her eyes flicker in fear and excitement at the prospect that they could taste honey fresh from the comb. When they climbed the stairs the attic smelt of whey on account of the rolls of cheesecloth that the cook had left to dry. Goodcole remembered the iron hooks screwed into the beams from which hops had once hung and he remembered, too, his own fear when they first uncovered the hive – the thrum of the bees loud and threatening in the timbers of the roof. He had led her away to the safety of the north-facing eave. There in the cool shadows he had lulled her on a low trestle bed and, afterwards, catching their breath they had listened to the sound of a cuckoo singing in a nearby copse. Why, he wondered now, had he gone through with it? All these years later it was hard to say. It was not purely a matter of lust for, although he enjoyed her company, Anne was a plain wisp of a thing and hardly full-grown. He surmised now that he had done it merely because he could and it was not really about her at all. He had been swept away by a notion of himself; perhaps it all just followed from that first moment when she had confused the sound of his voice with that of the master. But he wasn't the master and he had acted with malice aforethought, like a wolf in sheep's clothing.

The night before Eames's return the housekeeper had rounded up the missing servants and made them scrub the house from top to bottom. The master's arrival the next day restored his charismatic presence, instilling the regimen that had prevailed before. Now that he was back working in a routine, Goodcole avoided Anne. Guarded lest Bowyer pick up on any spark between them, he cold-shouldered her when served at mealtimes and avoided her gaze when they passed in the panelled corridor. So successful was he in expunging her from his memory that a month passed before he realised that she, that most diligent of servants, was no longer coming to work. In mid-June Goodcole was busy preparing for the exam that would win him a scholarship to Cambridge. The Monday before the exam he had attended morning prayers at church and was returning to his room, when a minister he had not met before introduced himself as Thomas Stafford. Stafford was the clerk of tribunals. He informed Goodcole that he had just made a house call to Brite's fisherman's cottage by the river where a complaint had been made against him; moreover, he told him to cancel his plans and attend a meeting of the Disciplinary Committee in the library at midday.

The meeting was as brief as it was to the point. Goodcole was called in to stand in front of a bench who included Stafford, two churchwardens and Eames, himself. When asked whether he had corrupted a maid, fornicating with her in the library, he had denied the charge only to be humiliated by Bowyer who, when summoned, lied under oath, saying that he had heard Goodcole 'carrying on with Anne in the library most every morning when he was trying to study'. During this hearing Eames was a changed man. Gone was the paternal concern and erudite banter. Now he was like a beak prosecuting the king's justice. Perhaps the worst moment came at the end of the hearing when, having dismissed Stafford and the churchwardens, Eames had looked searchingly at Goodcole. "I had such high hopes for you, Henry," he had said.

In the last week of June, while Bowyer and Bates were sitting their entrance exams, Goodcole's future prospects withered on the vine. Made to do penance in the local church he was told that he was now considered unsuitable for either university or ordination. His fall from grace was complete when a month later it became clear that Anne was with child. Rushed into a shameful marriage, Goodcole had to endure a chastising sermon from the local vicar who used the line from Timothy, '*flee the evil desires of youth and pursue righteousness, faith, love and peace, along with those who call on the Lord out of a pure heart*'. Although he had not appreciated the advice at the time, the passage was well chosen because, when Anne gave birth to Joan and when Goodcole had held his daughter for the first time, he was a changed man. If anyone had a pure heart she did and in learning to pursue righteousness he was really only following her lead.

Goodcole folded the Bible shut. Having plumbed the depths of his own guilt he knew now why that pamphlet had hit home: Ester was a servant, Anne was a servant, Joan was a servant and servants had to do their master's bidding. Goodcole was fearful for his daughter because he had himself experienced the aphrodisiac effects of power, so, within the confines of his study, he made a promise. He would do whatever it took to protect her; if necessary he would forego ordination and other earthly rewards and give himself over solely to the task of keeping Joan safe.

Day 6

On the morning of Elizabeth Sawyer's execution Goodcole rose early. He lifted his daughter's latest letter from the chest in the hall and inspected the dab of sealing wax to make sure it remained unread, then he placed the letter carefully in his bag and, leaving Anne and the boys fast asleep, stepped out into the darkness. A cold easterly was blowing that morning. It brightened the braziers outside the Mercers' Hall, rattled the awnings in Newgate market and pushed Goodcole west to the edge of the City.

Arriving in the guardhouse, he opened his bag. "How now," he said to the guard but the man ignored his greeting and waved him on.

Up in his study he changed the tallow and placed his daughter's still unopened letter high on a shelf where no intruder would think to look. He then settled down to leaf through his notes on the Sawyer case. When he was happy that these were in order, he placed them in a blue linen folder, which he disguised on a lower shelf under fragments of slate. He threw some chalk dust over these and, content that all was well hidden, gathered up his psalter, Bible, quills, paper and ink and locked the door.

Down in Limbo the air was as stifling as ever: fumes from the rush lights mixed with sweat condensing on the walls. Outside Sawyer's cell Goodcole took a moment. *No slip-ups*, he chided. *Handle today right and you will be able to celebrate Easter with an easy conscience.*

Inside he found Sawyer slouched in the corner.

He settled in at his desk and unpacked his things. "Are you ready?" he said.

"I'm ready as I will ever be," she replied.

"And when we reach the scaffold, will you stand and say the words you learned as a little girl?"

"I will do it."

Hearing Sawyer agree Goodcole relaxed and reverted to his familiar role. The words came easily to him – perhaps too easily. "Then you will find release for, as it says in the psalm, '*the sacrifice acceptable to God is a broken spirit*'." The silence that followed Goodcole's pronouncement curdled and turned sour.

"Have a care," she said.

"How so?"

"Be not proud when you lead me to the tree."

"I will be your guide."

"But be not proud… for you too will be humbled."

Though he heard her words he paid them scant heed. "Aye, for each must be laid low before they can be exalted." Again his words came easily and he was about to say more when there came three stout bangs on the cell door. "What is it?" Goodcole called to Maddox.

"An urgent message has come from Alderman Bull."

Goodcole cursed silently. He shoved his psalter and Bible into his bag and cleared the writing desk of his quills, paper and ink; then he thumped a reply and waited for the door to open.

Out in the dim light of the corridor he came face to face with Dicker. "Could this not have waited?" he said. Even on this lowest level of the prison Dicker was his bold self. He brushed away Goodcole's ire at being disturbed and pulled out a sheaf of papers.

"I have here a pair of warrants. Sign each so I can return them to the warden."

Goodcole examined the paperwork. The warrants were in fact release forms for a widow and daughter who had been admitted to the gaol on Tuesday, at the time of Deicrowe's execution. He flicked through the pages again and then thrust them back into Dicker's hands. "I can't sign these. Neither woman attends chapel and thus both are unknown to me."

Dicker's smile fell away. He proffered the papers again; this time his voice had a steely edge. "If Alderman Bull wants them signed, then you must sign," he said.

Goodcole noted the change of tone. "Is that what you meant when you told me to 'put my writing at the service of the company'?"

Dicker looked affronted. He jabbed his finger at Sawyer's cell. "God mend me, friend, this is for King and Country. Would you waste your time with the likes of her, when you could help these women find a new life across the ocean?"

Goodcole turned to his colleague. He took the forms and, folding them carefully, placed them in his bag. "I will talk to each of these women before the day is done. You may tell the warden that I will return the forms to him by the end of the dogwatch."

"This time they must be signed by *both* them and you," Dicker replied.

When Goodcole returned to Sawyer's cell, he realised his mistake for in his haste to answer the door he had left the lantern burning within. During his brief absence Sawyer had taken charge of the lamp, placing it between her knees as she knelt on the flagstones. Flooded in light she now looked almost holy.

"What are you doing?" he asked.

"I am praying. I have begged Grace for my children and now I will plead for yours."

Goodcole recoiled. "What know you of my children?"

"I know you have a daughter with fiery hair like the dawn." She pointed at the wick of the candle she held in her right hand. The candle was no bigger than a pebble. It had been moulded in her palm like a cake of lye soap and its wick glowed auburn in the light from the lamp.

"What have you there?"

"It is tallow made from the wax you spilled. The wick is twisted from a single hair that dropped from the pages of your book – it is blessed by the Word."

Goodcole advanced. He wanted to snatch the tallow out of her hand but he knew that those gnarled fingers would close into a fist. Instead, he spoke to her in a low, measured voice. "Give that to me, now."

Sawyer remained unmoved. "What's it worth?" she asked.

Goodcole shifted his stance and shrugged. He tried to sound calm and uncaring. "It is but one dead hair. It is worth nothing, of course."

"Well then, leave and let me pray in peace." She began to intone,

"Holy Mary, Mother of God,
Pray for Anne and her child,

That just as they are one blood now,
They may stay together in life everlasting.
Amen."

Sawyer released the door of the lantern and moved the tiny wick closer to its blaze. Lit by the raw flame her body lost its holy glow and became freakishly stark. Goodcole could see the lines of her bones through bruised flesh. He cursed himself for leaving the lamp unguarded. How foolish he was. He fought to stay in control of his nerves. "How do you know my wife's name?" he asked.

Sawyer held her hand steady. "A guess, I suppose." She paused, "Anne's a common enough name... as is Joan."

Goodcole took a step back.

Sawyer moved the wick to the flame and for a moment it stood apart; then, it flared as Joan's hair caught and the two wicks became one. Bitterness filled the room and Sawyer laughed. "Have a care now, one wrong word and your firstborn might slip away forever." She drank in his pain. "*Now* you rate me – *now* you care," she said.

"What do you want?" he asked, but she had already lost interest.

"There's a deal you could do for me, inkhorn, but I don't want a thing. Today, I will be with my mother."

"You will be with her where, in Heaven?"

"In Heaven or Hell – wherever she be. Now, leave me with the rats. They are better company."

But Goodcole did not leave. That final gibe fired his gall and allowed him to regroup. It was better, he reasoned, to have defiance now than later on the scaffold. "So you have prayed for me and mine, now let us rehearse Psalm

51 together, then I will leave you be until the Newgate bell tolls."

"Why? It makes no odds, anyhow."

"God is waiting to receive you."

"What know you of God?"

"I know what Jesus said before he was nailed to the tree."

"What said he?"

"He said 'do as I have done to you'."

At this Elizabeth Sawyer laughed. Her laugh was dry and mirthless – as dry as the reeds her father kept above the byre. Then she spoke plainly to him. "Jesus said 'do as I have done to you', whereas you, inkhorn, are like all the rest. You say 'do as I *tell* you to do', and there is a world of difference between doing and telling. It is why you are a scribbler and an inkhorn to boot. You may write what you like about me, it doesn't change who I am. I am a mother who has buried seven of her children and I have paid in blood and sorrow for every one. I don't need the Church to tell me that my babes lie in the bosom of Christ. I know it in my very soul. Just as I know you for what you are."

"And what am I?"

"You're an inkhorn with lechery in your heart."

Up in the chapel Goodcole stood in silent prayer. He asked God to show mercy to the penitent and chastise those who had no shame. He asked this to draw a line between his pure-hearted daughter and the caustic witch. 'Blessed are the meek for they shall inherit the earth,' he prayed, but he could not banish the thought of those gnarled fingers twisting his beloved's hair or of it catching in the flame of his lamp.

Goodcole sniffed the air. The smell in the chapel was worse, now. It was the same as in Sawyer's cell. In its odour the mud from the estuary mixed with the whiff of a graveyard after it had rained. He was about to leave when he remembered the uneven block of stone set into the end wall of the chapel and so, unable to resist, he lifted the lantern and walked the few short paces over to it. This time instead of kicking the block, he knelt down in the sawdust and ran his finger along the gap where the mortar should have been. Startled by a cold sensation against his fingertips, he drew back. He licked his finger and tried again. The airflow suggested that there was space behind the wall; moreover, it meant that that space was, however tortuously, connected to an outside wall. The flat toll of the Newgate bell reminded him that he had an execution to attend.

Down in the press-yard Goodcole listened to the roar from outside the City walls. The crowd sounded like an approaching stampede of cattle. He ignored their din and stepped over to where the lurch was being prepared. The hangman's boy was nowhere to be seen.

"No boy, just men," Simeon said, reading his thoughts. He pointed to the bench that had been fixed to the floor of the cart and to the rails that had been clamped on either side. "The voman vill sit. You vill ride vith her on the cart and this time ve take six men – two before and four behind."

Goodcole looked past the captain to the stables where guards dressed in the company's livery were leading out their horses. "You will ride at the back?" he asked.

"I have orders to stay," Simeon said. He shrugged as if to show that he had no choice in the matter.

Goodcole assented; he knew that from the company's point of view this was a sideshow. Sawyer would like Deicrowe be dispatched and the trade in live bodies would resume once more; meanwhile, he would have to steer this sour soul through her last moments on earth while the mob bayed for her blood.

They had struck off her irons and dressed her in a linen shift stitched by the women in the Stone Hold. In the cold light of day Elizabeth Sawyer looked spent. Barely able to stand straight, she walked alone across the press-yard. Her grey hair was crammed underneath a stained coif; her angled gait was the result of twenty years of giving birth and a week squatting on a cold stone floor.

Goodcole watched her faltering steps, then, concerned lest she fall, he took a pace forward and another until he stood with her by the cart. "Have you no blanket?" he said but she did not look up so he dipped into the tack room and pulled out a broad cloth used for rubbing down the horses. When he returned, Maddox the sergeant had already wound a cord round her, looping it in a hitch behind her back. Seeing that Sawyer was unable to step up onto the lurch, he linked arms with Goodcole to heave her backwards onto the boards and then he motioned to her to sit on the bench. Goodcole draped the broadcloth around her shoulders, but she shook it off, lifting her hands to her bonds. He watched her tug at the chord that tied her elbows tight into her sides and wondered whether she meant to wriggle free. "Do you want to say a prayer?" he asked.

Sawyer shook her head and pinched her blackened nails into the stiff rope. Goodcole watched her calloused fingers work the fibre. For a while he thought she meant to tear it but he soon understood that she meant to wear it in, softening its touch. Seeing she meant to make a friend of the hangman's rope, he signalled the sergeant to leave her hands and forearms free. "You may lash her around the knees," he said. Then, because the man was unwilling to stoop before her, he took the cord himself and pulled it tight and fastened it to the same ring in the floor of the lurch.

Goodcole knew it was time to move when Simeon left and so he took his seat by the driver. He looked up first at the leaden sky and then back at the nervous horses.

The gaoler swung the bell waiting for St Sepulchre's reply and when the great toll answered, the guards ratcheted up the portcullis, lifting the iron gate that loosed their cavalcade upon the crowd. The spectacle of people massing for anything other than church always alarmed Goodcole. Only in London could crowds gather or melt away so fast. He looked at the faces massing from Fleet Street to Old Bailey and repeated the Word from Revelation to remind himself of the righteousness of his cause: '*Blessed are they that do His commandments, that they may have the right to the tree of life, and may enter in through the gates of His city... for without are dogs, and sorcerers, and whosoever loveth and maketh a lie.*'

At Smithfield Goodcole was relieved to see that the livestock mart was much reduced for the traders had dismantled most of the pens for Easter. Seeing that a stage had been built for the Good Friday sermon in front of St Bartholomew's, he thought of the massacre that had brought men like Simeon to England and reminded himself that such things could yet happen in London if the kings of France or Spain gained a hold on the English throne. At the time of the massacre Sawyer had been a babe in arms, swaddled by the mill on the Lea. He looked back at her now and saw that she was skulking low in the cart: a hunched figure, tied to her seat and protected by the guard rails that had been clamped to each side of the lurch. The circuit around Smithfield was swift enough. With room to move and a greater escort behind it the lurch rattled over the ground giving bystanders little time to do else but gawp. Indeed, by the time the crowd had laid eyes on Elizabeth she was already being drawn away. They were leaving Smithfield and had crossed the Turnmill Brook when Goodcole remembered the barrel of pitch he had seen on Deicrowe's ill-fated run and, curious to see whether there had been another burning since, he leaned behind the driver and looked over the heads of the throng. The pole on the scorched col was barely visible. Draped with a bolt of canvas it now resembled a ship's mast on which a sail had been unfurled. Goodcole turned to the driver and pointed. "What is that on the Elms?" he asked.

"'Tis to catch the Good Friday rain," he said glancing up at the heavy clouds that massed from the west.

Goodcole frowned. He had once heard from a fellow in Ludgate that rain fallen in Holy Week was deemed lucky but he had presumed it was a country custom. It reminded him that in Sawyer's stories God's grace was deemed to be free-flowing through Creation. *There is no accounting for folk*, he thought: *they listen to the Word read to them from St Bartholomew's and turn to heathen quackery almost in the same breath.* They were 'the stony ground' and there was little hope for them.

At Holborn Bridge they crossed the River Fleet. The crowds were packed five or six deep here, but their party was moving at such pace that those by the stone piers of the bridge were forced to step back. Goodcole saw a street child moving amongst them. The girl threaded through the onlookers with the swift movements of a thief. For a moment Goodcole caught her magpie eye and then she was gone. He knew that today would provide rich pickings for the cutpurses for there was nothing like a witch to distract lay folk from their hard-earned coin. Goodcole was starting to feel in control when the lurch swerved and a stab of fear brought back Deicrowe's run and the memory of the dog twitching on the frozen ground. Life was fleeting and salvation had to be grasped; all had to atone for, whether quick or dead, no one escaped judgement.

Perhaps it was the near miss but their cavalcade had slowed a little now. They were close to Ely Place where tall facades signalled the start of the legal quarter. Here a high brick wall partitioned off the road from the Inns of Court, which meant that onlookers were stretched at its base in a thin ribbon along the highway. Goodcole could hear the guards talking ahead of him and wondered at their banter. He turned to the driver.

"Are we stopping?" he asked.

"Drinks for everyone but the witch," he said.

Before Goodcole could protest their party took a sharp right through a coaching arch and rattled down a narrow alley to where a bishop's hat hung on a pole. Goodcole looked up at the sign for the Mitre Inn, then at the faces that stared down from the tenements above. He turned back to the driver.

"Whose idea is this?"

The driver waved him away. "Loosen your joints, man." He pointed to the faces crowded around the windows above them. "These people have paid good money. If there's a drink in it for us, then so much the better."

A woman appeared with a tray of stirrup cups for the riders; meanwhile, a young girl approached the lurch with two tankards of ale. Goodcole was ready to refuse the ale, but in a quick move the girl placed both on the footplate and crept around the back of the cart. He watched her caught between curiosity and terror as she peered up at the witch. For a moment Sawyer's head turned and the two must have exchanged glances for the girl fled, unable to hold the countrywoman's gaze. A distant noise alerted him to danger and, when Goodcole looked beyond to the coaching arch, he saw that a mob had entered the alley. He elbowed the driver but the man was draining the second tankard of ale and seemed unconcerned.

The thugs were armed with staves and were backed by a group of women. The men advanced within a short distance of Sawyer then stopped, unsure what to do next. Goodcole looked around for protection but the guard was not worthy of its name; two were drinking, a third was urinating against the wall, whilst the others had disappeared inside the tavern. He told the driver to turn before they were hemmed in but again he waved him away.

"Let them have their fun," he said.

The crowd were now within ten paces of their quarry, blocking their way back to the Oxford Road. They nosed forward like a pack of hounds baiting a bear only to fall back when Sawyer so much as twitched.

"She's tied," a woman wearing a black shawl said.

"Her tongue's not tied – she can still curse you," another said.

"She can make herself small as flea, as swift as a wolf," a third said.

"Then why don't she?" the first woman replied.

Goodcole dismounted from the cart. He shouted at the guards in the alley to mount up, then ducked under the low lintel of the Mitre Inn to find the others. Inside he tried to ignore the welcoming glow, the malty warmth and the view of an ale wife leaning low as she proffered sudsy ale; he reminded himself that the tavern was like all taverns: a gateway to Sodom and Gomorrah. Finding the two guards fondling the girl who had brought the ale, he upended their table and kicked over a stool. "No more stops until Tyburn," he thundered.

Outside, the crowd was almost in touching distance of Sawyer. The men stood on the sidelines, while their wives pushed forward. The one wearing the black shawl was closest and seemed intent on settling a score. Goodcole mounted the cart; he could hear the guards grumbling behind. What happened next was hard to assess for cause and effect were closely intertwined: from his seat beside the driver Goodcole witnessed the woman hoist herself up onto the rear to spit in Sawyer's face. He saw Sawyer raise her hand and, though there seemed no contact between them, her assailant fell back onto the cobbles. A collective intake of breath followed the crack of her skull on the stones, then the crowd scattered. Two rushed forward to staunch the flow of blood from the woman's head, but most ran back to the mouth of the alley.

Sensing his moment, Goodcole grabbed the reins of the lurch. "Now, you drive this thing or I will," he said to the driver. And so with a crack of the whip they were on their way, but not before the guards, who were now crammed behind, knocked over one of the wives who had stayed to help her friend.

At St Giles in the Fields Goodcole saw the blind at work in the hospital garden. From a distance the coifs that tied around their eyes looked like nuns' wimples, a reminder of the St Lazar's Leper Hospital that had once run on this site. He watched them drift in from sifting herbs summoned by the clamour of the crowd and wondered about the old wives' tale that told how their eyes could be 'opened' by the death sweat from a freshly hanged woman. Banishing the thought he intoned the Word from Psalm 146:

> *"The God of Jacob, who made heaven, and earth, the sea, and all that therein is:*
> *Who executeth judgment for the oppressed: who giveth food to the hungry.*
> *The Lord looseth the prisoners.*
> *The Lord openeth the eyes of the blind: the Lord raiseth them that are bowed down: the Lord loveth the righteous.*
> *The Lord preserveth the strangers; he relieveth the fatherless and widow: but the way of the wicked he turneth upside down.*
> *Thy God, O Zion, shall do this unto all generations."*

The crowd were all around them now. They sat on the convent walls, hung on gateposts and stiles and, jostling for a good view, spilled into the road. The driver cursed as a mule train bound for Westminster caused him to veer onto the left-hand verge. In it some forty beasts were paired two abreast in strings of twenty. Having been driven through a downpour, they advanced in a cloud of their own heat. The lurch now had no option but to steer left into the ruts where the verge was breaking up. Goodcole could now make out the pox marks on children's cheeks. He saw milkmaids, tradesmen, families clutching baskets of wares and, behind them, constables, some brandishing cudgels cut from hazel rods and stained black with shellac. The cart was slipping sideways now but the driver had to wait for the mules to pass before he could steer back up onto the road's broken camber. Thus they passed through the musky steam from the animals' bodies and began the gradual descent to the Triple Tree.

From a distance Deicrowe's body shimmered underneath the triangular beam and it took Goodcole a while to realise that he had been stripped naked: Goodcole's coat, Deicrowe's shirt, his shoes, even his soiled britches had been torn from his body. Now only Goodcole's woollen cap remained. Smeared with white streaks from the gulls it made the rest of the body look more naked, from the pecked-out eyes to the sunken chest and long forlorn arms that dangled at different lengths on either side of his body.

At St Oswald's Stone Goodcole saw that a group of pikemen had staked out the scaffold and he looked with gratitude at Potts who stood with the court drummer behind their cordon. At least Potts, stickler that he was, was alive to what was going on; at least he appreciated the risk of a riot. "Is Topping not here?" Goodcole asked when the lurch ground to a halt behind the line of halberds.

Potts shook his head. "They are sending someone else," he said.

Goodcole surveyed the multitude and dismounted; his legs were almost numb. "How will anyone get through?" he asked.

"They won't, but we must wait – at least until midday."

"We may catch the bell from St Martin-in-the-Fields, if this wind is not too strong."

Potts looked up past where the hangman's boy was shinning along the beam. Above him a wall of clouds was advancing from the west, shutting out the light. "If the sun casts no shadow, we will call it noon," he said dryly. Casting a nod to the drummer-boy he added, "We may get the cart in position, the hangman will trim his line and you may prepare Sawyer, then I can execute the king's justice."

It has come to this, Goodcole thought when he heard the steady pulse of the drum. Sawyer was untied now; she sat in the back, legs apart, head slightly bowed. Aside from exhaustion she gave little away; she looked like a countrywoman taking a lift in a cart after a busy day at market and yet she was about to take her leave of this earth. When the lurch had manoeuvred around the three sides of the Triple Tree, Goodcole waited for it to reverse so the hangman could drop the noose. Looking first at Deicrowe, then at Sawyer, he wondered why the court had waited until now to make an example of them. A faithful servant and a defiant scold made an odd pair, but then Christ had died amongst thieves.

Goodcole watched the boy toss a line up to the hangman who now sat astride the beam. Above him the clouds loomed in sucking the warmth from the air and threatening a deluge. He watched the hangman climb down his ladder, then looked at Sawyer who was standing hands up to the noose. With the practised movement of one used to bending willow for baskets she was digging her nails into the fibre of the rope, softening the hemp to receive her neck. He thought of the moppet she held close as a child and the life lesson her father had taught her all those years ago. In spite of himself he could not help wondering how he would have behaved in her place: would he have had the nerve to keep mind and body together, or would he have been, like Robinson, a broken man?

When the hangman had checked the noose, Goodcole mounted the lurch and looked down at the crowd. And what of them? The first spits of rain were falling now. They blew in like a shower of spite, thwarting the promise of warmer days to come and causing the crowd to screw up their faces against the cold. Goodcole had just time to turn up the collar of his summer coat before the rain swept in. It soaked them all and made those that could bunch together like a herd in a squall. The rain knocked off hats, seeped down collars, bounced off boards and splashed against the raw wood of the Triple Tree. Goodcole looked down at the bobbing heads; most had turned inwards, waiting for the shower to pass, but one boy still faced Sawyer; he stood with his mouth agape, catching raindrops on his tongue. Watching his fresh face spattered by the downpour, Goodcole thought of the conundrum of Creation: when God's rain fell from the sky it was pure and yet the moment it touched mankind it became tainted; this was because man, led astray by woman, had defied God's Word and man free of the Word was a lost cause. Now, when he looked down at the huddled crowd, Goodcole saw hope, anger, joy and fear and yet behind all these emotions lurked sin; sin was defiance and it corrupted all flesh. Everyone in that crowd, everyone everywhere, was born of woman; all were 'shaped in iniquity' and, but for God's grace, all were destined for the pit.

As quickly as it had come, the shower blew over, the clouds rolling onwards to the City. Now rays of sun poked through; they glinted on the soaked bodies until full sunshine brought warmth, loosening the huddle that had clenched against the cold. Goodcole looked out over the gleam of wet heads. He sensed their energy coming back; soon that energy became a hum and it wasn't long before it was directed at Sawyer. She stood a pace behind him, wet fingers still working the noose. A voice called out, then another and another in a call and response.

"Save yourself, Witch."

"Aye, say the word."

A woman close to the scaffold pointed up at Goodcole. "Turn yourself to a fox and him to a chicken." General laughter was followed by a series of whistles and, emboldened, the crowd started to enjoy itself.

"Ho Witch, no curses for us now?"

"Cat's got her tongue."

"Dog, more like."

"The bitch is on the leash!"

"Show us the mark, where the Devil suckled you."

"Aye, show us your arse." More laughter, then someone threw a lump of manure.

Sawyer's face was set like flint. Goodcole surmised that she had heard these taunts before, perhaps at her trial where she had been strip-searched by women hurriedly pulled in off the street. Then another voice called out and he saw her face change; first surprise, then hurt softened her features and she mouthed her own name. "Lysbeth," she said. For a moment Goodcole was confused but then he remembered the parish register that Dicker had copied; Sawyer had baptised a daughter 'Elizabeth' on Christmas Day, though she had died a year later, worn down by the terrible cold. He looked into the crowd and saw a girl pushing through. She was perhaps thirteen and poorly dressed with mousy hair that fell in ringlets about her shoulders. He thought again and recalled that Sawyer had named another daughter 'Elizabeth'; she was a later child, born after that terrible time when she had lost five of her brood in as many years. The girl was calling out to her, but those close by were blocking her path, unwilling to give up their spot at the front. Goodcole saw Sawyer's features resolve; he watched her look away, sensing she did not want to draw attention to her own flesh and blood at the foot of the tree. Goodcole bid the driver step down and moved to the back of the cart where Sawyer waited with the noose around her neck. They stood together now and faced the crowd.

"Let us start this," he said.

"Start this?" she murmured.

"Aye, start your end." Goodcole nodded to Potts who stepped forward. He checked over his shoulder in case another squall of rain was driving in but the worst of the clouds had blown over and sunshine brightened the faces of the crowd.

Ever dependable, Potts read the words; as he did so he enunciated every syllable. "For this Mother Sawyer did witch to death a neighbour of hers, one Agnes Radcliffe, after she struck Sawyer's sow with a stick, the sow having eaten a bar of soap which the same Agnes Radcliffe was using to wash clothes at the stream that runs at the back of Sawyer's toft in Winchmore near the bounds with Enfield Parish…"

The crowd was quiet now, the hecklers silenced by Potts' authoritative voice. They listened with rapt attention to the exact circumstances of the argument that had led to the denouncing of this mother of eleven children. Goodcole watched the upturned faces. Freshened by rain, warmed by the balm of sunshine after a long winter, they knew that but for the grace of God they too might be standing there, the object of gibes and ridicule. All had told lies, most had stolen food; all had cursed, whether silently or profanely out in the street. The difference was that they were bunched together with their feet on the ground while she was up here facing their ire. Today she would die while they could at least look forward to another summer in which they took their chances in this uncertain world.

Goodcole opened his psalter at Psalm 51.

"Speak from the heart and as loud as you may," he advised.

"And if I cannot?"

"Then I will be there for you."

So she began. "O God, wash me thoroughly... and cleanse me from my sin."

Sawyer's mouth was dry, so Goodcole supplied the prompt. "For I acknowledge my transgressions..."

She gained heart from the sound of his voice and recovered some of her spirit. "My sin is ever before me. Against thee, *thee only*, have I sinned," but then she faltered.

Again Goodcole supplied the missing line. "Behold, I was shapen in iniquity and in sin did my mother conceive me," he said.

"Behold I was shapen in my mother who did conceive me." Elizabeth's voice had regained some of its usual vigour. "Purge me with hyssop and I shall be clean: wash me and I shall be whiter than snow." Perhaps she was thinking of her cousins, Meg and Eve, because she smiled before stopping again.

This time Goodcole raised his voice. "Make me to hear joy and gladness; that the bones which thou hast broken may rejoice," he said. Then sensing that she was either unwilling or unable to say more, he continued. "Cast me not away from thy presence and take not thy holy spirit from me." He was about to reel off the rest of the verse, when he caught the eye of Sawyer's daughter Elizabeth. She was standing three rows back, hemmed in by a family group who clutched baskets of heather. Now, ambushed by a sense that his own daughter Joan could be watching, too, Goodcole needed to get this over with. He managed another line before bringing the psalm to a premature end. "Restore unto me the joy of thy salvation and uphold me with thy free spirit…world without end, Amen." Shaken, he turned to Sawyer. "You have done well. Mind what you said at your catechism. You are a child of God. Go to Him, now." For a moment they stood close; he took in her frail warmth, the turned-in shoulders, her calloused hands and newly sewn shift, then he stepped away and dismounted to make room for Potts.

When the lurch lunged, Goodcole saw only blue sky. He was standing in mud and could hear the Tyburn Brook. Fed by the downpour it surged with spume, running through the culvert and past the farm where it joined other streams on their way to the sea. The crowd were silent now, spellbound by the spectacle that was unfolding behind Goodcole's back. He heard the creak of the rope, the stifled attempts at breath. Only when he turned did he see Sawyer fighting for life: first she trod air, then she kicked; then she went into spasm. Goodcole saw her right forearm rise while her mouth foamed. There was a cheer from somewhere far off; then the girl broke through. She jumped up and caught her mother's legs at the knee and swung on them. It was not, Goodcole realised, an embrace, it was a tug and it broke her mother's neck.

* * *

The evening of Maunday Thursday Newgate smelt like a drain backing up during a flood. Pushed by a spring tide the stink seeped upwards from the mudflats; it spread through Limbo on the lowest level and rose up through the flue of the stairwell to the chapel; here it collected in a great fug. Up in his study Goodcole hardly noticed the smell. It was now the end of the dogwatch and he was ready to return home. He had just spent two hours rewriting his tract on God's 'discovery' of Elizabeth Sawyer. Though his eyes smarted from candle smoke he felt heady, as if a great burden had been lifted, which in a way it had for the guilt that had pressed him on his return from Tyburn had now melted away. Goodcole kicked away the old manuscript that lay at his feet and perused his new copy under the glow of the lamp. His two drafts could not be more different. Instead of an inquisition, he had now written an inspired exposition of why Sawyer was righteous after all. Goodcole's hand trembled as he traced the letters of his title. According to this conception, 'The Wonderful Discovery of Elizabeth Sawyer' was quite simply that God loved her. God forgave everything: her diabolic curses, her ignorance, her slovenly ways, even the degradation of her body. And how did he, Henry Goodcole, know this? He had seen it with his own eyes; he had witnessed it at the gallows for in that moment when mother and daughter swung as one, their single nature was revealed to him. The two Elizabeths, young and old, were really one incarnation fused by God's love. To use Sawyer's own phrase they were 'one blood'. This was his epiphany.

Goodcole shuffled his papers into a single sheaf. Did he really have the nerve to take this draft to William Butler in the morning? A host of questions crowded his mind: would Butler print such a pamphlet and if he did, what would the consequences be? To steady himself Goodcole returned to the quote from Revelation, which had entered his mind during Deicrowe's ill-fated gallows run. That, too, was a sign; it revealed that he was in error because by pandering to powerful men he had turned his back on his personal covenant with God.

> *And the Son of Man showed me a pure river of water of life, clear as crystal…*
> *And in the midst of the street of it… there was the tree of life,*
> *Blessed are they that do his commandments for they… may enter in through the gates into the city.*

The Word reassured Goodcole but it also chastised him because, as he now realised, it absolved Sawyer, suggesting that for her 'the tree of life' was at Tyburn – 'the street' being the Oxford Road. He thought of her as a child standing by the Lea and as a young mother sitting by the Bleeding Tree. Although her ordeal was over now, he had a sense that his own was just beginning. Now he had to choose: he had to choose between this life and the next, between the earthly city in which he lived and that heavenly one described by the Word. He had to choose because if he did not he would forfeit Joan. Goodcole reached into his bag and pulled out his daughter's latest letter. His hand brushed over the broken seal as he held it to the light. The first time he had read Joan's words just two hours before he had felt shock, now, he felt resolve.

Dearest Father,

Please excuse my haste in writing but there has been much to do of late in our household. Yesterday the mistress suffered a heavy bleed but after a long night during which we offered up many prayers she has rallied. This morning she has woken and supped some remedy. The chief physic says we should give thanks.

Here there is much excitement with the news that the company's ship *Warwick* will sail from Gravesend for Virginia this summer. My companion Lucy Remnant has determined to make the voyage. Lucy will choose a husband amongst the fine men in Nova Britannia and has received a glowing testimonial from Alderman Bull. The alderman says that the Land of Milk and Honey lies over the ocean and Lucy now pities me for having to stay in 'this Babylon' with its threat of vice, fire and plague. I told her you are learned and have much to say on the subject.

Last night we sat together and read from the Book of Psalms. I wrote out our favourite line, which reads: 'for the Lord hath chosen Zion; he hath desired it for his habitation'. We now keep this saying pinned between our two beds. One day, if you would permit such a thing, I would travel across the sea, too. In the meantime there is Holy Week to observe and the mistress to serve. I will write again when I have more to tell.

Hold us in your heart.

In all obedient duty,
Your daughter,
Joan

The letter was now more than two days old and it spoke to his most secret fear: far from being safe, servants in the alderman's household were being lured onto the company's ships. Already Joan was implicated in the web of lies and deceit that emanated from St Sithes Row. A further thought struck home: since Dicker almost certainly knew about the voyage of the *Warwick*, Tuesday's trip to London Bridge may have been part of a plan to bring him on side.

Goodcole folded the letter and placed it back in his bag. He dared not wait until the feast; tomorrow, after he had concluded Good Friday prayers, he would make haste to Alderman Bull's house in Walbrook Ward. There he would prevail upon the steward to release his daughter, saying only that he wished to spend this most holy of days with his firstborn child. Once they were reunited he would lead Joan back to Newgate Street to talk sense into her: he would warn her about the company's scheme to procure breeders for its plantations; he would describe to her the perils of the voyage, the snakes of the Virginia jungle and the sort of men who awaited her poor deluded friend Lucy Remnant. It wasn't much of a plan but he had to act because, blind to the dangers, he had wasted too much time already.

Goodcole lifted his bag onto his shoulder and unhooked his lantern from its stand. It was the same lantern that Sawyer had held close when she had prayed for Anne and Joan. Remembering her then, crouching on the floor as she held his beloved's hair to the flame, he shuddered. In her own coarse way she had been warning him. 'One wrong word and your firstborn might slip away forever' she had said, but he had been too proud to listen. Now he must heed her and act.

Day 7

The morning of Good Friday Goodcole awoke late. So much had happened while he had slept: Jesus had faced the Sanhedrin, Judas had hanged himself and Peter had denied his Lord. Anne was at the hearth; she proffered a brew made from milk thistle and sage and cut the bread she had baked. The glint of the amber amulet around her neck reminded him that she had been right to worry about Joan. He glanced at the bag by the door and wondered how she would react if she knew what it contained. Perhaps he misjudged her because, up to now, she had hardly questioned her lot. She knew how fallible he was and yet still supported him in his difficult work. Although in the past he had assumed that she had no choice, the episode with the charm showed that this was not the case: she accepted that he had to work in that vile prison everyday; she accepted, too, that she had lost her daughter to another's household and would soon lose the twins to an institution of learning. Anne's attitude seemed to be, if God wills it, let it be. And yet now, even what little they had left might be spirited away.

Goodcole splashed his face with water from the pail by the hearth; he was drying himself when the shadow of a rider passed by his window. The jingle of spurs caused him to move towards the door. When he drew the bolt back, Dicker was standing before him.

The agent's steaming horse was spattered from the road. Dicker held out a gloved hand. "The warrants," he said without preamble.

"The warrants?" Goodcole repeated. Only when the words passed his own lips did he recall the papers that the agent had pressed on him outside Sawyer's cell before her execution.

"The warrants for Mistress Hampden and her daughter. You promised to return them signed by last bell. Warden Travers needs them on his desk, now." Dicker had no sooner delivered his message than he turned and mounted his horse. "Do not delay," he said before wheeling off. His horse's hooves struck sparks on the cobbles when he passed down the lane.

Goodcole hissed a curse into the cold morning air. He avoided Anne's gaze when he turned back into the house and reached into his bag to confirm what he already knew: it was empty save for Joan's letter and his pamphlet. He really had no memory of the warrants apart from receiving them in Limbo. Most likely they had got mixed up with his other papers and were lying torn and soiled on his study floor with the rejected draft. He would return now and search them out.

Outside the warden's chambers Goodcole stood empty-handed. He paused to catch his breath, then raised the heavy knocker and let it fall.

"Enter," the shrill voice answered. Inside the room was as he remembered it: the vellum map adorned the wall; the plush Turkic rug softened the floor. On this visit however, an ornate chess set was laid out on the heavy oak table. Goodcole regarded the ivory and ebony pieces on the checkerboard squares and saw that the game was carefully poised. He waited but Warden Travers was pondering his next move and did not look up. Eventually, still with his attention fully on the game, the warden extended his right hand across the table. "My forms," he demanded, snapping his fingers. When Goodcole remained silent, Travers looked up in irritation. "Did not Dicker deliver them to you? We need to complete the paperwork on the mother and daughter."

"I don't have them."

Warden Travers narrowed his eyes; a slight tremble entered his voice. "But the *Fortune* sails on tonight's tide. Without signed affidavits neither woman may travel." Inwardly Goodcole squirmed.

"I have lost them," he admitted.

"*Lost* them? But we brought you into the prison to expedite such matters."

Not for the first time in his life Goodcole was at a loss to explain. Like a schoolboy before the headmaster's desk he stood with his hands clasped and awaited his fate.

Warden Travers screwed up his face then relaxed; it seemed that he, too, was at a loss. He looked down at the chessboard. First his hand glided over his white pieces, then over the black ranks massed against him. "You play – don't you?" he asked in a nasal whine.

"I learned once but..." Warden Travers' smile was unnerving.

"Too frivolous for you, ordinary?" He drew in his breath. "Let me tell you there is nothing frivolous about chess. Chess is power on a board." He said the words reverentially as if divulging a great truth and leaned over and touched his white king. Again Goodcole heard the intake of his breath and again he prepared himself for the grating voice. "Say I am the king of England and you are the king of Spain. One move and I am yours. Go on, make it, now," he challenged. Goodcole looked down at the board. He was by nature a defensive player and bold attacks were not his style. His hand hovered over the black king which evidently gave the warden great satisfaction for he started to chortle.

"I thought you would do that. In fact the key to the game right now is the black queen." Demonstrating the move the warden lifted the black queen and, using her like a gavel, knocked out his own king. "Move her thus and, checkmate, the game is over," he said. The warden narrowed his eyes. The smile was gone but the sly look remained. Goodcole sensed that his superior was about to dispense another nugget; he forced himself to listen. "Do you understand what I'm telling you, Goodcole? If the infanta of Spain marries Prince Charles then England will become part of Spain." The warden turned and pointed at the vellum map. Far to the left, where a ribbon of land floated amongst sea monsters, the head of King James had been drawn onto the vellum. "And if that happens, then Virginia, which the London Company has toiled so hard to develop, will become part of the Floridas – another Spanish possession."

Goodcole swallowed. "I see," he said.

The warden was about to turn away but in an afterthought he added, "And where is the white bishop in all of this?"

Shaken, Goodcole checked the board once more and pointed to a square on the far right.

"Exactly: on the sidelines. Know where to place your loyalties or your tenure here will be short, indeed." So saying, Warden Travers reached to his right and pulled out two sheets of blank paper from a folder. "In the meantime, instruct each woman to sign, here and here."

Goodcole looked to where the warden's finger pointed at the base of each page. "But there is nothing to sign."

"Don't be stupid, man. First get them to sign and then you can add in the rest, afterwards. Now jump to it." He clapped his hands.

Outside the Stone Hold Goodcole found Dicker waiting for him.

"At last, Goodcole. We've been searching high and low for you. Have you been to the warden, already?"

When he waved the blank pages, Dicker looked askance but Goodcole ignored his ire. "Did you look for me in the chapel?" he asked.

"Yes, I thought you'd be giving one of your homilies. There is a queue of women waiting for their Good Friday prayers. Most are with child or heavy-breasted."

Goodcole pointed to the warrants and pulled Dicker with him. "Come they may lead us to these two," he said.

Dicker pulled away. "We don't need their help. Let us fetch the widow, directly," he said.

"No, feelings are running high in the Stone Hold and we will be safer with them," Goodcole replied.

"Because they are God-fearing?"

"Aye."

When they neared the chapel the two men found the corridor empty, although it soon became clear why: the door, which Goodcole had been careful to lock, was now swinging free. Strangely, the women were all grouped around the end wall. Disturbed by the entry of the two men, they stood up and formed a defensive line.

"The widow Hampden and her daughter – where might they be found?" Dicker said.

The redhead was suckling her newborn child and she spoke first. "My lady is in the Stone Hold with the rest."

"Take us to her now." For a moment the women stood firm but Goodcole knew they were hiding something.

"Do as you're told," he barked. When they had shuffled past, Goodcole looked at the black oblong space from which the stone had been removed. He held his breath against the fetid smell.

Dicker pulled him by the sleeve. "Come on. We must find these two," he said.

It took a while for them to reach the Stone Hold because the women were weighed down by their shackles and moved slowly. In that wretched place there were no discrete cells, only a wide corridor in which mothers and children sat in their own filth. Caught in the confusion of the passageway, Goodcole looked down at a wife who was embroidering a purse with an emblem of a heart. Drawn to the scarlet thread passing through felt, he thought of the keepsake of hair in Sawyer's second tale. He glanced at her emaciated child and moved on. Pushing on past a succession of glum faces, they searched in vain for the widow and her daughter but persisted until they reached the end of the corridor. Here the redhead pointed to a makeshift partition of wicker that had been lashed together to create a separate space. Dicker pulled open the screen and stepped onto the straw bedding. Inside the space a well-dressed woman of about forty stood shielding a younger girl on the cusp of adulthood.

Goodcole took in the bearing, the high-born features and silk dresses. It was like finding a pair of pearls stamped in the dirt; he was surprised they were not boarded in the Master's Side.

"Mistress Hampden and her daughter Rowena," Dicker introduced. He forced a smile and then presented the sheets of paper while motioning to the chaplain to provide a quill and ink.

A flustered Goodcole had neither, but the woman reached into a damask sweet bag and produced her own. She dipped the feather in a vial of deep violet, scratched her name and waited for her daughter to do the same. Her voice was crystalline. "Master Dicker, do I have your word that this will secure our release?" she said.

In answer the agent bowed and motioned for Goodcole to do the same. "You have my word, My Lady. We will escort you to Somer's Quay before the tide ebbs," Dicker declared. They left them then and, clutching the signed sheets, made their way back down that foul corridor.

Up in his study Goodcole sat at his desk while Dicker leaned on his shelves. "What exactly should I write?" he asked.

Now they had the signatures, the agent exuded confidence once again. "The warrant establishes that each woman has opted to undertake this voyage willingly and of her own volition. Although further testimonials will be provided, your job is to witness their assent, which I believe you have just done."

"Neither mother nor daughter has been forced in any way?"

"Not in terms of their decision to go. Mistress Hampden made an unfortunate second marriage. It seems that her new husband has parted her from her wealth."

"He put her and her child behind bars. Can he do that?"

"He can and he has. We can help her escape."

"But to what?"

Goodcole cut a new quill and refreshed his inkhorn. Thinking only of Joan, he scrawled his name under the violet signatures and passed the warrants back to Dicker before the ink was dry. "You fill in the rest," he said.

When the agent had left him, Goodcole took a deep breath and exhaled. A dark sense of foreboding now hung over him for if women as high-born as the Hampdens were powerless against the company's schemes, then what chance did Joan stand? He tried to remain hopeful; there was still the dean. He alone saw the trade in live flesh for what it was; consequently, it was imperative that Goodcole stayed on his right side. With this in mind he decided to check on the chapel. Since he now knew that there was something foul afoot down there, he should find out what it was. If he could solve that riddle, he might yet pull something out of the fire.

Downstairs Goodcole was surprised to find the chapel door locked. Inside the place was as pristine as he had ever seen it. The block had been set back into the end wall, the floor had been swept and fresh sawdust scattered; the fetid smell, he noted with relief, had dispersed. Once again he examined the end wall. How could those wives prise a heavy block out of its closely mortared surface; moreover, why would they bother? Dismissing the notion that such heavily pregnant women were bent on escape, he recalled what Stamp had told him about the history of the chapel. If the new stairwell was installed before Sawyer's cousins Meg and Eve had arrived in the gaol, then the latter may have suckled her newborn on this very spot. Goodcole thought back to the scene in Potter's

Field when the three cousins had watched the two brothers recover the remains of the shrine.

He knelt down by the wall and pressed his fingertips into the gap where the mortar should have been and then reached out to the row above. Comparing the feel of the two, he noticed that the block that had been removed was not as cold as the others in the wall, nor was it as rough to the touch. While the rest of the wall was made of chiselled granite, this block was somehow dryer and less rasping. Goodcole was about to explore more when there was a tap on the door. Unlike the repetitive thumps on Sawyer's cell door this sound was tentative. Goodcole was surprised to see the white-haired Stamp peering at him.

"My friend, how can I help you?" he asked. Stamp had the look of a surface-dweller that had been forced to descend to a subterranean world.

"I have received an urgent message from St Paul's. The dean wants to see you in his office, now."

Goodcole blanched. "Now? But I need more time. Besides, I have not yet taken Good Friday prayers."

Stamp's voice remained low and calm. "I strongly advise you to go *now*," he said.

Newgate Street was in full flow when Goodcole left the prison. Sidestepping the steady stream of those entering the City, he veered to his right and made to climb up Warwick Lane when his way was blocked by a mummers' parade flowing down from Amen Corner. The onlookers were so densely packed that he had no choice but to step aside and let it pass; so he backed off under the awning of a hosier's shop and watched the forerunners approach. First came the boys blowing whistles and banging drums, next a gang of men followed, their heads covered by pointed hoods of knotted hemp, then a loud cheer sounded as the focal point of the drama hove into view. The man was stripped to the waist and carried a great pole wound with cowslips and ivy. Interlinking the fingers of both hands, he clasped it at its base, balancing the shaft on his right shoulder. Every so often a runner would break from the crowd to relieve him of the weight. The pole thus bobbed up and down; sometimes it was nearly vertical, at other times so flat that the crosspiece was in danger of dragging along the ground. Goodcole sensed the hysteria mounting around him; the mood was infectious; it quickened his pulse and made him want to call out. When the drummers had passed, the man carrying the pole drew closer. His torso shone with sweat, his forehead was matted with dry blood where blackthorn spikes had pierced his temple. He had been whipped and scourged and was close to exhaustion. Without warning another face blotted out Goodcole's view. He recognised him as James Hudd, a debtor from Ludgate. Hudd was beside himself with excitement.

"Reverend Cod Oil," he shouted. "He died *for us*, Reverend. He died *for us*." Goodcole watched Hudd leap off after the limping figure. The procession was heading off in the direction of Smithfield where the Elms had probably been transformed into a makeshift Golgotha. The crowd around him was on the ebb now, drifting off to resume its business on this most bittersweet of days. Hurrying up the hill towards his meeting with the dean, Goodcole reflected that in this febrile atmosphere a single spark would ignite the passions of the mob; a row, a rumour, or a well-placed lie could send the whole city into turmoil.

Goodcole found the dean standing in the airy surroundings of the Chapter House. Fresh from conducting a service in the cathedral, his eagle eyes tracked him when he entered from the cloister. The dean folded his arms and waited for his messenger bird to approach.

"Well, Goodcole?"

"Good day, Your Worship on this most sad of days."

The dean made a perfunctory nod. "You promised you would keep me informed, did you not?"

"I'm afraid there has been little time, what with Sawyer's execution and my report."

"Good, you have written a script." The dean extended a talon. "I have decided that we may publish, after all."

Goodcole shuffled back a step; he clamped his arm tight against the papers in his bag. "I don't have the text with me," he lied. "May I ask why this change of heart?"

The dean spoke over Goodcole's head as if from a great height. "On reflection I have concluded that a well-worded denunciation of Sawyer would serve us well. It would allow us to move on an issue that still dogs us. You must know that parochial wives have been abusing the secular law for years."

Goodcole thought of the women in the record office; he thought, too, of Sawyer's cousin: Eve. "You mean the women who plead their bellies in court, demanding clemency for their unborn child?"

"Yes, a mother who behaves in such a way does not deserve to keep her issue. It's time the Church took their newborns off them. Know you, we have donors who will pay to place such infants in church schools?"

"But what has Sawyer to do with this?" Goodcole asked.

"Sawyer provides us with an excuse to carry out a sweep of the gaols. In the popular mind she is the mistress of all that is malign. Your pamphlet will explain how such a woman propagates evil, even from beyond the grave. It will present our actions as a matter of public hygiene."

Goodcole looked past the dean to where light flooded into the Chapter House. His mind went back to Tyburn: to the moment when the young Elizabeth broke through the crowd.

"But Sawyer was not a bad mother. She cared for her offspring and they cared for her," he said.

"Sawyer, herself, is not the point," the dean replied.

Goodcole recoiled. Set against the black plush of his robes the dean's flesh looked spectrally pale; he was like a vulture that has stooped to strip carrion. Evidently the Church had few scruples after all; now, there seemed little difference between it and the company since each was prepared to lie to get what it wanted.

At three o'clock in the afternoon Christ died. With his passing from this world the Sun faded and a void opened up in its place. The void was black and cold and it sucked the life out of everything. Then, when it seemed that spring would stop in its tracks and all would freeze over once more, the Sun reappeared and hung tepid in the sky.

Walking back to the prison, Goodcole felt his courage leave him. The urgency had gone out of his stride now and he felt defeated. Knowing he must take Good Friday prayers, he decided that, afterwards, he would rewrite his pamphlet. Perhaps he could blend the two versions into something more palatable to those in power. The dean's sudden about-turn had unnerved him; it combined with the warden's words to show him that he was out of his depth. To protect Joan it would be prudent to take a softer line.

On re-entering the prison, Goodcole noted the general malaise. He saw it in the hangdog looks of the guards and the maudlin mood of all he met. A sense of despair now hung over everything; despair is life without hope and without hope life in prison is too bleak to endure.

On his rounds Goodcole found the chapel empty and secure. He waited for first the men, then the women to assemble and gave each a short prayer service, leaving out the sermon he would normally deliver on Good Friday. Relieved that he had discharged his duties, albeit in a minimal way, he then returned to his study to mull over his next move. While the thought of rescuing Joan occupied his mind, he was unsure exactly how to secure her release. It would be risky to arrive at the alderman's house unannounced because the steward might simply send him away in which case he would lose face and his actions would rebound on her. The sound of eight bells signalled the end of the afternoon watch and told Goodcole that he should finalise his copy. He was pouring out ink when the scrape of leather on the steps outside announced another visitor. The door swung open and Dicker peered in. There simply was no escaping the man.

"I thought that we were done," Goodcole said.

"We are almost done. We require your signature one last time."

"Is the paperwork not sufficient?"

"All shipshape and Bristol fashion," Dicker replied.

"So, leave me in peace. I have my final draft to complete."

Dicker stood firm. "We've uncovered a snag. It concerns Mistress Hampden who, as you know, sails on tonight's tide." Goodcole recalled similar persistence before the trip to London Bridge.

"Is the lady having second thoughts?"

"The *Fortune* is not quite the vessel she had imagined. She requires assurances. You see a lady like that is used to servants and, given her straitened circumstances, none were available." Goodcole didn't know which version of Dicker he disliked more, the bold man about town or this wheedling snout. But the agent was in a hurry and knew how to apply pressure. "Have you not read your daughter's letter? She must have penned it *three* days ago, now," he said.

Goodcole stood up and reached into his bag. Willing himself to stay calm, he unfolded Joan's letter and scanned through the familiar script. When he came to the line, 'one day, if you would permit such a thing, I would travel across the sea, too', his thumb pressed the wax seal to powder. An alarm sounded in his head; it told him that there was an intruder in the nest. Dicker was behind this; he had clearly put Joan up to it; after all, how could the agent know what she had written unless he had been present when she had put pen to paper? Cold anger chilled his veins. "You whoremonger, are you now plotting to procure my daughter, too?" he said.

"Get a grip, man. This is not my idea – it's Joan's. She dreams of a new life."

"She is but a child. You *made* her write this."

"Joan is a dutiful daughter. She does not want to disappoint you by suggesting she wants to leave."

Goodcole knew he was being soft-soaped; he ignored Dicker's weasel words and returned to the heart of the matter. "Exactly what assurances is this woman demanding?" he asked.

"Mistress Hampden fears that her status will be much reduced on landing in Virginia. She will not marry again, which then puts the pressure on her daughter. She has demanded a number of costly provisions that show her standing, one being that a servant girl accompany her aboard the *Fortune*."

Goodcole shrugged. "I can do no more."

Dicker leaned in close. "Can you not?"

Sensing that further confrontation would only endanger Joan, Goodcole glanced back down at the letter. A spark of inspiration arrived just in time. "The solution is obvious," he said.

"Is it?"

"This Lucy Remnant has already expressed a desire to go. Alderman Bull could happily let her board the *Fortune* with the Hampdens. Then he can replace her – servants in London are two a penny."

Dicker eyed him warily then shook his head. "No, that wouldn't do at all. The maid Remnant is due to find a husband who must pay a bride price of one hundred and fifty pounds of tobacco for her. Her duties will be to him and him alone."

Goodcole felt his ire rising again. "Is that what this is about, *tobacco*?" he said.

"No, this is about your daughter Joan. She has expressed a desire to travel and, being too young for marriage, would make a fine maidservant."

"And… you want me to consent to this?"

"You do serve the alderman, do you not?"

"I am not his *slave*."

Goodcole waited for the agent to leave, then he sat down at his desk and held his head in his hands. He rebuked himself because his outburst was self-defeating. Now it would be harder to free Joan from Walbrook Ward because Dicker's account of their conversation would precede him. He had used some harsh words during their exchange and the agent would most likely repeat these verbatim, depicting him as disloyal and proud. He sank back in his chair and wondered what to do. Denied the prospect of taking control of his future he felt stymied. Instead of returning to Newgate, he should have pressed on east after seeing the dean because, if he had done that, he would have avoided Dicker and would be with Joan by now. This thought only aggravated his sense of grievance; his mind was full of wild imaginings so he tried to focus on the one question that really mattered: how could he keep Joan safe? A few hours earlier he would have answered, 'by bearing witness to earn salvation' but that was on Maundy Thursday and on Good Friday his courage had dried up. Goodcole's mind squirmed; he told himself that there was another way. Perhaps, using his skill with words, he could produce a pamphlet that kept him on good terms with everybody. He could be generous to Sawyer while still paying lip service to the alderman and the dean. So, he reached down to the darkness at his feet where the rejected first draft still lay. Here, instead of torn paper, his hand touched Deicrowe's mommet. Irked, Goodcole grasped the totem and brought it into the light.

The little figure was like a stillborn wrapped in its winding sheet but Goodcole forced himself to stare at it. This was, he reminded himself, a sign. It had been sent to him for a reason and yet so far he had avoided asking 'why'. The mommet was not about Deicrowe, Sawyer or the warden, but about him. Gingerly Goodcole unwound the bandage and regarded the crude cuts in its scarab sheen. This time when he pressed his thumbnail into the swelling belly he pictured

Joan: Joan, deflowered and defiled, Joan, left for dead in a swamp in a savage land. The mommet had been sent to him as a warning and, yet again, he had failed to listen. Far from being grateful, Goodcole felt nothing but hatred for the little figure. He would fetch her but first he must rid himself of this malignant tick.

Shortly before five bells on Good Friday Goodcole set off down Newgate's corridors with Deicrowe's carving tucked into the lining of his coat. Now that its true meaning had been revealed, the omen had become an ordinary object once again; it was a keepsake carved by one brother for another, nothing more. So, with few qualms, he opened a door before the Master's Side and climbed up the spiral stair that led up to the turret in the North Tower. In normal times he would have avoided this space, which was busy with guards using the latrine but now torpor had settled on the prison and all was a deathly hush. The turret was a hard climb. It was small and well suited to its function as a privy. To the keen-sighted observer who knew the prison it could be spotted from outside of the City, where it appeared as a crenulation high up on the wall above Giltspur Street. The turret was both exposed and confined at the same time but Goodcole had no intention of spending more than a moment there. Killing two birds with one stone, he aimed a stream of piss through the discoloured vent and took a boyish satisfaction in how the wind caught it as it passed into space. Next he reached into his coat and, pinching it between finger and thumb as one might a leech that has latched on during the fording of a stream, he flicked it through the hole. Goodcole resisted the temptation to peer down through the gap onto the rooftops; instead he contented himself with the notion that anyone looking up from the street below would see a black Madonna dropping out of the sky like a dart.

Afterwards, suffused with relief, Goodcole made his way back down the spiral stair. He had reached the landing above the Master's Side when footfalls from below made him pause; he heard a padding tread offset by a clicking, as of claws on stone. The footfalls passed by along the corridor and then diminished, slinking back into the hush of the prison. Keen to reach the sanctuary of his study Goodcole held back and then, in the drifting silence, stepped through the doorway. At first glance the corridor from the Master's Side was deserted but when he looked down its length, he saw a retreating shape. For a moment the rush lights illuminated a low lupine swagger but soon all was lost in the gloom.

Dread now filled Goodcole. That dread confirmed what he already knew; it told him that the prison was a malign place that was biding its time; soon it would swallow him up, just as it had swallowed countless men, women and children before him. Newgate was a well of ghosts; it was a mausoleum of stifled voices because over five centuries its dank walls had chilled the last breaths of the dispossessed – those who had been born into this world with hope and hunger in their hearts but had died stymied in the dirt.

Goodcole had climbed the stairs to his study and was about to engage the key in the door when he heard the loping stride return. Somehow he felt compelled to listen. The footfalls grew louder; they advanced from the corridor below and paused at the base of the stairs on which he was standing. He heard the grazing of a muzzle on flagstones, then a slow exhalation of breath from which he detected a rank smell: the tang of brimstone. Standing in the half-light, unable to see anything below, Goodcole recalled the legend of the Black Dog of Newgate. He remembered, too, the beasts from Sawyer's stories: the fox that, silver as shekels in the moonlight, had pinned her to her marriage bed and the wolf, that had leapt out of the mists to devour her firstborn child. He turned the key in the door and fled into the safety of his den.

Once he had secured the door and brightened his lamp, Goodcole sat down at his desk. He had spent the last week living on his nerves, which were now fractious and worn. Part of him longed to let go, to drift into slumber, but another part knew he must hang on because one slip now could lead to the ruination of all. For a while Goodcole sat and listened but that only fed his anxiety so he settled to the task of reformulating his pamphlet. This provided a refuge for his fevered mind; moreover, it allowed him to hope for better days ahead. He was midway through reading his second draft when an idea came to him; it was so simple that he struggled to understand why he hadn't already put it into effect. The copy that exonerated Sawyer was good; it was a little earnest perhaps but it could remain as long as he prefaced it with a section that emphasised the role of both the judiciary and the Church in first bringing her to book and then returning her to the fold. The pamphlet, then, could have it both ways: it could support the institutions of the land, while suggesting that personal miracles were possible, too. Far from encouraging dissent, such a text would suggest that no one was beyond redemption and that all should have hope. Thus by framing his pamphlet with a respectful nod to authority he could both bear witness to Sawyer's salvation and keep his job. Goodcole stretched in his chair. He would need to get his copy to Butler first thing in the morning because that way he could present the dean with a fait accompli. Since His Reverence had not parted with so much as a penny he could hardly complain, could he?

Insulated in his study Goodcole wrote quickly. Starting with 'An Apology to the Christian Reader', he developed the conceit that, although he had not intended to put pen to paper after the Robinson affair, his hand had been forced by the rumour and innuendo that had surrounded Sawyer's case. This 'ale house banter' trivialised the king's justice and distracted from the promise that each child makes when, at catechism, they are confirmed into the Church. 'Only when each of us forsake the Devil and his vain pomp can we reach the kingdom of heaven', he wrote.

Goodcole tacked on this beginning to the body of the second version and then concluded his copy with a short and simpering dedication to Mother Church. The institution provided 'the only path by which a sinner may find their way back to the Lord'. Gathering his papers into a blue linen folder, he slipped them into his bag and yawned. Then, overcome with fatigue, he dropped his head and fell into a deep sleep.

Darkness pushed in from every side. That darkness was dense as oily smoke and it tasted of burnt bones. Goodcole blinked, then searched amidst the black. He hoped for a chink of light from the keyhole or the gap under the door but there was nothing, only this miasma that rendered him blind. For a long while he slumped in his chair, unsure whether he was alive or dead. His body was numb: like an arm long lain on before the blood returns. He cursed the wick of his candle for sputtering out and felt a stab of regret when he realised that he had left his flint striker and tinderbox down in the chapel. When at last sensation did return to his hands, Goodcole looped the bag over his shoulder and grasped his keys. Somehow he was still unable to get up.

"You can't stay here." The voice came from inside his skull: it was Sawyer's.

"What can I do?" Goodcole said the words into himself.

"You hold the key. *Go.*"

"I dare not brave what's out there."

"But you cannot stay," she said.

"So, I am trapped."

"Aye, you are lost in a dark wood."

Mention of the wood reminded him of her final story set in the Lord's Grove. He was glad now that he had not used the first version of his pamphlet because, as he at last understood, no one summoned the Devil; instead, Satan came to you. When Goodcole next addressed Sawyer he did so out loud. This time he used the same unctuous tone that he reserved for prayer, as if trying to placate her. "I have written a faithful testament of your passing," he said. At this there was only silence. So he waited and in the quiet his minded drifted. He could see currents in the darkness now; they reminded him of the grainy residues in ink. He remembered the hawthorn cuttings fermenting in Butler's backyard; next, his thoughts sank into the ocean deep where leviathans swam amongst shoals of squid.

When at last Sawyer spoke, her words came direct from the Easter story. "*Why do you look for the living amongst the dead?*" she said.

"Why do you quote Scripture?" Goodcole replied.

"I mean, why do you care about the dean and the alderman? Go and fetch your child – if child she be." Goodcole noted the twist at the end. It showed that she saw through his sense of self: the doting father, paterfamilias and aspiring writer.

He held his bag close and made to stand up but his strength failed and he slumped back down again. "You think that I should ignore powerful men like the dean and the alderman? What then, are *they* dead already?"

"They have no power. In this world there are only the quick and the dead: the quick live through others so Satan cannot touch them; meanwhile, the dead live for themselves and are worm-eaten before they even die."

Goodcole leaned forward and cradled his head in his folded arms. Her words were cold comfort because they brought him no closer to Joan. "What is the point of this life if we cannot safeguard the ones we love?" he said.

"That is your pride talking. It is not for you to know."

"I take pride in my daughter. Is that such a sin?"

"She was God's before she was ever yours. I outlived seven of mine and others have suffered more. There's not a mother alive who could not tell you her woes. Besides, you told me that all women are unclean. How can your daughter be so pure?"

"She is a child, an innocent which means she is next to God."

"And she was sent to save you?"

"Yes. She is a mark of His love."

Mirthless laughter sounded in Goodcole's head. Sawyer was scathing. "This is not about her at all, it's about you. You simp, you are crying for yourself. After all, if God sent her then what do you really fear?"

That charge fired his gall. Anger boiled up in him and he stood up.

"You have spurred me on. I'm done with this and I'm done with you," he said.

"You will never be done with me."

When Goodcole opened the door, there was nothing there. He let out a sigh of relief and waited for his tired eyes to adjust to the half-light; then, he shuffled down the stairs. The sound of seven bells from the guardhouse told him that it was now half-past eleven at night. Leaden-legged, he forced himself forward cheering himself with the thought that, if he could just get through the dog-leg to the stairwell, he would be free of the prison in a few downward strides. He had turned the first corner and was heading to the next when he caught the sound of a melody whistled nearby. The tune's lilting air was so unexpected that Goodcole slowed, keen to catch more of the tumbling notes. With a pang he recognised it as 'There Were Three Ravens'. It was a tune he knew from childhood: a song about birds who found a dead knight in a wood. At first the descending scale seemed to fade, sucked into the stonework but when he turned the second corner, it grew bold once more. Goodcole looked towards the man who approached from the Master's Side. His manner and dress were as bright as the song was melancholy; indeed, he would have been more in place in the rose garden of a great house rather than the corridors of the condemned. Sensing that the stranger had spotted him, Goodcole raised a hand.

The man broke off his whistling and waved a greeting. He was too carefree to be an inmate; moreover, he was expensively dressed. When he drew close, Goodcole admired the lace ruff, the doublet embroidered with gold thread and his pristine silk stockings – all unmarked by the grime of the gaol.

"Hail friend. What brings you to the Whit this holy day?" he said.

The gallant was in his middle years, although time had been kind to him. He ran a gloved hand over his moustache and pointed beard, both of which were flecked with grey. "I am visiting, sir. Though the man I seek is nowhere to be found. He is the chaplain of this gaol. A man named Henry Good."

"The name is Good-*cole*. I am he."

At this the stranger beamed. "Then, we are well met and my visit has not been in vain."

Goodcole noted the West Country accent. Still scanning the corridor for a dark form, he shuffled forward. "Come sir, walk with me. Only it is late and I am ready to drop."

The stranger gestured for him to lead the way. "I'm told you are a writer of distinction sir, and yet I see from your attire that you are a humble man at home with the common sort."

Goodcole stepped into the main stairwell of the prison and half turned. "You keep strange hours. What do you want from me?"

"It's a delicate matter. Forgive me for not sending word but I prefer to conduct my business face to face."

"This is not a day for business, sir. It's the crux of Lent – a time of abstinence and prayer."

"The very thing, but just as Lent gives way to Easter, so our meeting may complete your rebirth."

Goodcole stopped on the stair. "My rebirth?" he repeated.

"The revelation of Revelation. It cannot be told and must be shown."

Goodcole felt a draft of cold air from outside the prison; it was deliciously fresh and told that the great expanse of the night sky was waiting for him. "In my experience, people who promise the world are apt to steal the crust from out of your mouth. Anyway, the last time I heeded talk like yours, I was dragged on a wild goose chase across London." Below him in the guardhouse they struck the midnight bell. Goodcole waited for the chimes to fade. "You didn't tell me your name," he said.

"My name is Nicholas Deicrowe."

Goodcole felt blood drain from his face. He shot a glance down at the guard; next, he turned back to face the man who stood a few treads above him. "One word from me and you will be thrown into the selfsame cell which held your brother," he hissed.

"In Limbo. Take me there if you would be so kind."

Goodcole was too tired for this carnival turn. Nothing about this man added up: he was a fugitive who had strolled into a prison; he was dressed like a prince, yet spoke like a jester and somehow he bore no malice to those who had hanged his brother. The man must be an imposter who was trying to gain a cut of the profits from his pamphlet. Clamping his bag tighter under his arm, he turned his back and was about to walk away when the man placed a hand on his shoulder.

"My brother William held you in high regard. He said 'go now to Henry Good. Show him the City of God'."

Goodcole almost choked. He pointed out into the night. "What, will you show me Rome, my Jesuitical 'friend'?"

"Take me to Limbo. It is through there that we shall enter the city."

Goodcole was about to walk away when an image flashed across his mind's eye: it was of the older Deicrowe naked apart from his woollen cap, twisting on the Tree. He knew that, but for providence, that could be him too. He turned. "Tell me your birthplace and I may yet oblige," he challenged.

"I was born in a hamlet called Minions on Bodmin Moor. Though I have no memory of it having been raised on Lord Arundel's estate at Lanherne."

Goodcole was now caught between his desire to learn more about the past and his need to break free of the prison. Strangely, it was the past that won out for it had a dead weight and dragged at him like the undertow.

The stranger could tell he was weakening. "Come, I will go first. That way you will have the whip hand over me." He made a gesture like he was driving the lurch through the uprights of the Tree and Goodcole dropped feet first as if from the scaffold. He came to rest, still breathing, down a level in the stairwell between the chapel and the Stone Hold.

"How did you do that?" he exclaimed.

Nicholas did not answer him at first; instead, he reached up to where a rush light flared high on the wall and rubbed his palm on the scorched stone. "I did nothing, friend. It is just a trick of time, which like an arrow flies faster with age. It seems only yesterday that my brother and I cut our initials into this wall."

Goodcole looked up to where the crude initials, 'W.D. and N.D.' were carved into a blackened block.

"You two brothers were here before?"

"Aye, as free men. We knew the masons that built this place after the fire. At Arundel's command we stowed holy relics from Queen Mary's time between the walls." He pointed at the newer stonework. "To this day, your prayers are blessed by the reliquary of saints and the Holy Mother, herself. The chapel was always dedicated to sancta mater dolorosa."

Goodcole had hardly heard these words when with a whoosh of air he plummeted to Limbo. Knowing that dark magic was sucking him deeper underground, he peered around to find its source: was it this clown or the Black Dog? Ahead of him, now on the lowest level of the prison, Nicholas Deicrowe was inspecting the cell where his brother had spent his last days. He swung the heavy door back and then moved on to Sawyer's cell, which was lying open and unused, too. He spoke with bitterness, now. "A miserable fate. Penned up with a witch and then hanged like a common thief," he exclaimed.

Goodcole felt a rush of blood to his head. He lunged at the lace collar but missed, grasping only dank air. "Lysbeth was not a witch," he said.

Nicholas Deicrowe faced him; the mask of bonhomie was gone. "Not a witch? Listen to yourself, man." He pointed down to the end of the corridor to where the barrel-vaulted ceiling framed a small doorway. "There," he said. "Open that, if you dare."

Against his will Goodcole moved forward; he was a sleepwalker, a dreamer drawn from the splashing shallows into the deep. When he turned the handle, a blast of air blew him through the door. It propelled him through the City's wall and along the length of its cavity, all the way to the next gate down. Here, it spat him out, leaving him dust-covered but otherwise unhurt, crumpled in a heap on Ludgate Hill.

Goodcole picked himself up and shook himself down. Somehow he was back on familiar ground, although only the gatehouse was recognisable because both the debtor's gaol and the surrounding houses had vanished. Above him the night sky glowed red. He looked down at the crimson river and struggled to find a landmark; across the Thames, where the Paris Garden and bear-baiting halls should have been, there was now only a ragged line of trees. The forest covered the near bank, too, just as it did everywhere else. In swelling groves of tangled trunks and roots, it stretched from Broken Wharf in the east to St Andrew's Hill in the west and then up the slope to Blackfriars. Indeed, aside from the wall and a few lumber paths, the City had ceased to exist – so overgrown was it with invading trees.

Goodcole shifted his stance on the sodden ground; he looked around for Deicrowe but the traitor was nowhere to be seen so he turned his attention to a raven that was ruffling its feathers close by. The bird was observing him from the flat of a tree stump. "What is this place?" he asked.

The raven spoke in a low croak. "It is the town of Lud: the same that you were born into, the one where you may yet be ordained, the place where you will die."

"Aye, Lud the pagan lies buried under this slope," Goodcole said. He looked back at the muddied banks of the Thames where a row of shackled figures stood in a snaking line by a makeshift pier. Noting the galley moored in the flooding tide, he watched the sailors ready the ship for its human cargo.

"Is this the City before it was built or after it was destroyed?" he asked the raven.

"It is the City now in the nineteenth year of King James, only you are seeing it stripped of all pretense."

"Stripped?"

"Yes, when vain pomp is stripped away, we see it as it is: a jungle of desire. The only way to survive in such a place is to sup with the strong."

Goodcole turned his gaze from the middle ground to the knoll of the hill on which he was standing. Here, in place of the great cathedral of St Paul's, a rickety tower had been constructed out of felled timber. The platform provided a roost for a great flock of birds. Their plumage was a mixture of black and white; some perched on its elevation, while others circled high in the sky where their piercing cries created a cacophony of sound.

He turned to the raven. "Are you one of *them*?" he said.

At this the raven let out a croak. "I was here long before they flew to these shores. They congregate on the high ground for with famine and plague in this port there is a feast of souls to be had."

Goodcole looked closer at the bird. He saw how the sheen of its feathers reflected the red of the sky. "What then is the difference between you and them?"

"They are functionaries and belong to the Church. Whereas I am a messenger sent to warn you."

At this Goodcole shook his head. "You are Satan shaped in a new guise, just as Deicrowe was a moment ago. You brought me to this place," he said.

But the raven fixed him with its brilliant eye. "No, Sawyer brought you here through her storytelling. Now, take a good look because here all is revealed," it said.

Day 8

Goodcole awoke within the confines of his study. He stood up, let the blood flow back into his legs and rubbed his eyes. Last night's dreams were still vivid: he thought of the messenger bird bathed in crimson light, the galley waiting for its human cargo and the Babel of St Paul's. The vision added to his resolve. He unlocked the door and let his eyes adjust to the flicker of the gaol. When he turned back to his study he saw it for what it was: a prison cell. Aside from the table, chair and dusty shelves, it was no different to the dungeons in Limbo. Like them it was a place where one spent one's last days and faced the reckoning to come.

Goodcole dropped the key on the table. Leaving the door swinging free, he shouldered his bag and descended the stairs; all around the sulphurous smell of marsh gas rose to meet him. It told him he must get out.

In the gatehouse the guards were passing around a jug of fortified ale. Moving through their midst, he caught a whiff of its strong liquor and stepped out into the biting cold of an April morning.

In Newgate Street he looked past the shadow of Christchurch into the morning sun. He turned right towards

Ludgate and, following a path parallel to his trajectory in last night's dream, he climbed as far as Ave Maria Lane. Outside Butler's print shop Goodcole regarded the poster on the shutter. 'Maids for the New Life of Virginia' he read and recalled the moment when the still-damp proofs had been pulled from the press.

The shop door opened and William Butler looked at him; the printer was bleary-eyed. "I expected you, yesterday," he said. He looked up the street, then signalled Goodcole to come in and locked the door behind him. "You have the transcript?"

Goodcole opened his bag and showed him his manuscript, but the printer still looked irked.

"You know most people pay me extra for working the holiday. You pay less."

Goodcole breathed in the dry scent of charcoal from the stove. He regarded Butler coolly. Truth be told he cared little for the pamphlet now, which he viewed merely as unfinished business. He would put this matter to bed, then return to minister to the women before he rescued Joan. Goodcole spread out his handwritten copy on the counter. "Did you find a woodcut for the frontispiece?" he asked.

Butler brightened. "I have the very thing," he said. He dropped down on his haunches and pulled a small wooden tile from the cabinet; this he placed beside Goodcole's copy.

The chaplain examined those parts of the stained surface left untouched by the artist's gouge. In reverse relief he saw the outline of a stout figure clad in a heavy skirt and straw hat: she carried a stick and was depicted stepping from the forest to the field. He inspected the grimy surface of the wood and sensed that the alchemy came from the materials rather than the image. Goodcole placed his hand on the tile, which was sticky and warm to the touch. He ran the pads of his fingertips over the grooves where the ink was like blood, which though clotted had not yet hardened to a scab. For a moment he was back in her story world. He thought of the tree cut during Rogation by the churchwarden's chisel. He heard Sawyer say words, which he knew by heart: "For a brief while, I caught hold of Meg and Eve and we three spun round, while the boys and girls of the parish beat the tree." Butler was speaking and Goodcole forced his attention back to the here and now.

"I trust this earns your approval?" the printer said.

"My approval?"

"I have the block from a friend in Fleet Street. It was used to depict a case of witchery in Leicester some two years ago."

Goodcole withdrew his hand. He glanced again at the image of the countrywoman striding forth. "It looks nothing like Sawyer," he said.

Butler looked at him askance. "It describes her *type*. You don't expect a true likeness – for what you pay?"

Goodcole backed off and avoided Butler's gaze. The printer's words were truer than he could know because his trade turned on making types out of originals; moreover, as author, Goodcole had instigated this process. He was about to monetise a woman by reducing her life to type. Those that had known Sawyer in the flesh would not read what was printed here and those that had only heard about her would now know her by these marks. And what were they, these squiggles on a page? At best they were a code for those who presumed to know her type but what did they really know, about Enfield, Winchmore, or her life in the Lord's Grove? Goodcole broke away from his own thoughts and forced himself to speak. "This will serve well enough: a countrywoman setting off for an honest day's toil. How fickle we all are," he ruminated, more about himself than her.

Butler shot him a curious look, then got back to business. Having scanned through his copy, he counted the words in Goodcole's title. "We can divide the page between the text on top and the block below. The pamphlet will be this big." He spread his ink-stained hand on the desk.

"Aye, pocket-sized." Goodcole agreed.

Butler looked satisfied. He motioned Goodcole to the back of the shop, then disappeared down some stairs before reappearing with a tray of bread, cheese and ale. The printer filled a tankard and placed it in Goodcole's outstretched hand. "To your pamphlet's success," he said. "I sense from your 'apology' that you have struck a less strident tone from our last publication about Robinson."

Goodcole was half-hearted. "It is an attempt to bear witness," he said.

Butler took a slurp and then cut the cheese and bread. "Well, there's already been interest. Yesterday, I took an advanced order for the first three copies."

"An advanced order?"

"From Master William Rowley. He insisted that the first copies should go to him and him only. He paid silver upfront, which is most unusual for a playwright." Goodcole could not place the name. He thought of the bills that apprentices had stuck up around the City, which advertised nights of sin and revelry at sinkholes like the Swan and Cockpit Theatre. The play *The Honest Whore* came to mind, but that was by a man who went by the dubious name, 'Thomas Dekker'. Then he remembered the cloaked figure with the grandiose voice that had stood before him in the queue in Stationer's Hall.

"But we don't want the players to get hold of it," he said.

"Why ever not? A sale is a sale."

Goodcole bit back his response. He pictured the spindly pile of timber from the dream and recalled the piercing cries of the birds that circled high above. How vain he was to believe that he could have the last word. The book trade of St Paul's worked by call and response. One pamphlet answered another and what was the point of this paper chain? The point was money because each pamphlet was really a promissory note. Amidst the clamour of the market it said, 'buy me, I will tell you the truth'. Yet such claims were false because only one book contained the Word of God and that was the king's Bible. Goodcole glanced around him at the ink cooling on the stove and at the paper that soaked in a tray. The alchemy practised here was a counterfeit art in which herbage culled from the forest – pulp for paper, galls for ink – was transformed into fool's gold. Perhaps one day all money would be made like this? After all, why dig for ore and mint silver and gold coins, if you can print a note for a fraction of the cost?

During this rumination Butler had taken a step back and was regarding him with concern. "Are you alright, my friend? You seem somewhat changed since the last time we met." He scratched his chin. "They have pestilence to the east of us, I hope you have not brought *that* to my door," he said.

Goodcole's mind was full of Revelation. "What is pestilence but the Lord's way of correcting us lest we come to nothing?"

Butler eyed him warily, then, drawn back to the job in hand, he glanced down at Goodcole's copy. "For us, the Devil's in the detail. Have you run your transcript past the warden and the dean?"

"Both approve my Easter theme of redemption," Goodcole lied.

Butler relaxed. "Then we're in business." He licked his ink-stained hands. "I will rack up the press today and print a first edition, tomorrow."

On the way back to Newgate Goodcole paused at Amen Corner to breathe in the fresh air. Watching the passers-by, he mulled over Butler's comment that he had changed. The printer was right of course but there was more to it than that, because specifically, he had changed sides. A week ago Sawyer had refused to sign a confession prepared by him, and now, he was withholding his consent too. "Do you think that I would trust you, a stranger, with the souls of my own flesh and blood?" she had said when he had pressured her to make her mark above his. How strange that he had expressed that same sentiment to Dicker when he had last approached him in his study. This change came as a shock but it was wonderful, too. It was wonderful because it freed him from the anxiety and indecision that had beset him all his life.

What a difference a day made! This time on Good Friday he had been scurrying around trying to please his 'betters', yet now on Easter Saturday, clarity had taken hold. This showed the way forward; moreover, it told him that however bleak the prospect, he always had a choice because no one could compel him against his will. Goodcole watched a cutpurse sidle out of an entry opposite Paternoster Row. On impulse he crossed over the cobbled slope and proffered a groat in his open palm. At first the boy hung back sensing a trap, then he pounced with quicksilver hands, melting away in an instant. Goodcole did this just to show that he could, much as one might toss a coin into a wishing well. He did it to acknowledge that his fate lay in the hands of providence.

Pressing on to Newgate, he made his plans for the day ahead. Only when he had conducted a full service for the men and the women would he make his way east to join Joan in Walbrook Ward. And why was he not fretting that he would arrive too late? It was because he finally understood that all was one because his blood tie with Joan was no different from the blood ties that the women shared with their own kin and in honouring them, he was honouring Joan. This, he knew now, was what it was to be meek. To be meek meant to put others first, to be calm in the storm of battle, to know that whatever happened, if you remained true, nothing could sunder you from God's love. Never before had he been able to live like this, yet now, somehow, he could.

Goodcole did not look up when he entered the gatehouse. Finding Dicker descending from the South Tower with the sergeant-at-arms, he stepped into his path.

"Did the Hampdens sail on the tide?" he said.

Dicker motioned for the sergeant to leave them. "After a deal of fussing, yes. We found a girl to accompany them and they took their place on the *Fortune*. I believe it is docked at Gravesend now and will leave our shores, tomorrow."

"And Joan?"

"What of her?"

"Is she attending to her duties, as before?"

Dicker took the measure of Goodcole's new-found self-assurance. "Absolutely. Mistress Bull wants her to remain by her bedside at all times. You must know that we need a signed affidavit from you, her guardian, before we can send her overseas."

"And that you will never have."

Dicker narrowed his eyes. "Where have you been? You should know that the dean has paid us a visit. He is with Warden Travers now and I believe there's a rumpus in the chapel."

For a moment Goodcole was thrown. "The dean is in the chapel?"

Dicker shook his head. "No, the dean is with the warden in his chambers; I believe they have reached an agreement. Meanwhile, you sir, have a shower of shrews on your hands."

"What do you mean by that?"

"You have an infestation in the chapel – something truly rotten," Dicker laughed.

Downstairs Goodcole found the chapel door locked. Hearing voices inside, he peeked through the keyhole and saw light. The voices were hushed in prayer and, although he could not catch what was being said, he could smell incense. Goodcole breathed in the resinous smell of the forest; then, he turned his key in the lock and entered. Inside he was confronted by the strangest of sights. At the far end of the cramped space a group of seven women knelt with their backs to him. In front of them a row of urns was arranged in a crescent around a small statue. Goodcole stared at the pots; the largest was the size of a flagon of wine, the smallest could have been held in the palm of one hand. Next he turned his attention to the statue that formed the focal point of the women's worship. No more than a foot high, it bore an uncanny resemblance to Deicrowe's mommet: he noted the slight incline of the head, the scarab sheen and the way the Virgin held her hands out at her sides. It was as if the black Madonna was blessing the flagstones of Newgate and drawing off the sorrow and hurt of five centuries into her own scorched form.

The women were reacting to him now. One clasped her suckling baby to her breast, while another tried to obstruct his way. Goodcole brushed past her and found himself face to face with a girl who was no more than nineteen years old. He looked into her fresh face, into green eyes, then down past her cropped hair to her belly, which, swollen with the child within, projected through her smock. Seen through threadbare linen the bulge had a miraculous quality, like a bubble of light rising from the depths of the ocean. Goodcole was caught unawares and he felt humbled. He was a witness to the miracle of motherhood, and overcome, he dropped to his knees in the midst of them. "Water, clay, forest," he mouthed whilst in his head Sawyer spoke the Word.

> "*In the beginning my womb was without form, and void;*
> *And the spirit of God moved upon the face of the waters.*
> *And God said let there be light and there was light.*"

As he knelt there on the cold floor, heady with the scent of the forest, he knew that He had willed it and She had willed it: from the darkness of the primordial waters to the separation of the earth to the growth of the fruiting trees. This was creation; creation was Genesis and genesis was happening right now before his eyes.

The girl backed away. Avoiding his stare, she hid herself amongst the older women who now banded in a clump facing the door. For a moment Goodcole didn't know what they were looking at, but then the heavy tramp of boots from the corridor made him turn.

The dean stood in the doorway. Holding up his staff to ward off evil, he took in the scene before him: the women, the makeshift altar and Goodcole prostrated before it. "GET UP OFF YOUR KNEES," he bellowed. Next he addressed the redhead who was nursing her newborn. "Enlighten me as to what is going on here."

The mother looked up at the dean and then down at the idol from Potter's Field. "We are praying, Your Worship."

"To whom or *what*, exactly?"

"We are praying to the Virgin to save our souls."

The dean surveyed the row of pots. Then he turned to Goodcole who was now on his feet. "I take it these vessels contain the remains of children born within the confines of the prison?" he said. Goodcole's mouth was dry.

"Your Worship, you must understand that a great injustice has been done…"

"An injustice – by whom, exactly?"

"By the Church. By excluding these children from the care of Christ, we have proved ourselves to be unfit."

The dean stepped forward into their midst. For a moment Goodcole thought that he would strike him, instead he pointed to the women and children. "But these souls are in *your* care Goodcole, yet, instead of protecting them, you have presided over this heinous ritual: this blood sacrifice with a necromancer's stone."

Goodcole let the epithets fall around him. Facing the back of the chapel, he saw the scene as the dean saw it: the women with their bare backsides to the altar table, while he prostrated himself before the black Madonna. Of course it was heinous, but appearances were deceptive because what was truly chilling was the neglect that had allowed this situation to fester for so many years.

Over the next hour the guards carried out a thorough sweep of the Stone Hold. First they prised the sucking babies off their mothers and then they bundled the infants into a wagon bound for an almshouse. For Goodcole the speed of the action combined with the shock in the chapel to alienate him further from those who wielded power. Two years before, the London Company had impounded more than one hundred vagrant children off the streets, transporting them to Virginia for 'their better improvement'; now, the Church was doing something similar within the confines of the prison. Thus one injustice compounded another and the whole sorry tale continued. While part of him understood the actions of Mother Church in reclaiming these souls, another part identified with the mothers' grief and doubted the institution's motive. Wasn't Sawyer right, after all? He remembered her statement that 'in this world, the poor always lose'. Those women had been stripped of everything but their infants and yet, now, even their own flesh and blood had been taken too. In his head she rolled out the words from Scripture: '*unto every one that hath shall be given; but from him that hath not shall be taken away even that which he hath*'. He recalled his joy at first holding his daughter and thought how he would have felt if she had been ripped from his arms. What the dean had perpetrated today was a type of theft; moreover, this theft was part of a pattern. Just as the courts had labelled Deicrowe a common thief to deprive him of the true course of his life, just as he had appropriated Sawyer's story to boost his own standing, so the dean was now working hand in glove with the warden to erase every worthwhile thing about these women's lives. They would be called 'godless' by the authorities and their children – 'the lucky ones' – would grow up knowing nothing of their mothers. Except, they weren't godless, nor would Mother Church succeed in erasing their faith. God the Father would know and there would be a reckoning. Again Sawyer spoke in his head: 'at Last Lammas, when wrongs are put right, all these forgotten ones will rise and take their rightful place with our Lord'. What then for Mother Church; what then for the dean and the warden?

While the guards turned the prison upside down, Goodcole returned to the chapel. Leaving the idol where the wives had placed it, he concentrated on the urns. One by one he carried each to the safety of his study, turning the little room into a charnel house, a crypt where those who had been born and died in captivity might be kept until such time as he could transport them to sanctified ground. Praying before them there, he felt the same reverence as he had when he had dropped to his knees in the chapel. He recalled the bubble of the girl's belly and compared it to the shrivelled remains in these jars. The briny wetness of one contrasted with the sad dryness of the other; it was a reminder that the body is a vessel into which the spirit is poured – a reminder, too, of how grace flows through us leaving only dust in its wake. To console himself against the finality of this, Goodcole spoke the passage that Sawyer had told him in last night's dream. Characteristically her memory of the Word was not as it was written in the Black Book.

"Now, early in the morning, the women came to the sepulchre, bringing spices.

> *And they found the stone rolled away.*
> *When they entered in, they found not the body.*
> *And, behold, two angels stood by them in shining garments:*
> *And as the women were afraid, they said to them, 'Why seek you the living among the dead? He is not here, but is risen: remember how your son was delivered into the hands of sinful men, to be crucified, and on the third day to rise again.'"*

When he mouthed these words, something connected in Goodcole's mind. The first word that triggered this was 'spices', which reminded him of Deicrowe hiding myrrh, and the last was 'rise', which related to Sawyer's comments about Last Lammas. Together they suggested the sentiment that connected the brothers Deicrowe with the three cousins, Elizabeth, Meg and Eve because, although much separated the two camps, there was a deal they held in common. Of course on the surface they could not have been more different. The brothers grew up far to the west in the Duchy; they were literate, educated papists. The cousins, on the other hand, were reared here in the east; they were illiterate country girls, nominally Anglican by religion. Here again, however, appearances were deceptive because both the Deicrowes and the Meads had been born landless; moreover, their poverty had been ground in by loss. Goodcole knew that there was nothing unusual about this. He had experienced want, as had most people in the realm but that was the point.

Returning to the Easter story, he now understood the gospel in a new way. Because what the Deicrowes, Meads, Cronwells and many other commoners took out of it was something quite contrary to the teachings of the Church. Now, when Goodcole heard Sawyer repeat the words spoken by angels in his head, he savoured that difference. "*Remember how your son was delivered into the hands of sinful men, to be crucified, and on the third day to rise again.*" In practice it didn't matter whether it was 'your son', 'your daughter', father, or mother; just as it didn't matter whether the sinful men were Roman soldiers, or thugs from the London Company, or even the Church. What mattered was that ordinary people believed that in an unjust world where force triumphed, loss would be rewarded with eternal life; this was why the meek would inherit the earth. This was the consoling thought that was giving England succour, while driving it towards a revolution at the same time.

When all was tidied away, Goodcole readied himself for the journey across the City to the alderman's house in Walbrook Ward. Sensing that he should confer with Stamp first, he turned left into the record office after entering the gatehouse. There, instead of his friend he found Dicker standing proud as a peacock at the counter. The agent held a vellum scroll in his right hand. Goodcole recognised the sign of the cat pressed into the wax seal and knew that Dicker was holding the Burghley Appeal. He assumed that he meant to return it to the Cecil family in Hatfield and, though he knew he should be civil for Joan's sake, he couldn't resist a dig.

"You never did tell me about the connection between Deicrowe and Sawyer," he said.

After the debacle in the chapel, Dicker barely masked his contempt. "Do you need to know for your pamphlet; I was trying to guess what you might call it?"

"It goes by the title, 'The Wonderful Discovery of Elizabeth Sawyer'."

"Wonderful in what way?" Again, his tone was sneering.

Goodcole focused all his energy on the agent. "Wonderful in the way that God finds us *all* out in the end." When he said the words, Goodcole knew that he was repeating Sawyer's exact phrase from their first meeting a week before in Limbo.

Dicker nodded his head slowly, confirmed in his suspicion. "My sense is that, though dead, that woman still holds you in her thrall," he said.

"Her thrall?"

"You spent far too much time with that witch. I warned you but you let her talk you round and now you are under her spell. Did you ever ask her how she lost the sight in her right eye?"

"Lysbeth is not a witch."

Dicker ignored his denial. He was now poised like a duellist who has cornered his opponent and is about to inflict a mortal wound. "I asked her neighbours in Winchmore where it is common knowledge in the village. Her youngest boy poked it out with a stick; it was when Sawyer was nursing her mother Ma Cronwell shortly before the old woman died."

For a moment Goodcole was thrown by this revelation; his mind struggled to reconcile Sawyer's description of Grace Cronwell's early death in childbirth with Dicker's findings in Winchmore but then the voice in his head reassured him. 'Tell him,' she said.

"She told me that her mother died giving birth to her," he said flatly.

Dicker leaned forward; he had Goodcole skewered. "I know what she *told* you. She spun you a yarn. Perhaps she told you the story you wanted to hear because it is what she's known for in the village. A woman like that does not confess to anything. She makes up stories that ensnare her audience."

"Is that why you forged her confession – to save my blushes?"

"Yes, to move things along. You were brought in to speed things up, not spend five days chewing the fat with an ignorant peasant." Goodcole bridled at the word and, somewhere deep in the core of him, something broke free: a loathing for those who treated the poor with contempt coursed through his veins.

"You prating ponce. What do you know? You ride the shires, poking your beak in where it doesn't belong. You judge others while pandering girls to the port." Goodcole was about to say more, but a scornful look from Dicker caused him to return to his original point. "You think I'm just a witch's mouthpiece, so tell me."

"Tell you what?"

"The real reason you stopped off at the Arundels' house in Tottenham Wood before travelling on to Edmonton."

"The truth is quite plain and I make no apology for it: the king has sequestered that entire forest. For a small exchange of land Alderman Bull has offered to appoint the Arundels' house as a hunting lodge."

Goodcole noticed that Stamp had joined them now; he was standing in the aisle between the shelves and listening to every word. He turned back to Dicker. "A hunting lodge, you say?"

"Aye, the Arundels have retreated to the Duchy and good riddance to them. Tottenham Wood has always been a refuge for outlaws and priests, so now we may finally flush out these vermin." He waved the scroll and continued. "Though Sawyer was not named on the indictment it is well known that she was present that day in Potter's Field thirty years ago when the Enfield women broke down that fence. But for her escaping to the forest afterwards she would have been brought to book. It seems that no one pursued her and it's my guess that people were too afraid to do so – listening to you now, it's no wonder."

After Dicker left them, Stamp poured out grog for them both and ushered Goodcole into his room in the back of the archive. He raised a beaker. "Tomorrow will be Easter and not a moment too soon," he said.

Goodcole raised his cup. "Aye, it has been a long week; a baptism of fire no less."

Stamp looked at him with concern. "You know, it's best not to rise to men like Dicker. They are hirelings and have no being beyond the cause they serve."

Goodcole drank deeply; then he wiped his lips. "Is this brandy?" he asked.

Stamp nodded. "It's French, but worry not, I got it off the Huguenots." The two of them laughed and Stamp put a friendly hand on his shoulder. "I hear you told the dean a few home truths," he said.

"Well, the ordinary is universally despised so I had little to lose."

Stamp refilled his beaker. "Except Joan," he said and raised an eyebrow.

Goodcole savoured the mellow fire of the brandy. He pictured the barrels being exchanged for bundles of wool in a cove beyond the reach of the Cinque Ports. "I will fetch her presently," he said. For a moment he scanned the shelves of ledgers and scrolls, then he turned back to Stamp. "Why now?" he said.

Stamp looked at him quizzically. "Are you referring to Sawyer and Deicrowe?" he asked.

"Yes, why send them west after all this time?"

"Well, you heard Dicker. If the alderman is to curry favour with the king then he must start with a clean slate."

"So getting rid of Sawyer and Deicrowe was sound housekeeping?"

"In one way but there is more to it than that." Stamp gripped Goodcole by the shoulder. "You know, there is a well of sorrow attached to this case. I advise you to leave it now and look after your own."

Goodcole could tell that Stamp was holding back, weighing up whether to say more.

"John Dicker was right about one thing," he said after a while.

"Spit it out."

"Sawyer was a dissembler. Her words had a way of snagging people like briars and before they knew it they were ensnared. Even in the grave she is a dangerous woman."

Goodcole pushed his chair back and stood up. "Lysbeth is righteous. She is not in the grave. She lives," he said.

Stamp stood up, too. He faced Goodcole, toe to toe. "I have checked with Potts. The pressure to convict Sawyer came from her neighbours – mostly the other wives. They have wanted rid of her for years. In the end it took a local beak from Tottenham to act on their behalf."

"And the alderman thought he would kill two birds with one stone?"

"Well, you know the judiciary. Nothing happens for one reason, alone. It takes a coincidence of interests to seal a person's fate."

"And this is justice?"

"This is life, my friend. Come, I will show you something." Stamp walked back to the front of the archive; here he positioned a stepladder. When he could reach to the top shelf, he gripped a heavy tome.

Goodcole helped him lower the volume onto the front counter. It was covered with grime and had leather straps to hold it closed. "What is this?" he asked.

Stamp first wiped the dust off with his neckerchief and then he unbuckled the fastenings and let the book fall open. He smoothed out the page. "This register was compiled in the last years of Gloriana: our good Queen Elizabeth. It was drawn up on the orders of Cecil and enacted by Wroth. It records all those convicted of vagrancy after they changed the poor laws. Most of those listed here were sent to the Bridewell Prison to beat hemp."

"To beat hemp?"

"Aye, to soften it for rope."

Goodcole glanced at the thickness of the binding; there must have been thousands of names contained within. He swallowed. "Why imprison so many?" he asked.

"Because after a succession of failed harvests England was in uproar. The roads were clogged with starving people and the parishes could not cope."

Goodcole moved closer; he looked down at the columns of names listed by the county courts. He turned the pages from Essex to Hertfordshire, from Middlesex to Kent.

Stamp drained his cup. "This is what the powerful really fear – more than popery or invasion. It is the rising from within because when people have nothing they have nothing to lose." Goodcole struggled to clear his head.

"So, why choose Holy Week to hang Deicrowe and Sawyer – it turns them into martyrs," he said.

"You, my friend, are the first person to remark on that. You see, most people would say that by putting them together the authorities sounded a warning. A thief on Holy Tuesday and a witch on Maundy Thursday mean the same thing."

"And what is that, perchance?"

"Be vigilant. There are tricksters in your midst."

Goodcole turned away from Stamp to the shelves of the record office. The warmth of the brandy was gone now and all he could smell was dust. All that parchment and old vellum put him in mind of the urns in his study; it was all so dry and dead. Aside from parish registers, these records represented the only evidence that some people had ever lived. He took a last look at his friend and raised his hand in farewell. "I will leave you to your paperwork: you must note down those who have left a prison they never entered."

Stamp raised his hand in reply. "Go you and get your girl. I will see you after the feast," he said with a smile.

Stepping out of the gatehouse and into the City, Goodcole felt that sense of release that always came from leaving Newgate. He listened to the peel of St Sepulchre's bells and the answering call from St Augustine and felt his heart lighten. Soon he would celebrate Easter with his family but before that he still had one last errand to run. Just beyond Newgate market at the place they call the Shambles Goodcole stepped aside for a yoke of cattle that pulled a cart towards Billingsgate. It was a reminder that the port of London never slept, that the ceaseless pursuit of trade trumped the ecclesiastical calendar and that the work of the London Company would continue through hell and high water. It was a reminder, too, that he should not dawdle on his way to free Joan from the clutches of the alderman.

Goodcole wondered which steward he would face when he reached Walbrook Ward. He started to pick out words he might use to secure her release but then gave up, deciding instead to embrace the Holy Day and act in its spirit. So buoyed up was he at the thought of being with his daughter that he raised his hand in thanks as he passed under the Eleanor Cross. Ahead in Eastcheap the shell of Mercer's Hall reflected gold, silver and bronze. *How the world shows us a false face*, he thought and looked up to where a coat of arms was painted on a shield above his head. Goodcole took in the bust of the Virgin wearing a crown and read the motto 'Honor Deo' that floated underneath. He wondered that the same image could mean such different things to different people. The Virgin had meant one thing to Deicrowe, perhaps another to the women in the prison and something quite different to the 'Worshipful Company of Mercers'. The thought of Joan, alone and vulnerable, quickened his pace.

The light was turning amber, now. It flattered the Italian facades suggesting that England was building a new Rome and in a way it was for whatever the watchword of the Worshipful Company, England had chosen Mammon over God and its ships were like those Roman galleys before them; they were intent on conquest. The bell from Mary Woolchurch told him that it would soon be dark. Goodcole looked forward to the moment when he grasped Joan's hand to lead her away from servitude. Then, when they had celebrated Easter together, his family would seek fresh lodgings outside the City. Perhaps he would break with his present job and take his family back to Clerkenwell where he knew people. There, they might live a pious life outside the orbit of powerful men.

Goodcole turned down Bearbinder Lane only to find his way barred. Two constables armed with staves stood in front of a makeshift barrier. The barrier was made up of a pole hung between a pair of sawhorses and in the centre a board marked with a red cross hung from its length. Goodcole carried on walking towards the roadblock; he took in the daubs of paint and saw the two men stiffen as he drew near. He stepped into the centre of the road and approached the pole just to the left of the board.

The foremost constable was tall with a bushy beard of brown like the pelt of a bear. He raised his stave when Goodcole drew near. "Ho, sirrah, Walbrook Ward is closed. You may not pass," he said. Goodcole decided to plead ignorance.

"Why ever not?"

"This ward is infected with pestilence. By order of the mayor, no man, woman or child may enter or leave."

Goodcole drew in his breath; he was a man set on a course and nothing would stop him from reaching his goal. His heart was beating, gall coursing through his veins. He felt more alive now than he had done in the past seven days and was glad to be rid of that stink-hole Newgate. He ducked under the pole, brushing the board with his shoulder as he did so; then, making a leap for freedom, he slipped through the grasp of the constable and ran hell for leather down the street. Goodcole kept running until the shouts behind him grew faint.

In a doorway in St Swithin's Lane he caught his breath and listened for sounds of pursuit. When none came he looked about him and, seeing that the doorways were free of red daubs, he breathed a sigh of relief. To close an entire ward in this part of town was a severe step but perhaps the lockdown was precautionary. The smear of wet paint on his right shoulder told him the measure was fresh in which case there would still be time to smuggle Joan out. They could slip away by Budge Lane and then climb up St Sythes to Poultry. The thought made him smile because if they went this way they would pass directly in front of the offices of the London Company. The prospect underlined his hope that he and his family would soon be free of their influence forever.

Goodcole knew that he was close now; he looked down the cobbled street. Below, between the towers of Rose Manor and the spire of All Hallow's, he could see the Thames. The river was that bright bar of silver that Joan had described in her letter to him from before Holy Week. Now, on the cusp of Easter Sunday, it glinted beguilingly, suggesting an untold future that was just beyond their grasp. Goodcole walked down the hill; he could hear his boots smack off the hard stone; he could hear the jingling of his keychain. Together the sounds broke the hush of the City, which was holding its breath before Easter. The houses at the bottom of St Swithin's Lane were grander than those at the top of the hill and Alderman Bull's house was the largest of them all. Goodcole checked for a guard dog on a leash and finding none he strode under the overhang of its floors, past its white stucco walls to the black-timbered porch.

On the weathered oak of the door a red cross warned him off. 'Plague House' a hand had scrawled underneath. For a moment Goodcole stood and gawped. This was the work of vandals like graffiti or libels left on walls but then his mind cleared and he grasped that the house was indeed infected. Again, his will bent the facts to suit his purpose. If the house was diseased, it was more important than ever to get Joan out of there. He didn't care what the steward said; he would reclaim his child. He lifted the heavy knocker and let its thump go through to the hall. When no answer came, Goodcole decided to try his luck around the back. Moving to the brick arch that led to the garden, he found his way barred by a wrought iron gate.

To his surprise it opened and he stepped through into the green space that spread deep and wide into a bloom of trees. Remembering the orchard from his last visit, he thought to find a shady spot and sit for a while if only to still his beating heart. The trees were mostly apple but there were pear and a few cherries in blossom, too. Lit by the glow of evening their flowers beckoned, soft and cloud-like after the hard-edged streets.

Goodcole wandered for a while and then sat down on a clump of tree roots. They rose like varicose veins from the soil at the base of an old medlar tree that twisted up above him, blackened and old. The house seemed distant from here; its lime-washed walls tilted like a chalk cliff in the evening light. Goodcole gave himself to the beauty of the place. The April warmth was cooling and a blackbird's song filled the air. He took in the piebald plumage of a magpie. It perched on a branch and then flapped noisily to the ground where it dispatched the nestling it had stolen with quick stabbing motions of its beak. He looked up and noticed that someone was walking towards him from the far end of the orchard. It was he surmised a constable or gamekeeper; he would wait for him to approach, describe the nature of his business and request access to the house. Goodcole watched the man duck under an arbour of hawthorn and then turn. For a moment his tall striding form was silhouetted against the sun and then he disappeared, lost in iridescence.

The shadows were lengthening and yet the evening retained a balmy brilliance that promised summer days to come; it suggested long twilights when dusk merged with dawn, when the insects hovered through the small hours until the Sun rose, blazing over the horizon. So he luxuriated in the glow. Joan was close by and that knowledge filled him with wellbeing. After a while, Sawyer spoke to him once more.

"Know you the gardener?" she said. He guessed that she was referring to the man he had seen ambling amongst the trees.

"The gardener, is that what you call him?"

"He is keeper of the Lord's Grove. Here, he lets all things grow wild – except the beasts, they bow to Him."

"There are beasts in this place?"

"Aye, there are beasts everywhere – two-legged, four-legged."

"Snakes?"

"That, too."

Goodcole felt the years fall away. He was like a child that has somehow stumbled upon an enchanted garden. Now that he had found his way within, he felt in some way charmed because although everything was strange, it was also familiar. The trees were fruit-bearing and had a cultivated look that showed that throughout the winter, from All Hallows to Hocktide, they had been cared for.

Rocking back on the tree, Henry kicked off his boots. Looking at them lying there tumbled on the grass, he saw they were like objects of stone. Scuffed and chipped by London's paths they were things from another world; they did not belong here and he would not wear them again. For a while he aired his stockinged feet and then restless, he thought to climb the tree. At first, he regretted his choice because this medlar appeared to be the most diseased in the grove. The bark was brittle and blistered and the trunk, which turned like a screw above his head, was riven with splits and knots. After a few failed attempts, Henry clamped his feet against the twisted stem and, using the strength in his arms, pulled himself up to where gnarled branches spread out like the fingers of a scorched hand.

"This tree is dead," he said out loud.

"On one side it is dying, yet on the other it lives. It grows through suffering," Sawyer answered him.

Henry balanced on the crook of the branch. The wool of his stockings was torn now, his bare feet rasping against the bark. All around the grain was oozing amber blood. The resin stuck to his fingers; moreover, it had a sickly perfume, like mandrake root and myrrh. That smell reminded him of a tomb and it made him sleepy. Forcing himself to stay awake, he reached to the upper branches, where to his surprise, he found green shoots growing.

Henry felt his world tilt. He was like a boy climbing a mast on the high seas. He clamped on tighter but the hypnotic fumes were strong. "What if I fall?" he said.

"Taste the sap," she told him.

Somehow he felt compelled to obey and so, summoning his courage, he loosened one hand off the nearby branch and pressed it into the crook of a bough. The resin here was viscous as tar. He raised his finger and touched it to his tongue. In his mouth the sap was the texture of gum arabic, yet it tasted of frankincense. Henry felt the globule pass against his teeth; he rolled it around his mouth and swallowed. For a moment he felt nothing but then warmth radiated from his core. The sensation was a tingling energy, which spread out through his limbs until it reached the tips of his fingers and toes. It was as if the sap rising in all the trees in the whole orchard was somehow circulating through his body, too. That feeling was blissful and it made him feel immortal. Without thinking, he released his grip and fell.

When Henry Goodcole woke, the sun had long set and it was cold in the grove. Above him the paschal moon was arching towards the west and from nearby came the hooting of an owl. He stretched in the darkness and for a long while lay on his back, giving himself to the sensation that flowed through his body. In spite of the wet grass the darkness around him was like a blanket. It insulated him against the chill of the April night; moreover, that darkness pulsated with life. Tiny gnats whined past and amongst the trees spirals of white moths rose like smoke. Life was underneath him too: below his prostrate form the larvae of beetles, worms and bugs were moving in the soil.

The footsteps came from the direction of the house and he felt them through the ground as soft padding tremors that grew stronger with each impact. When he was sure they were close, he sat up and stretched. At first all he saw was the light. It hovered above the ground, swaying slightly as it approached. The lantern stopped a couple of paces from him and only then could he see the figure behind. She wore a woollen cloak and had covered her auburn hair with a white coif. Her manner was that of an older sister come to fetch an errant child before bedtime.

"Come, the mistress is concerned about you. You should come in out of the cold," she said.

"But I am not cold," he said.

"Come now, Father. We've been told you're not well. Come now with me and take your rest."

Henry took Joan's hand and let her lead him into the house.

For writing and publishing news, or
recommendations of new titles to read,
sign up to the Book Guild newsletter: